H. Philip Birdsong's ESP

H. PHILIP BIRDSONG'S ESP

BY

Harriet Lawrence

WITH DRAWINGS BY

Sandy Huffaker

NEW YORK

William R. Scott, Inc.

Library of Congress Catalog Card No. 69-14568.

Contents

1.	Birthday Blues	7
2.	Secret Diplomacy	16
3.	More Problems	23
4.	"Dr. Birdsong's Office"	34
5.	The Peckham Threat	42
6.	The Ancestral Recorder	50
7.	Sensations New And Strange	64
8.	Groping Around In Bozo's World	74
9.	Bozo Starts Transmitting	85
10.	A Little Light On A Dark Subject	98
11.	The Plot Thickens	112
12.	An Encounter With Miss Peckham	131
13.	Light Through A Burning Glass	140
14.	A New And Reluctant Pupil	151
15.	Thwarted Efforts	160
16.	Balloons For Buoyancy	174
17.	A Cat On Horseback, A Dog On Wheels	185
18.	A Weasel At Miss Peckham's	201
19.	Sam's Hereditary Affliction	210
20.	Miss Peckham Is Buttered Up	219
21.	A New Plan For Peckham Persuasion	229
22.	A Soggy But Successful Rescue	242
23.	More Well-Laid Plans	251
24.	Operation Bloodhound	263
25.	Miss Peckham Gets Her Goose Cooked	277
26.	A Song Without Words	291

1. Birthday Blues

I dropped my books on the last desk next to the windows in Room 3 and looked glumly around. I was about to start an hour's detention for being late for school that morning, and so far I had the room to myself. It was not a cheering sight. Room 3 is in the old part of Haunceton High and is a dreary waste of wall-to-wall blackboards, heavy old screwed-down desks that always smell of varnish, and one long row of tall sash windows that look out on an alley closed to traffic. It's principally a math and detention room and is known as the Morgue. The blackboards were covered, as usual, with squares and triangles and numerals. I turned from them to the windows without much hope of seeing anything interesting there either. Still, cats and dogs and even people walk through the alley occasionally, and this time I was in luck, for there, marching briskly along, was the tall, lean figure of Haunceton's champion walker, Major Featherstone.

The Major is a special friend of mine; he's the most cordial and in some ways the most sensible adult I know. I opened the window and leaned out. "Hi, Major!" I said.

The Major jumped and looked up, smiling as he recognized me. When the Major smiles, his whole narrow face crinkles up. "Hi, Phil!" he replied in his deep, pleasant voice. "Many happy returns of the day!" I guess I didn't look awfully happy, because he added, "It *is* your birthday, isn't it?"

"Yes, my thirteenth," I replied, "but I don't know that I want it to return, thank you; it's been terrible so far. You know that automatic grain hopper I made for the ponies? Something went wrong, and it dumped a lot of extra oats into Jones's stall in the night, and Father is wild. I had to tell him in case Jones got sick. He says it's hard enough to be a vet to all the sick animals in the county without having me contribute one at home."

"Tough luck!" said the Major. "How did Jones seem?"

"O.K. this morning," I replied, "but I don't know just when he had his feast. I had to take down the hopper in case there were any more oats it could let down, so I was late for school, and now I have detention."

"You *are* having your troubles," said the Major. "If Jones is all right, why don't you bring him over to the track later to work off his oats?" In the Major's back pasture there is an old racetrack that comes in very handy. I brightened at the thought of it.

"One good thing," I said. "I got that saddle I wanted for my birthday. It's a beaut. I'm going to shorten my stirrups like a jockey and beat the stuffing out of Jane and Evans." Up till then my sister Jane and I had had only one saddle between us, and when we rode together I had to go bareback. It's a good way to ride, but you can race better with a light saddle.

The Major started to say something, but was interrupted by a deep, melodious, bloodhound howl. We both turned our heads to watch Bozo, the Major's dog, lumbering toward us.

Though Bozo has a full-blooded bloodhound yell, he isn't a full-blooded bloodhound, but some mysterious mixture in which, though he is long-haired, bloodhound predominates. His most peculiar and engaging feature is a feathery tail that revolves as if it were attached by a ball-and-socket joint. Caleb Polewhele, the Major's man-of-all-work, had brought Bozo home from his annual vacation and presented him to the Major, who, a few weeks later, appointed me co-owner since Bozo spent almost as much time with me as he did with the Major and Caleb. I was especially pleased with this arrangement since our own old dog had recently died and was not to be replaced till spring. This week, though, I hadn't been to the Major's, and Bozo hadn't called on me.

"Hi, Bozo, old boy," I called. Then, after taking a quick look behind me to make sure that no teacher had come in yet, I pointed to a closed bulkhead door just below the window and added, "Come on up!"

To my surprise Bozo merely wrinkled up his wrinkled face more than ever and sat lackadaisically down at the Major's feet. "Oh, come on, Bozo," I repeated. "It'll hold you." He gave me a long look and started slowly up the sloping door.

By the time Bozo reached the top of the door, I knew there was something wrong with him. I had hoisted myself up so that I was balancing across the window sill on my stomach, with one hand stemmed against the bulkhead. With the other I shook hands with Bozo, and he made his usual swipe at my front cowlick with his tongue, but in such a halfhearted way and with such a melancholy expression that I was alarmed. "He must be sick," I said to the Major.

"Bozo sick? What makes you think so?" he asked.

"He's different," I said, "—droopy; his tail's all limp. And look—his legs are trembling."

"Caleb did say this morning that he didn't think Bozo was up to snuff, but he ate well and seemed all right to me. He wanted to come walking with me; but if you think he's sick, too, I'd better take him to your father. We'll take a taxi out to the hospital." That's one reason I like the Major so much. He's such a determined walker, he'd never order a taxi for himself if he could drag one foot after the other, but for Bozo, or any other ailing creature, he'd never hesitate to call one.

By this time Bozo was sprawled out on the bulkhead, and I was examining him. "His gums are good and pink," I reported, "but his nose is hot and dry. I bet he has a fever."

The Major looked worried. "Come on, Bozo," he said. "We'd better get going." But Bozo merely raised his head and let it sink again.

I looked him in the eye and said firmly, "Get up, Bozo, and go with the Major. You're not *that* sick." Bozo got to his feet and hobbled carefully down the door.

The Major smiled his crinkly smile again as he straightened up from snapping the leash to Bozo's collar. "What's your magic formula, Phil?" he asked. "Bozo will do anything you tell him to."

"Gosh, I don't know," I replied. "I guess I just concentrate on getting something across so he knows it's important. But how did you happen to have a leash? I've never seen one on Bozo before."

The Major's smile faded and he looked more worried than ever. "I've been having a little trouble—" he said; but before he finished his sentence, he stepped back and lifted his hat apologetically. At the same moment somebody grabbed my belt and pulled me back into the room. Titters and a guffaw in the background warned me that the other detention victims had assembled and had doubtless been enjoying at least some of my conversation with the Major and Bozo.

As my feet hit the floor, I did an about-face and looked up, grinning uncertainly as I recognized a large pair of tortoiseshell spectacles and a neat head of graying red hair. It was my English teacher, Miss Norcross. She's also assistant principal and a number of other things at Haunceton High, where she's been teaching for over twenty years. She's certainly not the type to stand nonsense from anybody, but she's always fair, and I didn't think she'd consider hanging out the window before detention started a very serious crime. Some people say she never smiles in school. That's not true, but you have to watch for her smiles or you'll miss them; the corners of her lips just twitch once and she lowers her eyelids. I guess that's what's called a ghost of a smile. She gave me one now and said, "Sit down like everybody else, Philip. Your ESP isn't working."

"My ESP?" I said blankly as I sat down. I'd come across the expression somewhere, but with half a dozen faces smirking at me, I couldn't place it at all.

"Your extrasensory perception," said Miss Norcross.

I didn't get this either and I must have still looked blank, because Miss Norcross let her eyes travel quickly over the other faces in the room and then said, "Tell him, Sam, what extrasensory perception is."

Sam Paine had taken the seat in front of me. He's a freshman like me, but he's tall and gangly and he wears big spectacles that give him a scholarly look. He's not at all scholarly, really, and I was surprised that Miss Norcross picked on him to enlighten me. But then, she always seems to be able to tell who knows and who doesn't.

"It's seeing something you can't see," announced Sam with a grin.

"Or something that people can't see with their ordinary senses," said Miss Norcross. "I have ESP," she continued matter-of-factly. "In teachers it used to be called 'eyes-in-the-back-of-your-head,' but now it's ESP no matter who has it—at least it's one kind of ESP. And any pupil in this school who plans to go in for gymnastics out of the window between classes had better cultivate it."

At this recommendation there was another guffaw from Sam and a general tittering among the girls, except for one senior girl who inquired seriously, "What other kinds of ESP are there?"

"Oh, many more than I know about, doubtless," replied Miss Norcross. "Several things we used to know by different names, such as hunches, mental telepathy, clairvoyance, and a sixth sense, tend to be called ESP now. And before those words were in common use, the same ideas were lumped together under witchcraft."

"Then it's really true there is such a thing?" inquired the senior girl, wide-eyed.

"Well, that's still debatable, I suppose," replied Miss Norcross. "The existence of ESP hasn't been proved to the satisfaction of all scientists, but there's a widespread belief in it that's growing as evidence accumulates."

"Can't you do card tricks with it?" chimed in another voice from across the room.

"I suppose it would be a help, George," replied Miss Norcross, "but what you're probably thinking of is card *tests* for ESP. You try to guess what's on the reverse of identically-backed cards, and if you have a high average of correct guesses, your ESP is working well. Of course it doesn't have to be cards," she added, glancing over the desks. She took a yellow pencil from my desk and a green one from Sam's and then collected a red and a blue one from two other pupils. With these she sat down at the teacher's desk and said, "I'll hold three of these pencils in my left hand below the desk where you can't see what I'm doing, and I'll take one in my right. You all concentrate and see if you can guess which one."

We did this about ten times and then checked scores. The senior girl claimed the highest and seemed quite excited about it. Sam did creditably too, but I failed miserably. When I announced my score, Sam said, "Poor old Hippo! His ESP has gone to the dogs," and he made a silly *oo-hoo-hoo* noise meant to sound like Bozo.

Miss Norcross fixed Sam with her tortoiseshell gaze, and as if impelled by some invisible hand, he turned around in his seat and opened a book. "You had better get to work on that book report on *Kidnapped* that you didn't pass in today, Sam, if you want any credit for it at all," she said.

"But I haven't got the book," protested Sam. "My mother thought I'd finished with it and took it back to the library, and there weren't any copies in the school library this morning."

"I have a copy he can borrow," I offered, holding it up. I had chosen *Kidnapped* for my report, too, and had brought it to school to use during a study period.

"Very well," said Miss Norcross. "Give it to him."

"My friend!" exclaimed Sam dramatically as he turned and snatched it from me. "Classy!" he added in a whisper as he noticed the binding. It was a Christmas book I had received several years ago from my Great-aunt Serena. She had lived in California and had died recently, so I had never seen her; but as long as she lived she always sent me an expensive edition of some classic for Christmas. Sam examined the outside of this one minutely, handling it with exaggerated care and delicately blowing some imaginary dust from the gilt edges of its leaves.

"Sam," said Miss Norcross, "get to work! But first bring me that candy bar you have in your pocket. You may collect it when detention is over." There were more titters, but no guffaw this time.

Sam got slowly to his feet and began rummaging

around in his pockets—there were several since he was wearing a jacket—and examining dredged-up odds and ends on the palm of his hand before shaking his head and returning them. Just as Miss Norcross said "Sam!" again, he produced the candy bar, and after showing it to me with an air of intense surprise, he took it up to the teacher's desk and presented it to Miss Norcross. She received it gravely and with one sweep of her tortoise-shells across the room stifled all giggles and set everybody to work—or at least a good show of work—except the senior girl, who had her hand raised.

"What is it, Anne?" asked Miss Norcross.

"Isn't ESP hearing sometimes instead of seeing—like Joan of Arc or Dick Whittington?"

"Yes," said Miss Norcross, "hearing, smelling—any sense can be so heightened, I believe. And often it's just knowing without knowing how you know."

"She *smelled* my candy bar," declared Sam in an indignant undertone that made me snicker.

Another look from the tortoiseshells silenced us both, and I slumped down behind an opened history book to consider what might be going on at home. I wasn't too worried about Jones. Welsh ponies are tough, even the ones like Jones and Evans that are almost as big as horses; it didn't seem as if a few extra oats could do them much harm. But I didn't like the look of Bozo. I wondered, too, what the Major meant about a little trouble that caused him to carry a leash. If only I could get out of the Morgue and look into these important matters! What a day! And, I added sourly to myself as I gave up all pretense of reading and let my book slide down onto its back, what a birthday!

To my grand-nephew,
Hilary Philip Birdsong
II
Christmas 1960
Serena Chillingworth
Birdsong

2. Secret Diplomacy

Without the screen of the history book before me, I became suddenly aware that Sam was strangely uneasy. He was rhythmically hunching first one shoulder and then the other in what I finally realized was an attempt to attract my attention without turning around. I sat up straighter and peered over his shoulder. My heart sank as I saw his forefinger pointing to the old-fashioned handwriting of the inscription with which Aunt Serena invariably provided each Christmas book. It read: "To my grandnephew, Hilary Philip Birdsong, Christmas 1960. Serena Chillingworth Birdsong."

I had forgotten all about that inscription when I offered to lend the book to Sam. The four years I had lived in Haunceton, I had managed to keep my first name a secret, and now Sam, of all people, had discovered it. Not that Sam isn't a good friend of mine, but he's a born clown, and I shuddered to think what he could do with a name like Hilary. He tapped his finger under the *Hilary,* then suddenly turned around and pointed at me with questioning eyebrows. I shook my head, not so much in denial of the name as in warning.

Miss Norcross, who had apparently been absorbed in correcting papers, said in an ominously quiet voice, "Sam, move up to this desk in front of me and don't oblige me to speak to you again."

Sam moved, and I propped up my history book again and sank behind it to consider this new trouble. There wasn't much to consider really; I'd just have to get hold of Sam after detention and swear him to secrecy about my name. It wouldn't be easy, but if I could make him realize I was in earnest, it could be done. And it would help matters if I could think up some effective counterthreat to control him with. By the end of the period a possible one had occurred to me.

I was right behind Sam as he passed in his paper and collected his candy bar, and I stuck close to him with the idea of steering him into a quiet place and getting the business of my name settled. But to my annoyance, he handed me back my book in the hall and said quite loudly,

"Who is this Hilary bird? I never heard of him before."

"Oh, do be quiet," I said. "I'll tell you who he is if you'll promise not to tell. Wait till we get outside where we'll have some privacy." And I hustled him out the front door, which was the nearest one, though it's supposed to be reserved for faculty and seniors.

Once we were outside, Sam, finding scope for his dramatic talent, took charge, and pulling me behind one of the clumps of bushes that flank the front walk, hissed "Silence!" in my ear, and after a short period of spying around and listening, said in a hollow tone, "We are alone. Produce the family skeleton."

"First," I said, "you've got to promise not to tell a soul about it."

"I promise," said Sam with a solemn air, "on the honor of Samuel S. Paine III."

"Well," I said, "it's not exactly a skeleton; it's me."

"You?" said Sam. "You mean you are Hilarious Hilary?"

I nodded glumly.

Sam was immediately all righteous indignation. "You denied it when I asked you; you shook your head. My promise is not binding under these conditions."

"I only shook it to warn you to turn around," I said.

"I took it for a denial and you knew it," said Sam. "You extracted my promise on false pretenses, young Hippo—Hilarious Hippo," he amended with a grin.

"What about the honor of Samuel S. Paine III?" I asked, and then playing the trump card I had been saving, I added, "What does the *S* stand for?" I had asked him once before and he had been evasive. He was now.

"Oh, it's a family name," he said.

"Obviously," I said, "since you're the third. It ought to be easy enough to find out. I can just take a walk in the cemetery and read the tombstones." Sam's family has lived in Haunceton for a long time.

"Oh, well," said Sam with a sigh, "a lot of old people know what it is anyway, but they don't talk about it—don't even think about it, I guess." Then, looking cautiously around, he lowered his voice and said, "It's Serafino."

"Gosh!" I said. "That's worse than Hilary." Then, smiling happily, I tried out Serafino. Rendered as "O, Serafeeno-o-o!" with a sort of yodel on the *o,* it seemed most effective to me. Then I murmured dreamily, "Seraphim and cherubim—Sam the Seraph—Seraphic Sam III, or perhaps you'd prefer to be Cherubic Sam, or just plain Cherub? What's the difference between a seraph and a cherub anyhow?"

For a long moment Sam glowered at me and I grinned back. Then he gave up. "You win," he said. "We'll *both* have to keep mum now."

I nodded contentedly. "How did the Paines ever get such a name?" I asked.

"My great-grandfather went to sea for a while when he was young," said Sam, "and he got shipwrecked and somebody called Serafino—an Italian, I suppose—rescued him from cannibals. So he named his first son Samuel Serafino in gratitude. The Paines are still grateful. They're a very grateful family."

"So are the Birdsongs—at least this one," I said as I eagerly accepted a generous half of Sam's candy bar. Sam and I are sympathetic about the food problem; like dogs, we are both always hungry.

"I suppose yours is a family name too?" said Sam between bites.

"No," I replied, "it's my mother's fancy. She likes the name Birdsong, believe it or not. She says it's cheerful, and she wanted to give Jane and me cheerful names to go with it. She'd have called me Felix—it means *happy* in Latin, you know—if Father hadn't put his foot down. He said it was bad enough for a vet's family to have the name Birdsong without adding something to it that made everybody think of cats. When she came up with Hilary, which means *cheerful,* he couldn't make the same objection, but he insisted that at least my middle name should be an ordinary one and gave me his own. When we moved here from Massachusetts, I was darned glad to use Philip and shake the Hilary. I was tired of being called Hilarious Songbird. You know what my singing's like."

Sam was so uproarious over this tale of woe that I had to laugh myself; but then he annoyed me by saying, "You haven't done much better with Philip. I'll never forget that day in the sixth grade when you announced that your name meant Hippo. You were even smaller then than you are now; your head barely came above the desk."

"Nonsense!" I said. "You don't have to exaggerate so. And I never said my name meant Hippo. I said that it meant a lover of horses and that the *-ip* came from *hippos,* the Greek word for horse, and it does, though I admit I was dumb to say so; I'm stuck with Hippo now."

"Cheer up!" said Sam. "For my money it's much better than Felix and you don't have to sign your name Hippo. Imagine having all the teachers calling you Felix!"

"It was a lucky escape," I admitted, "but Jane got it when she came along."

"You don't mean to say *her* name is Felix?" asked Sam, aghast.

"The feminine form of Felix, Felice," I said. "That's confidential, of course. We agreed not to give each other's first names away, but I don't think she really cares much. She's always been called Jane and nothing but Jane, except by me when she gets too fresh. Little sisters can be pests if you don't keep them in their place."

Sam ignored this comment; he has no idea what sisters are like, since he has none. All he has is a much older brother who works for the state forestry department and is very obliging about giving us lifts in his jeep. Sam was interested in Jane's name, though. "*Jane* is your father's contribution, I suppose?" he asked.

I nodded. "He's a sensible guy most ways. He is a little unreasonable about some of my inventions, though," I added glumly. "He sure was on the warpath this morning because one of them didn't work and Jones got too many oats. I've got to get home now and find out how both Jones and Bozo are. And if Jones is O.K., we'll be going to the Major's."

"You're lucky," said Sam. "I've got to wash the car—*wash* it."

I knew what Sam meant by his bitter emphasis on washing. He doesn't object to cleanliness, but it galls him that washing is about all he is ever allowed to do to the family car. If only he could fiddle with its insides and take them apart, he'd be happy, but parents seem strangely reluctant to encourage mechanical talent by letting their children do things like that.

I felt for Sam in his predicament, but that word lucky was too much for me just then. "Lucky!" I snorted. "Detention and everything else on my birthday? I'm glad I can't be thirteen on Friday more than once."

At that Sam began to sing *Happy Birthday* in a silly sort of voice. He hesitated when he came to my name, but I looked him sternly in the eye, and he contented himself with "dear Hippo."

"Thank you, dear Samuel," I said. "So long!" And I made off across the lawn before he could think up anything more.

3. More Problems

Haunceton High School with its grounds occupies a short block on Main Street, bounded in the rear by the alley where the Major was walking, and on the sides by Emerson and Mapes Streets, which here, where they begin, look very much alike; each has a filling station on the corner, a couple of new stores farther on, and then old houses. About a mile from the school these same two thoroughfares bound the Birdsong property, but there they are so unlike each other that they seem to belong to different worlds. Emerson remains a straight and stodgy residential street with a tar sidewalk all the way to our house and a little beyond, but Mapes Street has long since straggled into the pleasant dirt road that veers obliquely across the valley through farming country to Appledore. Our property comes under the influence of both these boundaries. It's a thin rectangle sliced from a farm in the 1880's to make a house lot on Emerson Street; but the paddock and hayfield behind the stable clearly belong to the Appledore road.

I usually walk down Emerson Street to school in the morning because it's quicker, but often come home by the Appledore road because I like it better. High school students don't get bus service if they live in the residential district, which just includes our house since it's the last on Emerson Street to be supplied with town water. Though none of my school friends happen to live on either route, I seldom lack company on my walks, for I've gotten to know every dog and cat along the way and often collect quite a retinue. But sometimes I'm glad to get a ride with one of the farmers who use the Appledore road, and this afternoon when I sighted Tom Vickery's old green pickup truck at the Mapes Street filling station, I made for it like a homing pigeon.

Tom was just heading for home with a load of empty milk cans from the dairy, and cordially offered to drop me off on his way. We were soon past the paving; and as we joggled comfortably along the Appledore road, we chatted as best we could above the hollow clanging of the milk cans. We admired a herd of Guernseys as we passed them and discussed the results of too many oats for ponies. As we drew up at the lane that leads along the hayfield into the back of our paddock, Tom grinned at me and pointed across the field. "Your pony's all right," he said.

Both ponies had seen the truck stopping and were running toward the lane gate, their tails flying and their chestnut coats gleaming in the sun. "Handsome pair," said Tom. "Your dad knows horses. You'd better feed 'em by hand from now on."

"Father's seen to that," I answered with a grin as I jumped down to the road. "Thanks for the ride!"

Jones and Evans always give me a rousing welcome to their part of the Birdsong estate whenever I come home by the back way. I kept exchanging joyful whinnies with them as I hurried down the lane. Once inside the paddock, I changed my calls to answer the boisterous greetings of the kennel dogs, whose parallel runs reach as far as the paddock fence. The ponies, paying no attention to this uproar, poked and prodded me along the deep-cut, crumbly path to the back door of the stable. I opened the door a crack and slid through, taking care not to pinch Jones's nose in it as I shut it again.

I walked on through the stable, relishing its good, horsey smell and pausing to run my hand down the back of our black cat, Pounce, who was having a nap in a rickety old porch chair placed near enough the open front double doors to catch the sun. He yawned and blinked in acknowledgment of my attention and promptly went to sleep again. I didn't expect any more enthusiastic a welcome from Pounce. He lives in the stable by choice and prefers the society of the ponies and the kennel boarders to that of human beings.

I scooped up a handful of lump sugar from the box we keep on the shelf with the curry combs and the saddle soap and then stepped out onto the driveway. The dogs were still noisy; so I turned toward them and hushed them with a special sharp whistle I've cultivated for the purpose. Then I turned the other way and approached the spot where the ponies, who had lost no time rounding the stable, were jostling each other and stretching their necks impatiently over the paddock fence. This fence extends from the front corners of the stable to the side boundaries of our lot and consists only of a line of wooden posts joined together by two rows of horizontal boards; but it's so blocked by dog runs on one side and by spruces and a tall rose hedge on the other that there are only a couple of yards adjoining one end of the stable where ponies and people can reach each other. Here I divided the sugar between Jones and Evans and then turned to see what might be going on at home. I had a good vantage point because our driveway is U-shaped, and the stable is on the underside of the U. The carriage house—now a small-animal hospital—is just around the bend on one side, and our house is around the other bend nearer Emerson Street.

Father calls the Emerson Street end of our property a "gentleman's town residence of the gingerbread era." The gingerbread appears on all the buildings in the form of wooden scrollwork along the edges of the roofs, but the house has a few extra touches—ornate back and front porches and a skimpy little turret on one front corner. It's a fairly big house and tall, but the thin porch posts with their attached gingerbread give it a flimsy look, and like the stable and the hospital, it's painted a dismal coffee color, though there are plans for having it painted white.

A quick glance toward it this afternoon told me only that Mother was home, for her red Volkswagen was in the small parking space near the back porch.

I next checked the hospital. There were no signs of life there—no cars in the drive, and none in the parking space as far as I could see; but since Father's office hours were not over yet, I assumed his old jeep station wagon was parked out of sight in the last space as usual. This was all to the good; if no outpatients were being treated, I'd be able to ask Father about Bozo right away.

My inspection over, I stretched luxuriously in the warm sunlight, glad to be home again with everything serene. But suddenly an uneasy feeling stirred in my mind that I had missed something in my survey of the premises—something that should be there and wasn't. I looked again; everything seemed normal. In my perplexity I even inspected the deep lawn with its handsome maples which fills the inside of the U-shaped driveway. Since it's the most impressive feature of a not very impressive property, we call it "the park." Some leaves had turned red and yellow already, I noticed; we'd be raking them soon. And I recalled that I was due to mow the grass tomorrow—probably for the last time this year. But that was all I was reminded of; nothing was missing. I decided I was imagining things and started off toward the hospital.

As I rounded the bend in the drive, the collie in the first run kept pace with me to the hospital and propped himself up with his forepaws against the fencing. I said "Hi, Angus!" to him and then stopped short. The run behind him was empty. Houdini had done it again!

Houdini's folks, the Molloys, say he's a cross between a Dalmatian and an Irish setter. That may account for his short, foxy red coat, but it leaves his acrobatic ability a mystery. He can climb a fence as easily as a cat and can make tremendous and accurate leaps. The Molloys have to go to Boston at regular intervals; so every couple of months he's with us for a few days. His first stay lasted less than twenty minutes; he climbed out of his pen, jumped through a small, high window in the operating room, and went back home. Father retrieved him in the jeep and then stowed him for safekeeping in a double-decker pen with a cat cage on top; but the next day I found him hobnobbing with Pounce in the stable. He had somehow managed to open the door of his pen and had escaped through another window. At this point Father said he was too busy to spend any more time matching wits with one superbly healthy dog and turned the problem over to his assistant Mike and me. I suggested that since Houdini seemed at home in the stable, he might as well stay there, but Father was afraid he would stray off; so I've spent a lot of time and ingenuity during the last two years working on Houdini-proof devices.

My biggest success to date had been some tautly stretched chicken wire hooked securely over his run. Mike helped me with it and we all but welded it on. Father was especially pleased with it because when Houdini isn't with us—and of course most of the time he isn't—it makes an ideal yard for cats. But Houdini was supposed to be with us today. I could see, on closer inspection, that the chicken wire was loose on the paddock end of the run. Houdini might be anywhere, but he probably was somewhere near. After that first time, he has never attempted to run back home. He seems to like our place, and I believe he breaks out of confinement just to show off.

I knew he wasn't in the stable or the paddock; I'd just been there, and Houdini never hides. He picks a comfortable spot and takes what he seems to feel is a well-earned rest after his triumphs. It's useless to call him under these circumstances, however; he plays deaf till he's found. So I turned and ran down the drive toward the house. I kept an eye on the park in case Houdini might be lying behind a tree, but I was headed for the porches. Houdini likes porches.

A glance at the back porch assured me that Houdini was not there, so I ran on beside the drive to the front one. This required more thorough investigation because the porch extends right around the turret. I went its whole winding length, but still found no sign of Houdini. I vaulted the porch railing, dropped to the ground, and kept on along the narrow strip of lawn between our house and the privet hedge that marks our boundary on that side, pausing once to peer through the hedge at the empty lot next door. Once more in the back yard, I thought of inspecting the Volkswagen. One window was down about three inches, but even Houdini couldn't slide through that. If he was still on the premises, there was just one place left to check, and I made for it.

It's a rectangular plot enclosed by a rose hedge, one of its long sides bordering the paddock. We think it must have been a garden once, but it's grassed over now and used principally for drying laundry; but since it's a nice sheltered place to sit, we keep a couple of deck chairs in one corner along with one of those huge spools they wind electric cable on. This spool, given an occasional coat of paint, makes a good outdoor table. It also makes a good sunbathing platform for a medium-sized dog. When I opened the gate of the enclosure, I saw that Houdini was taking full advantage of it.

"Houdi!" I exclaimed reproachfully. Houdini sat up and grinned at me. It was no use scolding him. Mike says he has no conscience, but I don't think that's true; he looked awfully ashamed once when I caught him eating Pounce's dinner. He and Mike just have different ideas of sin.

I said "Come!" and he came, and "Heel!" and he heeled. He's quite biddable once he's had his fun.

As we came out of the clothes yard, I saw Jane, dressed for riding, coming up the drive from the house. Our paths converged near the stable.

"Has Houdi done it again?" asked Jane.

"Yes," I replied. "He was sunbathing on the big spool this time."

Jane giggled. "Does Mike know?" she asked.

"Not yet," I replied. "I'm just going to tell him. Where are you going? Have you finished the kennel chores already?"

"I'm going to Still Waters," said Jane—she meant the Major's farm—"and I haven't finished the kennel chores because it's not my turn to do them."

"But it's my birthday," I said. "I did them for you on yours."

"You *had* to," replied Jane. "I was having a party, and I've taken your turn several times since then. You owe *me* kennel chores."

Before I could make an indignant reply, Mother came hurrying toward us from the hospital. "Phil, dear, where have you been?" she said. "Oh!" she added as she noticed Houdini, and without waiting for further explanation, went on, "Your father's been called out to a cow, and he's taken Mike with him, and I have a dentist's appointment. So you'll have to tend the office till he gets back. I know it's your birthday, dear, but it can't be helped. He probably won't be long now."

"But what about the kennel chores?" I asked. "I can't do both."

"Oh dear! I'd forgotten them," said Mother. "Jane dear, I guess you'll just have to put off your ride and do them."

Jane gave an outraged yelp, but Mother was full of instructions for me and paid no attention. "There's nobody in the waiting room now," she said, "and I've left a sandwich and a glass of milk in the office. And Mrs. Johnson's Doberman is ready to go when she comes for him. The bill is on the desk."

Father's office hours are from one to four o'clock and during this time he doesn't often get emergency calls where he needs Mike; but when he does, somebody has to answer the phone and try to keep people in the waiting room happy till he returns. Since these sudden calls to duty are almost always inconvenient for at least one member of the family, I once asked Father why he didn't get a secretary. He said he didn't need one with such an efficient family, and anyhow he'd rather support two ponies than a secretary. I've made no protests about tending the office since then; but the extra kennel chores were too much for Jane today.

"I'm always having to do the kennel chores," she protested. "It's Phil's turn. If I have to stay, why can't *I* tend the office?"

"Well, dear," said Mother, "Phil's a little older and

knows more about the business. And you're not always tactful, you know. Remember what you said to Miss Peckham."

I snickered. Miss Peckham had phoned one day to inquire for the health of her Pekingese, who was in hospital at the time, and Jane had taken the call. In response to Miss Peckham's questions, Jane had reported, "Oh, she's all right. All that's wrong with her is that she's too fat anyhow." Miss Peckham had required some soothing.

"Well, it was the truth," said Jane with a disgusted look at me. But she knew it was no use arguing and stamped off toward the hospital with as much dignity as she could muster.

"Since you're going to the kennels anyway, please take Houdini with you and make sure he's locked up tight, will you?" I said.

"He won't come with *me,*" replied Jane, taking another step toward the kennels.

"He will if you take his collar," I said.

Jane turned and glared at me, then looked at Mother, and without a word, stepped back and took Houdini's collar.

"Go on, Houdi," I said. Then *he* gave me a dirty look and went off with Jane.

"You'd better run along too, dear, before the telephone rings," said Mother. "And do wash up before anyone comes; you don't look very tidy. If you get bored, you can open Aunt Serena's box. The expressman left it in the office with some kennel supplies this morning." We had been notified at the time of Aunt Serena's death that we were heirs to a box labeled "Family Items," but it had taken some time for it to reach us.

I said, "O.K., thanks," without much interest. Then I added, "Good luck with the dentist," whinnied mournfully at Jones, and followed my sister. Jones's answering whinny verged on a shriek and he rolled his eyes in a way that suggested I'd better exercise him soon and thoroughly if I didn't want to take a spill or two.

4. "*Dr. Birdsong's Office*"

A few minutes later Jane stuck her head into the office where I was sitting at Father's desk, thumbing through a card file. "Hippo the Drippo, think you're smart, don't you?" she said. Then with further inspiration, "Hilarious Hippo the Drippo!"

"Plain Jane the Pain," I retorted promptly. I've always found that a neat phrase, but it wasn't very satisfying; I'd used it too often. So I tried "Felice the Fell Feline," which is a little less stale, but she merely made a face and chanted contentedly, "Hilarious-arious Hippo."

It doesn't seem to matter to Jane what I call her; being a fell feline merely amuses her, and Plain Jane has no sting, because she's a very pretty little girl, blonde and blue-eyed like Mother.

So to the repetition of Hilarious Hippo, I merely replied, "You'd better get to work. Have you got the water pans out yet?"

"Yes, Sir Hippo, I have," she replied. "They're in the steamer. And guess who's in the hospital?"

"Bozo," I replied. "I was just looking up his card."

"Oh, you knew," said Jane. "You got second sight?"

I ignored this and extracted Bozo's file from the drawer in front of me on the desk.

"Did you know he's in isolation too?" asked Jane.

"Oh no!" I replied. "Not something contagious!"

"It's probably just a precaution putting him there. It usually is," said Jane. She came to the desk and read out loud over my shoulder, "Admitted September 30, 3:00 P.M.; temperature 103°; heart and lungs O.K.; no visible injury; lassitude. Diagnosis?"

"So Father doesn't know either," said Jane. "What's lassitude?"

"Languor," I replied, feeling sure she wouldn't know that word either. But, as often happens, she fooled me.

"Oh, you mean he's dopey," she said. "He does look that way."

"Poor old Bozo! Let's go see if we can cheer him up," I said.

"Since he may be contagious, we'd have to get disinfected," said Jane. "I only looked through the glass door before." At this I remembered thankfully that I had not touched Houdini, and that as soon as I entered the hospital, I had washed the forehead that Bozo had licked and the hand that had explored his gums with the antiseptic blue soap provided in the operating room. I was wondering if I hadn't better go disinfect the doorknob I'd used, when I realized that Jane had said something else, which my mind had recorded automatically: "Anyhow, you can't leave the phone and I can't take it for you because I'm not always tactful."

I was about to argue this point when the phone rang. "Dr. Birdsong's office," I said in my most businesslike voice. Then, "No, ma'am, he isn't in, but he's expected back shortly. Can I take a message?" As the answering voice went on and on, I grinned at Jane and silently mouthed the syllables "Do-lor-es," which make up the ridiculous name Miss Peckham gave that Peke of hers.

Jane had been quoting Father when she said the dog was too fat; but nothing could stop Miss Peckham from overfeeding her darling. Consequently Dolores was forever getting sick and having to stay in the hospital, where her treatment consisted mainly of exercise and a rigid diet. She did not enjoy her visits with us, and neither did we; she was such a hysterical yapper and nipper. Only Mother sympathized with her. "Imagine giving the poor creature a name that means pains and sorrows!" she said. "No wonder she's sick so much." Mother doesn't have to handle the animals. She says running the house and answering the phone and taking the office in a pinch is enough to keep her out of mischief.

The voice on the phone finally stopped, and I replied,

"Yes, Miss Peckham. Of *course* a thumbtack is very serious. I'll have my father call you the minute he comes in."

Jane was giggling as I hung up. "Has Dolores sat on a thumbtack?" she asked.

"Worse than that," I replied. "Miss Peckham thinks she's swallowed one."

"Oh-oh!" said Jane. "Father will be up all night with her. That Peke! She's so used to being stuffed, I suppose she'll swallow anything she can get in her mouth."

When Miss Peckham phoned, she often phoned more than once; so I decided I had better wait till later to see Bozo, but I did get a paper towel and antiseptic from the operating room and wiped the doorknob I'd used, just in case. Jane had returned to her chores, but a few minutes later when I was back in the office, I saw her peering through the small glass in the door leading to the kennels. I paid no attention to her, but continued to slowly remove the cord from a good-sized carton I had hoisted onto the desk. Jane promptly bounced back into the office demanding, "What's in that box?"

"Aunt Serena's things," I replied. "Mother said I could look at them."

"I'll help you," said Jane, advancing eagerly upon the box. She can never resist a package of any kind.

"Oh, no you won't," I replied. "Look at the clock." The afternoon kennel chores are supposed to be completed by four o'clock, and they generally are. My father is an Englishman and believes in discipline for children. His motto is "Make 'em mind when they're little, and make 'em work when they're old enough." He says this is an infallible formula for the prevention of juvenile delinquency and he regrets he can't apply it more widely, but Jane and I, he promises, shall never suffer for lack of it.

Jane looked at the clock, which said ten minutes to four, and then mutinously back at me. "It's not fair!" she protested. "Here I am stuck at home doing your work, and you sit here just—just wallowing in idleness! You ought to be doing the magazines at least." Jane referred to the various animal magazines that Father subscribes to mostly for the entertainment of people in the waiting room. Since I'm a quick reader, I have the job of skimming through them and noting down any articles of possible interest to him.

"The magazines can wait," I replied. "I should think I might have some fun on my birthday, if you can call this fun. After all, I'm stuck at home too, and I wanted to try out my new saddle."

"Why didn't you have a party if you wanted some fun?" demanded Jane.

"I'm too old for that now," I replied grandly, and then added not so grandly, "Anyhow all my friends are too busy to come; they're all at football practice—except Sam Paine."

"Oh!" said Jane. "Sam's too gangly and wears glasses, and you're too small for football, I suppose. I hate being undersized, too, but I guess it's worse for a boy. You've just got to put up with it, though, if you're a Birdsong."

"Not necessarily," I replied. "All Birdsongs aren't midgets. And don't forget, I'm not only the smallest boy in my class; I'm the youngest too. I've plenty of time to grow yet."

"But look at Mother and her family," said Jane. "Oh well," she added, "perhaps you won't mind being small when you're grown up. Father doesn't seem to; he makes out all right."

Father is not really a midget, of course, but he's not much over five feet tall, and that's an inconvenient height for a man, especially for one who has to deal with large animals. That's why he picked a giant like Mike for an assistant, though he really makes up for his smallness more through his own skill than Mike's help. His ability to control high-strung horses without force is so remarkable that the grooms at the racing stable are superstitious about it, and even the owners won't employ other veterinarians, though they used to call them in from all over the state and beyond before we moved here. As Jane said, Father does make out all right despite his size; but all the same I'd like to be a normal height, and on this day of troubles I was depressed by Jane's calm assumption that I never would be. So, without replying to her last remark, I went on opening Aunt Serena's box.

Jane watched me quietly for a moment or two and then said briskly, "I'll tell you what. I'll hurry and finish the chores and then I'll saddle both ponies. Then as soon as Father gets back, you come out to the paddock and we can start right off for Still Waters. You don't have to change your pants, do you?"

"No," I said, looking down at my rather grubby slacks, "these are ready for the laundry."

"Good!" said Jane. "Dinner'll be late tonight since it's a birthday dinner. We should be able to get around the race track once and still be home in time unless Father's awfully late. O.K.?"

"O.K." I replied. "And I'll only take a quick glance through some of the old documents that Father said would be in this package. We can look at the other stuff after dinner."

But the phone rang even before I could get to the documents. This time it was the Major. "That you, Phil?" he said. "Will you just tell your father that Bozo *hasn't* had a distemper shot as far as we know? The one we thought was for distemper turned out to be for rabies. Caleb has a certificate for it."

"Oh-oh!" I said. "That'll turn Father's hair gray. Distemper in the hospital is one thing a vet can do without—and hepatitis and leptospirosis are two more. Dogs are immunized to all three in one shot now, but distemper's the worst. Still, it's easier to cure than it used to be, and Bozo was put right into isolation anyhow."

"That's a blessing," said the Major. "Caleb's very much upset about the mistake; he thought Bozo had everything he needed in the way of shots. Those things are so complicated nowadays. How's Jones?"

"Fine," I replied. "Raring to go. Jane and I are coming over as soon as Father gets back from a call. I'll bring you the latest on Bozo."

"Good!" said the Major. "See you later."

As I hung up, I heard a car in the drive and looked out. Mrs. Johnson had come for her Doberman. I had to get him because he snarls at Jane. While Mrs. Johnson was paying her bill and I was receipting it, a new client with a kitten came into the waiting room. I asked her to wait and was just making out a file card for her when the phone rang again. It was Miss Peckham. The thumbtack had been found in the vacuum cleaner bag. I congratulated Miss Peckham and crossed her message off the desk pad just as Father and Mike drove into the parking space.

Father was not as disturbed about the Major's message as I had expected. "We'll have to take every precaution, of course," he said, "but it just doesn't seem like distemper—or hepatitis or leptospirosis either—to me. Time will tell. You can come out with me on late rounds if you like and see how he is then, but meanwhile just leave him alone; the quieter he is the better."

When I got to the paddock, Jane complained that Jones had sneaked up behind her and butted her so hard with his head that she had fallen over. "He seems to think he's a goat," she sputtered, "except that he laughed like a hyena. I'm glad I'm not riding him today."

"You'll wish you were when you see us sweep past you and Evans on the track," I said, and then added as I swung into the saddle and Jones started off on his hind feet, "if I'm still one of the party."

Jones did a few more dance steps and then settled down to tossing his head as he tried to get the bit in his teeth.

"That must be a good saddle," observed Jane. "You sit a horse just like Father today." For the first time since early morning I felt really pleased with myself and the world.

5. *The Peckham Threat*

The Major lives about two miles across the valley from us at the foot of the mountains. To get there we start off toward Appledore and then take a crossroad that comes out on Foothill Road only a few hundred feet from his house. The crossroad ends with a downward slope where the ponies are always inclined to pick up a little speed. Today, with Jones so full of oats, they really were hard to hold. Still Waters is a second home to them, just as it is to Jane and me, and they like the racetrack as well as we do. It's an old track that's been private property now for many years and has gone back to pasture; but it's still level, the turf is firm, and the Major's stock, with some help from our ponies, keep it mowed.

The Major calls his animals his stock; so the rest of us do too, though I'm never quite sure whether the name is meant for a joke or not. They were all lined up along the front pasture fence to greet us with a strange mixture of cries as we passed. The two white geese had spotted us first. They were the noisiest of all, and though they were the first in line, they left their place and tried to keep pace with us, pushing their way around or under the other animals. Placid old Betsy, the retired roan work horse whom the Major had rescued from a life of drudgery, hung her head over the fence and nickered softly. The spotted Nubian goat—she was a gift—thrust her head through a square of wire and bleated in a bass voice, her two kids, one on each side of her, following suit with their heads a couple of squares lower and their voices a couple of octaves higher. The shaggy little Highland cow, whom the Major had imported from Scotland with some idea of propagating the breed in New England, stood with her head stretched protectively over her calf and lowed plaintively. And finally some belated ducks came quacking up busily as if congratulating themselves on having arrived in time for the fun after all.

The only one missing was Moonlight, a tall and knobby dappled gray mare whom the Major had bought at a riding school auction for fifty dollars. She and the Major were waiting for us at the racetrack. Moonlight is not a racer—she rarely goes faster than a long, shambling trot—but with her assistance the Major often acts as track supervisor, starter, and timer for Jane and me. He does the job in style with a cap pistol and a stopwatch.

Jones and I not only won the race that day, but broke our previous record for the course. I was so pleased with the victory that I let Jane blame her defeat on Jones's extra oats without argument. But as we walked the ponies around the track to cool them off, with the Major and Moonlight between us as usual, I began to realize uneasily that the Major was not himself at all. Ordinarily he's about the easiest adult to talk to that I know, but now he was silent and unresponsive. I thought he must be worried about Bozo; so I tried to set his mind at ease. "I wouldn't worry too much about Bozo," I said. "He really doesn't seem very sick, and Father doesn't think he has distemper or any of those bad contagious diseases. A hundred three isn't much of a fever for a dog, you know."

"I know," said the Major with a sigh. "And perhaps it's just as well he's confined at present anyhow."

I turned toward the Major in astonishment, recalling as I did so his mention at the school of "a little trouble" he'd been having—apparently with Bozo; but he gazed straight ahead and his long nose drooped so mournfully over his mustache that I hesitated to question him. Jane saved me the trouble. "Why, what's poor old Bozo been doing?" she asked.

"Miss Peckham says he's been chasing Dolores and made her sprain a hock," replied the Major despondently. "I can't understand it. Bozo's not a mischievous dog."

"Oh, that Peke!" said Jane. "She's a pain. She sprained her hock all right—we had her on our hands for several days last week—but she's so fat she's always spraining something. I don't believe Bozo ever went near her. He wouldn't be bothered."

"I wouldn't think so either," replied the Major, "but Miss Peckham says he did. So the last few days I've tried to keep him with me—on a leash some of the time—when I could, and I've had to confine him when I couldn't, and I hate doing that."

"I should think so!" said Jane. "Poor old Bozo! But why do you pay any attention to Miss Peckham? She's always fussing about something. Nobody bothers about her except Father, and he has to because he's her vet."

"I'm afraid I have to bother about her too," said the Major. "She's my landlady and can put me out of Still Waters."

We looked at him aghast. "But I thought you *owned* the farm," I said.

"Not quite," replied the Major. "I have a five-year lease with an option to buy, but it's a queer sort of option. It's really Miss Peckham who has the option to sell. It's the old Peckham home, you know, and she's sentimental about it. She said she wanted to be sure it went to a suitable person who'd take proper care of it; so she decided to try me out for five years before signing away her rights. She's found me satisfactory till now, and she told me last spring at that birthday party she gave for Dolores—you remember I took Dolores a blue satin bow and some chicken livers on your advice? Well, she told me then that she would sell to me when the lease expired so that it was safe to make any improvements I wanted to, and of course I *have* made the workshop and the pond for the stock. But she hasn't signed anything but the lease, and she said the other day that Bozo was a disgrace to the neighborhood. Of course I didn't have Bozo last spring, but I have him now and I won't give him up; it's unthinkable. Even if I could bring myself to find him a good home on some distant farm—and really I couldn't—Caleb would never forgive me. I don't like the look of things at all."

Neither did we. We knew Miss Peckham. Even Jane was struck dumb for a few moments. It was I who finally spoke. "When does the lease expire?" I asked.

"In about two weeks," replied the Major. "October thirteenth."

"Gosh!" said Jane. "That's simply awful!" Then we walked on in stricken silence.

As the Major dismounted in front of the barn, Caleb came limping out to meet us with a broom in his hand. He has an artificial leg that seems to work pretty well, but he can't walk quite normally. The natural expression of his face is serious, even severe, but today it looked anxious besides as he questioned me about Bozo. I repeated what I'd told the Major, emphasizing that Father didn't think it was a case of distemper.

"Ah," said Caleb consideringly. Caleb's *ahs* are weighty. He speaks slowly and he listens slowly and you have to know him a long time before he gets conversational. This habit, together with his square, serious face, his squarely clipped, kinky gray hair, and his steel-rimmed spectacles give him a forbidding appearance which made me uneasy when I first met him; but when I saw him working with the animals, I knew he was really a very gentle man. Jane claims she knew it all the time.

Caleb gazed at me earnestly as he digested his *ah* and then said, "What do *you* think, Philip?"

"Me?" I asked in surprise. "Why no, I have a hunch it's not distemper—or any of those things—either, but how would *I* know?"

Caleb merely smiled faintly and nodded his head as if that settled something. Then without another word, he led Moonlight into the barn.

The sun was already sinking behind the mountain and the still air of the valley felt suddenly cold as Jane and I set out on our ride home. We were too dejected to talk at first, but as we topped the rise on the crossroad, we stopped of one accord to look back at Still Waters. The shadow of the mountain had fallen on the neat white farmhouse and the huge red barn, but the golden horse weathervane on the barn's ridgepole still sparkled in the last rays of the sun, and half of the quiet old pond in the side yard still gleamed with daylight. We could see the Major busily rounding up his stock and urging them toward a side door in the barn, where Caleb stood awaiting them.

"That horrid old Peckham!" said Jane. "I'd like to stick her *full* of thumbtacks."

"Well, here she comes in the glass chariot," I said. "If you've got your tacks handy, we can hold her up and get to work. I'd be glad to help."

Miss Peckham's house was nearby, across the road from the Major's and about the same distance from the crossroad, in the opposite direction. Jane turned that way and said, "Ugh, that creepy, crawly thing! I hope it doesn't turn up here."

"That creepy, crawly thing" was Jane's disrespectful name for Miss Peckham's venerable but well-preserved electric car, one of the wonders of our countryside. They say that Miss Peckham inherited it from some relative who had kept it under a tarpaulin in a barn for fifty years. It glided about our valley with stately deliberation and ghostly silence, displaying Miss Peckham and Dolores to the best advantage through its oversized, highly-polished windows.

"It won't," I replied. "She's heading past the Major's toward the state road. She gets off the dirt roads as soon as she can. I suppose with those hard tires, she and Dolores feel every pebble. But it would be fun if she did come this way. We could escort her all the way to the Appledore road. A steady trot would do it nicely. She'd love it."

"Well, I wouldn't," said Jane. "Remember what happened last week when she sneaked up on us." We had been waiting to cross the state road when the glass chariot had glided up beside Evans. He had been a little skittish and I had grabbed his bridle so he wouldn't bolt with Jane.

"You weren't really scared, were you?" I asked in surprise.

"No, not really," said Jane, "but you know how she went into town and told everybody she met that we were too young to be riding on public roads."

"So what?" I said. "She's always telling somebody something like that. You say yourself that nobody pays any attention to her."

"Except Father," amended Jane. "He heard about it and asked me yesterday what happened. When I told him, he said I was to watch out for the glass chariot and keep out of its way until he had a chance to train Evans not to mind it."

Father had trained both ponies to be unconcerned about all normal traffic, including airplanes, but it hadn't occurred to anyone that the "creepy, crawly" glass chariot might present a special problem.

It had passed the crossroad while we were talking and was rolling majestically past Still Waters as we turned home again. The sight so exasperated Jane that she shook a fist at it in parting and spent most of the ride home thinking up extravagant plans for thwarting Miss Peckham and saving Still Waters for the Major. She wanted to kidnap Dolores and make the ransom Miss Peckham's signature for the sale of Still Waters, or to keep Bozo under cover at our place and make Miss Peckham think he was dead so she'd sign of her own accord. But I knew that wouldn't do. As I pointed out to Jane, the Major is an honorable man.

6. *The Ancestral Recorder*

As Jane and I were closing the stable doors at home, Father came out of the hospital and joined us. He was sympathetic but not reassuring when we told him about the Major's plight. "I remember now that Miss Peckham *was* sputtering about Bozo when she brought Dolores in with that sprained hock," he said. "But I was busy and didn't pay much attention. Of course I didn't know that she was the Major's landlady. I never heard of a reversible option before," he added, "but trust the Major to get involved in something like that."

Jane bristled at this. "Don't you *like* the Major?" she asked. Jane is always ready to stand up for her friends, and she's especially defensive about the Major because some people call him a nut and laugh about his fad for walking and his stock and the model boats he makes and sails on his pond. Jane says they're just jealous people who don't know how to enjoy themselves and should be ignored. But she doesn't ignore them; she always has to give them a piece of her mind, and she was prepared to do battle even with Father if necessary.

Father, however, just smiled and said, "Of course I like the Major. I like nothing better than innocent children and animals."

"But the Major isn't either," said Jane. "Phil says he's an honorable man."

"And Phil's right for once," replied Father. "I'm glad you listen to him now and then. The Major is an innocent child and an honorable man and therefore a ready-made victim for more artful natures. But right now Miss Peckham is stirred up about something she can't blame Bozo for. She called again to announce that she thinks the thumbtack she found in the vacuum cleaner is *another* thumbtack and that the first one is very likely in Dolores."

Jane and I groaned. "Is she bringing her in?" I asked.

"I hope not," replied Father. "She said Dolores was resting comfortably; so I said to let her rest. Of course if she shows signs of pain, she'll have to be X-rayed. We may have her with us yet."

We had been walking toward the house as we talked

and were now greeted at the back door by Mother and instructed to wash quickly because dinner was ready. I did pause to tell her briefly about the Major; but the dinner that followed soon took my mind off him and all other troubles of the day.

Mother is the best cook I know, and she had cooked all my favorite foods for me, including a fancy kind of chocolate cake that nobody else in the family likes much. Jane brought it in from the kitchen, holding it high and walking with a stately slowness so that the lighted candles on it would keep burning steadily.

Jane lowered the cake carefully to the exact center of the oblong table. It was also the exact center of the space between her place and mine, since we face each other across the table's width. Then she hustled Mother through the rest of the table setting for dessert, and as soon as they were both seated, said briskly to Father, "Time for the count!"

Father started, "One . . . two . . . three . . . four . . ." The numbers fell at long, regular intervals with the maddening slowness of drops from a barely leaking faucet. Jane squirmed and whispered, "The candles will burn out," but they were all still shining brightly when the count ended at thirteen. A moment later they were all out and I was glaring at Jane through writhing wisps of smoke. "Why did you have to go and blow too?" I demanded. "You're not supposed to. It's not *your* birthday."

"Oh, I just had to," replied Jane. "We've never had so many candles before; you needed help. And anyhow you really needed two wishes. I had to do the other one for you."

As I scowled at her with that helpless feeling arguing

with Jane so often produces, I saw her lips form the words *Bozo* and *Major*. How did she know what I'd wished? I wondered what Miss Norcross would think of Jane's ESP.

Meanwhile Father was saying, "Wishes are all very well, but you know what makes them come true."

"Work!" said Jane in a weary tone.

"Discipline!" said Mother in a stage whisper.

"Responsibility!" I crowed.

"Elbow grease!" shrieked Jane.

"Application!" said Mother with a splendid imitation of Father's voice and manner.

"Perseverance!" I shouted, flourishing the cake knife. We were all laughing by now, Father the loudest. I cut a good-sized wedge of cake and offered it to him. He shook his head, but I kept holding it out and started to intone the familiar sentence, "In *this* house—"

Then I stopped, scared by my own recklessness; but Father reached for the cake and finished for me with a grin, "—everybody eats what he's given without fussing." Then he added, "I've heard of eating humble pie, but this is my first experience with humble cake." He ate it all as we cheered him on. We've called that kind of cake "humble cake" ever since.

At the end of this riotous meal I was pleased to learn that, even though I'd escaped the kennel chores, I was to have a birthday exemption from helping with the dishes. At Mother's suggestion, I went out to fetch Aunt Serena's box from the back porch where Mike had put it. As I stepped from the kitchen entry onto the porch, I drew a sudden deep breath. The chill that had settled over the valley with twilight had turned frosty, and in the light of a full moon, the drive gleamed white except where the sharp shadow of the house fell across it. And everything was uncannily still. Not a leaf stirred. Softly I closed the door and crossed the porch. With my hands on the cold railing, I looked up at the sky above the stable roof. There is a cupola on the stable and on its peak a wrought iron weathervane—a pointer with a forepaw bent and a streak of a tail straight out behind. Tonight the pale sky glowed behind every sharp black edge of the weathervane so that I could see it more clearly than in the daylight. A distant dog barked. Then the whole valley seemed to hold its breath and I with it as I strained to catch some faint sound in that deep and secret stillness. It seemed to me that there must be something yet—some small thing usually lost in the noise of the world—that at last I had a chance of hearing. And I heard it—distant, tiny, but clear and joyous—a high trill; then a cascade of notes without melody but wonderfully rich and sweet; then the trill again, fading away as if some fabulous singing bird had flown past high, high above the valley.

Suddenly the spell was broken as the world about me came to life with a whicker from the stable, a bloodhound bay from the hospital, and a soft thud on the railing beside me as Pounce joined me. I returned the whicker softly, but I felt obliged to answer poor Bozo with my sharp whistle for fear he'd set all the dogs in the kennel barking. Pounce I spoke to quietly and ran my hand down his back and tail as he walked past me on the railing. He stopped at the corner post and stared at me a moment, his yellow eyes glinting copper in the moonlight. Then he dropped to the ground and disappeared among the shadows.

The haunting music I had heard still tingled through me. Where had it come from? Had I imagined it? I shook my head decidedly to that. I had sensed it was there when I listened for it, and, in a way, it had sounded familiar as if I had half heard it before. It had been there all right; it was just a question of being able to hear it. And wasn't that the way ESP was supposed to work? But what did the music mean? Faced with that unanswerable question, I suddenly realized that I was shivering and, glad of some exercise to warm me, started to haul Aunt Serena's box indoors.

It was a long, deep carton and quite heavy, but since it was narrow, I wrestled it through the doorways without much trouble and hoisted it onto the dining room table. While I waited for Jane to finish in the kitchen, I sat down and pored over a browned old manuscript I found in a manila envelope near the top. The title puzzled me. It read, *History of the Birdsong Family of Dorset*. I had always understood that Father's family in England lived not in Dorset, but in Shropshire near the Welsh border. The old-fashioned curlicued handwriting of the manuscript was hard to read, and the history it related proved to be very dull—it was really just a list of names copied from parish registers—until I came to the last page. There I sighted a familiar name heading a long paragraph.

Just as I finished reading, Father came into the dining room. He is not interested in ancestors; he says they're for people who have no descendants to keep them busy. But I had found something so remarkable that I thought it might impress even him. "You know what?" I asked, stopping him on his way to the kitchen.

"No. What?" he said with a smile.

"It's no wonder you're so set against magic."

Father's face registered exaggerated patience. "I'm not

set against magic," he said. "I'm only set against *believing* in magic. There's nothing wrong with nonsense if you don't mistake it for sense."

"I know," I said hastily, anxious to forestall a lecture I'd already heard many times. "I mean it's no wonder you're so set against believing in magic."

"Of course it's no wonder; I'm a sensible man," said Father. Then he grinned and said, "O.K., I'll bite. *Why* is it no wonder?"

"Because an ancestor of yours was convicted of sorcery in 1640. That's how the Shropshire Birdsongs got started, according to this family history. He had to leave Dorset in a hurry."

"How did he manage to if he was really convicted? I should think he'd have been hanged or burned or whatever they did," said Father.

"Listen to this," I said. "It's a quotation from some old record:

> 'Two sturdy knaves dragged him to the stake and began to bind him thereto with chains, when a mighty tumult arose among the beholders, for that they were set upon by three raging beasts, a screaming black pony, a monstrous slavering dog, and a fearful hissing cat. These demons blasphemed in human voices and kicked and bit and scratched all who came in their way, until they reached their master at the stake, who, as those who bound him fled in terror, leapt free of his chains with hellish laughter, and sprang upon the pony's back. Whereupon the pony rose into the air above the heads of the multitude, and galloping northwards, soon faded

from sight together with the great dog who bore the cat upon his back. So vanished the little black man with his familiars from Dorset and never was seen there more.' "

"But they were seen in Shropshire, I gather," said Father. "How were they received there?"

"It doesn't say," I replied. "But what do you suppose the sorcerer's name was—besides Birdsong, I mean?"

"Hilary?" said Father.

"Oh, you knew all the time!" I said. "Why didn't you ever tell me?"

"I didn't know he was almost killed for sorcery. If I had, I'd have told you the story as a horrible example of what can happen when people believe in such nonsense, wouldn't I?"

"Yes, I guess you would," I admitted. "But how did you know his name?"

"I didn't," replied Father. "I guessed. When you were born, Aunt Serena wrote me a letter to congratulate us not only on your birth, but on your name too. She said she was glad to learn that I took an interest in my ancestors after all. So of course I knew you weren't the first Hilary Birdsong."

"Oh!" I said. It was just like Father to leave it at that. He never says much about Aunt Serena, though he lived with her a couple of years when he first came to this country. The most we have ever heard about her was his statement, "She was a very worthy and generous old lady, but we could not agree on several matters." One of the matters was apparently the importance of ancestors. But the coincidence of this ancestor's name was more remarkable than he knew, and I was determined that he should appreciate it. So, as he was moving toward the kitchen, I added, "His name was Philip too."

"What?" said Father. "Another Hilary Philip? That's odd," he added with a frown. "I thought people didn't have two given names in those days."

"Well, I'm not sure he used them both at once," I answered. "Perhaps Philip was an alias. Anyhow, he was Hilary in Dorset and Philip in Shropshire, 'though undoubtedly the same person,' the *History* says."

"A sensible precaution, considering his record," observed Father.

"There's a footnote in newer-looking ink on the 'little black man,'" I said. "It says, 'the *black* refers to the swarthiness so common among the Birdsongs, which is said to stem from a Celtic or possibly a gypsy strain.' Gosh!" I added as I looked up at Father and as we grinned at the sight of each other's black hair, black eyes, and dark skin. "Do you suppose we really *are* gypsies?"

"If so, we must be exceedingly diluted ones," replied Father. "But who cares? There have always been what the villagers at home called 'black Birdsongs,' and I suppose there always will be, but it's hopeless to try to find out why. Save your brain for something else." He tapped my head with his knuckles as if to reassure himself that it housed a brain, and went on to the kitchen from where I heard him announce that he was going to "take another look at that cow." A couple of minutes later I heard the hum of the old jeep station wagon leaving the hospital, as Mother and Jane came into the dining room.

My mother, of course, showed more interest in the coincidence of the two Hilary Philips. "I remember that

kind she calls silly. So I replied, "Oh, skip it. I'll keep this one."

I worked the cover off the labelless tube and discovered a roll of large, heavy papers curled inside it. I pulled them out and peeled off the top one, spreading it out on the table to examine it. It proclaimed in magnificent lettering that Serena Chillingworth Birdsong had been graduated with honors from Miss Stoughton's Academy for Young Ladies. I let it bounce back into a roll and looked over at Jane. From the other case she was pulling something swathed like a mummy in a long strip of oily cloth. This she carefully unwound and then stood frowning perplexedly at the slender black tube in her hand. There was a line of holes in it and one end curved to a point.

"What is it?" asked Jane.

"I think you blow it," I said. I had picked up its case and was deciphering the label glued to it. The handwriting and ink were like those in the *History,* but were almost worn away. I was finally able to read out, "Flute à bec or recorder said to belong to Hilary (or Philip) Birdsong, and conveyed by him, concealed on his body, in his flight from Dorset to Shropshire."

"Well, fancy that!" said Mother absentmindedly, as she continued to rummage among the things on the table. I did fancy it if fancy means imagine, and I went on to wonder who had later put the flute in the metal tube and labeled it and whether he and other Birdsongs had carried it about with them. That label certainly looked as if it had had more wear on the backs of galloping horses than it could ever have gotten lying around in trunks. A piercing squeak interrupted these conjectures; Jane was blowing into the flute.

I put my hands over my ears and groaned, but she went on blowing. When I tried to snatch the flute from her, to my astonishment I lost my balance and had to clutch the table for support. My head was swimming, and the high squeals that Jane produced seemed to swell and vibrate strangely inside it. I slid into a chair, and propping my elbows on the table and my head in my hands, I looked hopefully across at Mother. Surely, I thought, even she couldn't stand such a noise for long. But Mother was still heedlessly busy with the lace.

"Mother," I said, purposely speaking in a low tone. "What does *bec* mean in *flute à bec?* It's French, isn't it?"

"What dear?" said Mother. "Jane, dear, do stop that noise. We can't hear each other."

I shot Jane a triumphant look and repeated my question.

"Yes," said Mother, "I think it means *beak*."

"The blowing end does look like a beak," I said. "And what an appropriate instrument for a Birdsong! But those awful screeches Jane makes are no birdsong. They make me feel sick."

"Too bad about you, Hippo," said Jane. "It's the sour grapes that make you feel sick. Why don't you read your nice rolls of paper?"

"What do you mean, sour grapes?" I demanded. "It's my flute; I drew it."

"Prove it," said Jane.

"Why, you know its tube was the one with the label!" I said indignantly.

"Prove it," said Jane with a wicked smile. "And anyhow," she added, "you said I could keep it."

"I did not!" I fairly shouted. "I said—"

"Hush, children!" said Mother. "Don't quarrel about that pipe. You can take turns at it somewhere where it won't annoy your father. Let Phil have it now, Jane. I want you to try on this darling little old-fashioned dress. If it fits you, it will be just the thing for the play. You'll look sweet in it."

The look Jane gave me was anything but sweet, but she did need a costume for a school play; so she let me escape upstairs with the flute. As I took the stairs two at a time, I had forgotten all about my strange flash of dizziness.

7. *Sensations New And Strange*

The stairs in our house zigzag continuously up, landing by landing, from cellar to attic. The cellar and attic flights, which are plain and bare, live a private life behind closed doors, but the staircase in between is on display and rises from the front hall in gloomy grandeur. Its wood is very darkly stained and the banisters are quite ornate. A crimson stair carpet enlivens the gloom a little, and the landing, where the stairs turn, has a stained-glass window and a window seat with a tufted crimson velvet cushion, though nobody has sat there since the telephone was removed from the landing to the hall below and an upstairs extension added beside Father's bed.

Jane and I, unawed by all this splendor, used to leave the doors open and race the whole way from cellar to attic, arriving at the top breathless and dizzy after the five right about-faces necessary to reach it. Memories of these races spurred me on tonight as I sped up toward my pleasantly secluded quarters on the third floor. But my speed was checked on the second floor as I turned right toward the now closed attic door; and even as I put my hand on the knob, a glimpse of the window on the landing recalled another memory so strong that it stopped me completely. I even stepped back down a couple of stairs to get a better view of the figures in the stained glass.

The chief of these is a young Pan sitting on a rock under a tree and playing on a reed pipe. Against his goat legs a lamb is curled up asleep, and all around him on the ground are attentive animals—a fox, a deer, a rabbit, a sheep—and up in the tree are two oversize squirrels and a strange creature that seems to be some kind of wildcat. Mother says this window, as an unusual and well-preserved relic of the Victorian age, is probably the most valuable thing on the premises, but it's not what you'd call a work of art; in fact, the numerous figures are so roughly outlined and so peculiarly colored that they make most people grin. So the fascination the window had for me when we first moved into the house became a family joke.

After I had been found a couple of times sitting on the

stairs or kneeling on the window seat examining the scene, it occurred to Father that the subject might be puzzling me; so he had me look up Pan in our big dictionary. When I finally located him and read out that he was the Greek god of flocks and wild animals and had invented the shepherd's pipe, Father thought the matter was settled; but what really fascinated me about the window was the odd sensation it gave me. I once asked Jane, when we were both inspecting it, if she didn't feel as though somebody in the picture was looking at her. She replied, "How could they be? Pan's looking at the lamb, and all the animals are looking at Pan."

Jane's argument was so unanswerable that I felt foolish and deliberately avoided looking at the picture for a time. Soon, like the rest of the family, I came to accept it as one of the oddities of the house and passed it several times a day without giving it a thought. But tonight I remembered vividly that feeling of strangeness the picture had given me, and I examined it closely again for the first time in years. I quickly spotted what had attracted my attention; it was Pan's reed flute. In the window it's a bright green (Father says, "Why not? Reeds are green, aren't they?"), but otherwise it looked remarkably like the recorder in my hand. I looked from one to the other, thinking how oddly memory works, when I heard Mother and Jane below. A glance over the banister showed them approaching the stairs, weighed down with all they could carry of Aunt Serena's things. Before I could be detailed to carry the rest, I stepped back to the second floor and slipped through the attic door, closing it softly behind me.

Tonight, as usual, I felt a kind of secret satisfaction in shutting myself into my own private domain. Of course I can't claim the whole attic, but since my tenth birthday the best part of it—the bedroom and bath—has been mine, and I've acquired by squatters' rights the space under the eaves where I store useful odds and ends. All that's left is the trunk room and some open attic.

As I turned from shutting the door, I couldn't resist jerking the bellpull that dangled invitingly beside it. The resulting clang of the cowbell fastened outside my bedroom door was reassuring. That's one of my inventions that goes right on working. My mother summons me to meals with it; my father summons me to work with it; and my sister—well, Jane is really too enthusiastic a summoner. She contributed the handle of an old jump rope for the bellpull, and she takes such a proprietary interest in it that she ducks in and gives it a tug almost every time she passes by.

I have been forbidden to lock the attic door since the time I forgot to unlock it and couldn't be roused for breakfast; but I could lean over the stairwell and raise the bellpull beyond Jane's reach. I considered resorting to this strategy for a moment and then gave up the idea; Jane would have a real mission tonight. If she couldn't reach the bellpull, she'd come up and bang on my door to demand the recorder, and she'd be within her rights. It even occurred to me that if my birthday hadn't been entirely satisfactory to me, it had been no picnic for Jane either, and I resolved to pay back my kennel chore debts promptly and in full.

There was no need to turn on the old overhead light to find my way about my bedroom that night, for slanting bands of moonlight from the rounded turret windows lay upon my desk, which just fits within their semicircle. And through the dormer window the pale radiance of the sky lightened the space near my bed. I could have shivered again at the sight of that frosty light; but it wasn't really cold in my room. I could hear the comfortable hiss of the old steam radiator against the front wall as it spread its warmth about. I sat down at my desk and switched on the lamp, noting that my desk clock said 8:30; that gave me half an hour before late rounds when I could see Bozo. Then I turned my attention to the recorder, which I still held in my hand, though I had dropped its case and oily wrapping on the foot of my bed as I passed by.

The little instrument was made of a black wood that I thought was probably ebony, and was worn to a buttery smoothness delightful to the touch. As I rubbed my thumb lingeringly over its surface, the thought came to me that the flute might be terribly old—older even than that Hilary in the sixteen hundreds. But perhaps not, either, for there on the back, inlaid in yellowed ivory, a piece or two of it missing, was an odd insignia that surely identified it as his property. Within the outline of a five-pointed star was an H-P monogram and on the peak of the star perched a tiny bird, its head raised and its beak parted as if in song. Above this hieroglyph was a hole like those in front. Carefully I adjusted my fingertips over the front holes and a thumb over the back one and blew into the "beak." To my disgust the note I produced was not much different from Jane's shrill squeaks. But I kept trying, lifting my fingers from the holes one at a time and in different combinations until I produced some sweet, soft notes. I did not succeed that first night in playing even one octave of a scale, but I made a start on *Silent Night* and played the first four notes over several times.

I would have tried harder and gone farther if I hadn't been prevented by a return of that strange dizziness I had felt earlier in the dining room. The more I played the worse it got. I began to feel weak and trembly, and sharp pains shot up and down my left leg. Uncomfortably reminded of how scarlet fever had felt—that was the only sickness I had ever had—I put down the recorder and stumbled over to the bed. I lay down and closed my eyes, but opened them again almost immediately, for I had not closed them on total darkness but on some dim place full of sharp smells and strange yells, where I had a frightened feeling of being shut in. I decided that I must be very sick indeed and was wondering what to do next, when I began to feel better. I tried closing my eyes again and this time I closed them on total darkness.

I lay still for a few moments recovering and listening to a bewildering, muffled hubbub that might have been a faraway version of what I had just heard, when the cowbell clanged vigorously. I got up cautiously, but felt perfectly all right; so I opened the door and looked down the stairwell. It was Jane, but instead of demanding the recorder, she said, "There's a frightful row in the kennels, and Father isn't home yet. Mother says will you please see what's the matter. I should think you'd have heard the racket even on your side of the house."

"I hear it now that you've opened the door," I said, "and I thought I heard something before, but I didn't know what it was."

"Well, for Pete's sake!" said Jane. "I should think you'd know what a kennel sounds like by now."

"It sounded different somehow," I said perplexedly, as I started downstairs.

Jane stepped back, holding the door for me and then shutting it as I turned my back on her and continued on down to the ground floor. As I turned again at the landing, I looked up and caught her eye. "I've got to go to bed," she said, "but let me know if it's anything exciting."

"Like what?" I asked.

"Oh, burglars or something," said Jane.

I scoffed at the idea of burglars, but I detoured through the living room and borrowed the poker from the fireplace, just in case. It didn't seem much of a weapon, but it's apparently the favorite of people who have to deal with burglars.

The moon made it so light outside I took the short cut through the park and stopped in the shadow of a maple to reconnoiter. My teeth were chattering with the cold, but still I lingered a moment or two to check for any signs that somebody else was about. There were none that I could see. The old building looked peaceful in the moonlight, its slate roof almost white, its fancy cornices extended by their own sharp shadows on the front wall. The noise coming from it, however, was terrific. Apparently every boarder and patient had joined in the wild chorus, and Bozo's voice led all the rest. But as I listened, I noticed that, for all its power, it quavered strangely; its higher notes sounded like a cry of pain. Completely forgetting the possibility of burglars, I hurried into the hospital and made straight for the isolation ward, snapping lights on as I went.

When I opened the door and spoke to him, Bozo stopped baying immediately and began to revolve his tail; but before the full cycle was complete, he hit the side of his metal pen with a resounding bong, gave an anguished cry, and slumped down on his side. I started toward him, but then remembered this was the isolation ward. "You wait, Bozo," I said. "I'll be right back."

I turned toward the main kennels and whistled my special shushing whistle, but it was only partially effective; Bozo's yells must have been extraordinarily exciting. So I had to make a special tour past all the pens, admonishing a couple of persistent barkers, a musical tomcat, and a cairn terrier who seemed to be practicing bloodhound yells and not doing so badly considering her size. Houdini, I noticed, was lying relaxed and he greeted me with a virtuous air, though I felt sure he had contributed generously to the noise. When I had checked and hushed them all, I returned to Bozo, on the way hastily slipping into the long-sleeved, zippered coveralls and the smooth, light rubber boots that are required costume in isolation.

Bozo's eyes were shut and he was breathing very fast. When I spoke to him, he jerked and twitched a little as if he were dreaming. When I opened the door to his pen, he raised his head and looked about him in a bewildered way. Then he sank back again with a moan and closed his eyes. He was plainly very sick and I was worried, but there was nothing I could do for him. I knew that Father would notice the lights as soon as he turned into the drive; so I settled down to wait for him. There isn't any chair or stool in isolation—it's a very bare place because of the disinfecting problem; so I sat on the floor with my back against the wall and my feet almost against the door of Bozo's pen.

As I sat there watching his uneasy sleep, I was dismayed to feel some of those peculiar sensations I had had earlier when I was trying to play the recorder. This time I didn't feel so sick—just dizzy and uncomfortable—but I was plunged again into a world of unfamiliar noise and smell. I didn't hear any yells and barks now; instead a faint background noise of rustling and high-pitched hums and squeaks was dominated by three musical notes of a strange richness. They were successive notes on a descending scale and were repeated again and again. The smells were overpowering, but different from the former ones. Before, a strong smell of disinfectant had predominated, but this time the only one I could attempt to describe was like a mixture of damp woods on a warm day and a freshly-cut lawn; but the vague smell of decay I had often noticed in woods was now divided into several sharply defined smells, and there was even more than one kind of grass smell. I was reminded of the little boy in Jane's class who had recently gotten glasses and had astonished everybody by exclaiming enthusiastically, "Why, I can even see the leaves on the trees!" I felt as if I had magnifiers on my nose and ears, but I couldn't quite tell what I was smelling and hearing. My attention was distracted, too, by some vague shapes before my eyes. They were something like the afterimages you see when you've been gazing toward a bright light, only these weren't colored.

Suddenly a new smell, some kind of animal smell, overwhelmed the rest. I closed my eyes in order to concentrate on it and, if possible, identify it. Immediately I was in different surroundings. The vague shapes came into slightly better focus and took their part in a complete picture, for my eyes now saw what my nose had been smelling and my ears hearing, but they saw poorly and colorlessly. Television must have looked like this to that boy before he got his glasses. And strangely I seemed to be acting in the picture myself. My head was down near the ground beside a big bush—*hanging* down, apparently, though I felt no discomfort; it seemed as much at home in that position as a quadruped's. As a movement some feet away to the left caused me to look up, I saw a large, squarish, glittering object, and beside this and partly behind it loomed a tall, solid human figure from which projected a thin, shiny thing pointed toward me. At a rustle in the bush and another wave of animal smell, my eyes turned back again. Then almost simultaneously I heard a pop, a dreadful howl, and an ear-splitting shriek, and saw a small object hit the ground a few feet in front of me, and felt something like a bee sting in my left leg.

I opened my eyes with a start to find Bozo closing his mouth and looking at me sadly. Then his head flopped down on the floor, and a voice said, "Just what's going on here?" Father, his black bag in his hand, was standing in the doorway looking from Bozo to me.

I started again and scrambled painfully and dazedly to my feet. "It's Bozo," I said. "He's awfully sick."

"So I see," said Father, "but what's wrong with *you?*"

I smiled what must have been a sickly smile and replied, "Oh, I was waiting for you and I just had a nightmare, I guess." I knew I'd not been asleep, but it was the handiest explanation I could offer at the moment.

"You look as if you were still in it," said Father. "Too much birthday dinner, I suppose. I noticed you were feeling peckish tonight, but I thought *your* stomach was proof against anything. For heaven's sake, move about a little and pull yourself out of that nightmare. I may need your help with Bozo."

8. Groping Around In Bozo's World

While Father went to put on his isolation togs, I paced up and down the small room trying to pull myself together. The mysterious pain in my leg had disappeared and I felt quite normal physically, but my mind was still in a turmoil. I kept frantically trying to make some sense of my evening's experiences. They had been eerie and frightening: first the dizziness in the dining room, then that awful feeling of sickness and pain in my room, and now this crazy, dim television show I'd just been taking part in. Suddenly I caught myself muttering, "Three Blind Mice," and realized that I had identified those three persistent musical notes that were still echoing in my ears. Had somebody been playing the beginning of *Three Blind Mice* the way I had played the beginning of *Silent Night?* If anybody had, it was Jane, of course. But how could I hear her way out here in the hospital? The recorder's sound was too light to carry that far. But what else could it have been?

A clank in the hall and a loud exclamation cut these speculations short and made me alert enough to dodge a collision with Father as he lurched suddenly into the room. He steadied himself against Bozo's pen with one hand and with the other brandished something at me accusingly as he shouted, "Phil, what in—in thunder is this doing here?" It was the poker, which I had left leaning against the door frame in the dimly-lit corridor.

"Oh-h-h!" I gasped guiltily. Then, as I felt my face reddening, I mumbled, "Mother sent me out here because there was an awful racket, and Jane thought there might be burglars."

Father looked from me to the poker and back again. Suddenly he laughed. He has a large, melodious laugh for so small a man, and I have always found it irresistible no matter what mood I'm in. For a moment or two we both leaned against the wall and laughed to our hearts' content. That laugh scattered the anxieties of the day as a romping dog scatters a flock of feeding crows, so that when Father took his thermometer from its case and said, "Get a good hold on his head and shoulders; he's only half-conscious and may be startled," I knelt beside Bozo intent on my job and comfortably convinced that Father would cure him of whatever he had.

Bozo's temperature was just below 106°. As Father thoughtfully shook the thermometer, I surprised myself by saying decidedly, "It's his leg—his left hind leg. It hurts like sixty."

Father looked at me perplexedly. "How do you know?" he asked. "Did you see him limp?"

"N-no," I replied. "But when he bonged his tail on that side of the pen, it hurt him."

"Perhaps it's his tail," said Father.

"No," I said with conviction, "it's his leg. He lies on his right side all the time and spares that leg."

Father's gentle, skillful fingers slid under the coarse, wavy hair on Bozo's leg. Bozo moaned, jerked his leg, and howled. "You're right, Phil," said Father. "There's inflammation there. I'll have to shave the spot to tell what's what, and that will mean anesthetizing him." He looked at his wristwatch and added, "I was late tonight, but it's not quite 9:30 yet, and you don't have to go to school tomorrow. We'd better do it now. While I'm getting things ready, get your mother on the intercom and report what we're doing. She's probably wondering what's become of you—and me too, for that matter."

I paused uncertainly at the door. "What about these clothes?" I asked. "Can I wear them to the office?"

"You can if you want to," replied Father, "but you might as well take them off for good unless you're cold. You spotted the trouble, and whatever caused it, it's pretty certainly not contagious, thank heaven!"

When I returned from the office, Father was waiting

with his syringe, having already clipped a spot on Bozo's foreleg for the injection. I held Bozo again, but he offered no resistance and was soon out cold. He is a heavy dog, and unconscious he was a dead weight and seemed to be all legs, but the hospital equipment is designed to deal with such loads when Mike isn't on duty. All we had to do was ease Bozo onto a low-slung baggage truck, wheel him into the operating room, and then ease him onto the operating table, which can be lowered almost to the floor. Actually Father did the wheeling, and I followed along with the electric clipper.

Under the bright light of the operating room I stood and stared in fascination at Father's hands as they worked. Anyone can use an electric clipper with a little practice, but he uses one so quickly and deftly that it seemed as if poor old Bozo could hardly have felt it even if he'd been conscious. The shaved patch revealed a dark red lump, the size of the long half of a large egg, and in the center of the lump a darker speck. "You see that?" Father said, pointing to the speck with the delicate point of a probe. "Something entered there and caused an infection."

"What? A thumbtack?" I guessed, remembering Dolores. Then suddenly I remembered from my "nightmare" the thin, shiny thing pointed toward me, the pop, the bee sting—and I knew. "Oh, it was BB shot!" I said. I didn't quite say, "Of course," but the way I spoke must have implied it. Father looked at me with a puzzled frown and then said dryly, "I'd thought of that. Perhaps I'll find out for sure."

A few moments later he held the upturned palm of his hand toward me. A tiny discolored ball, obviously BB shot, rolled on it. He said nothing at the time, for Bozo was beginning to show signs of life, and the wound had to be tended. But when Bozo was back in his pen (Father said he might as well stay in isolation where he'd probably be less noisy than among the other patients), and I was cleaning up the operating table, he stood in the doorway smoking his pipe and watching me quizzically. "I wish you'd tell me," he said, "why you were suddenly so sure there was BB shot in that lump. Anybody'd think you'd seen it go in."

"It was just a hunch," I muttered, spreading antiseptic on the table with elaborate care.

It wasn't the right answer; Father doesn't believe in hunches. He claims all his bright ideas are reasoned. "You wouldn't have put it there yourself by accident, would you?" he asked.

I looked up at him indignantly. "Of course not!" I said. "I wouldn't shoot toward Bozo or any other animal. It was that ghastly Peckham woman."

"How do you know?" asked Father. "Did you see Miss Peckham do it?"

"Well," I mumbled, "she has a BB gun and she claims Bozo chased Dolores."

"Have you seen the gun?" asked Father.

"Well, yes I have," I answered hesitantly. "At least," I amended, "I *think* I have."

"So," said Father, "you *think* you've seen Miss Peckham with a BB gun, and it follows that she shot Bozo. Really, Phil, I thought you had more sense than to jump to conclusions that way. You mustn't make such groundless accusations. And Miss Peckham is *Miss* Peckham. Do you understand?"

"Yes, sir, I understand," I replied, scrubbing away industriously.

A few moments later I cast a sidelong look at Father. He was grinning. As I caught his eye, he said, "I'd like to see Miss Peckham with a BB gun. I shouldn't wonder if she's a good shot."

I restrained myself from saying, "She is." I merely grinned.

We went back to Bozo before we shut up the hospital for the night. He was conscious and moved his tail when I spoke to him.

"I'll give him a pill to keep him comfortable for the night. And I'd better phone the Major and tell him what we found," Father said.

"Bozo'll be all right, won't he?" I asked.

"I hope so," replied Father. "He's a pretty sick dog. That infection has been developing for some time, but he's strong, and penicillin does wonders."

It was still quite light as Father and I walked back across the park, but there was a difference in the air. The cold and the shadows were not so sharp, and I could hear a little rustling in the trees, "A breeze coming up," said Father, "—east, probably. Today has been a weather-breeder. We're in for rain, I expect."

As I was on my way upstairs with instructions from Father to go to bed immediately and sleep as long as I liked in the morning, a hushed hail from the darkness of Jane's room stopped me. I stepped inside and, standing by her bed, gave her a whispered account of Bozo's operation. Then I asked, "Were you playing the recorder while I was out there?"

"Sure," said Jane. "Why not? It was my turn."

"I thought you were supposed to be in bed," I said, sounding as severe as it's possible to sound when whispering.

Jane made an exasperated sound like "pooh" and then added complacently, "Mother was in the sewing room and never noticed a thing. I went up to your room and closed both doors so I'd be soundproofed. I sat at your desk and played a tune."

"What tune?" I demanded.

"*Three Blind Mice,*" she replied.

"All of it?" I asked.

"Well, no," she admitted. "Just the beginning."

"Just three notes?" I asked.

"No, six," said Jane.

"Three," I said. "You just repeated them."

"Six," said Jane.

"Then I played eight," I said. "I played the first four notes of *Silent Night* and they're repeated too. It's more of a tune anyhow."

"It is not," said Jane.

I realized that our voices had risen; so I said "Sh!" and then asked, "Did you feel all right while you were playing?"

"What?" asked Jane, apparently puzzled.

I repeated my question.

"Of course I felt all right," replied Jane. "Why not?"

"I've felt sort of funny myself this evening," I said.

"You ate too much," said Jane. "You just stuffed yourself at dinner."

"The same to you and many of 'em," I replied. "You had—" I paused as I heard a voice downstairs say, "Do you hear voices somewhere?" This was followed by footsteps; so I took off my sneakers and went upstairs as silently as possible.

That uncanny recorder was lying in the center of the blotter on my desk. I eyed it doubtfully for a moment, then picked it up gingerly, hastily rewrapped it in its oiled rag, put it in its tube, thrust the tube to the back of the bottom drawer of my desk, and shut the drawer with a good, hard push. I then went to bed with commendable speed, but not immediately to sleep.

As I lay on my back with my eyes closed, the wonderful feel of the flute's wood was still on my fingertips and the first three notes of *Three Blind Mice* echoed in my ears, reminding me fleetingly of the strange yet half-familiar music I had heard on the back porch. That had been light and quick and gay, of course, in contrast to Jane's monotonous and flat-footed production, but the richness of tone was curiously similar. On this night of mysteries, however, I dismissed that first marvel from my mind to consider the startling discovery that twice while the recorder was playing I must have heard, smelled, seen, and felt with Bozo's senses. Or was it three times? I had certainly felt rather sick when Jane blew a few notes in the dining room, but I hadn't heard or smelled or seen anything unusual; it must take prolonged playing to get the full effect. And just what was the full effect? Had I actually *been* Bozo twice? What a spooky idea! And yet how else could I explain what had happened?

Suddenly I sat up in bed and rubbed my head till my hair stood on end the way I always do, to the amusement of any onlookers, as I near the solution of a difficult problem. Then I remembered. I had not been Bozo because *I had not bayed*. I had heard with Bozo's ears, I had smelled with his nose, I had seen with his eyes, and I had felt with his nerves, but I had not given that awful howl. I lay down with a sigh of relief and grinned to myself. Perhaps after all there was some scientific explanation for my eerie experiences, even though that *flute à bec,* which I couldn't help thinking of as a magic flute, must be responsible for them.

Somewhat reassured, I settled down to consider calmly this most recent sample of Bozo's sensations I had experienced. The reason I had not felt sick as I had before was obvious; I had tuned in on a feverish dream memory. My guesses about Miss Peckham and the BB shot were wild in a way, but when I made them, I felt convinced I was right; and now, as I reviewed what I had witnessed with Bozo's senses, I realized that my guessing was inspired by real, though imperfectly grasped knowledge. The large, angular, glittering object I had dimly sighted to the left was, now that I recalled it at leisure, unquestionably Miss Peckham's glass chariot. I remembered its sharp odors of wax and glass polish. And of course the tall, solid human figure pointing something shiny, which popped like a BB gun from the ambush of the chariot, was just as unquestionably Miss Peckham.

Stimulated by this confirmation of my guesses, I now recalled what must have been the mountain ash in Miss Peckham's front yard. Yes, and across the drive at about the spot where Bozo must have been, there was a large lilac bush. Well, then, that settled it. Bozo had been innocently sniffing about the lilac bush and that horrible Peckham had potted him, deliberately, and as a teacher of mine who is studying law would say, with malice aforethought. And now look at the state he was in!

For a few moments I was overcome with anger, and nursed thoughts of revenge. I ought at least to report Miss Peckham to the A.S.P.C.A. But then there was the problem of proof—proof that Miss Peckham had shot Bozo and proof that Bozo was innocent of chasing Dolores. Proof was hopeless, of course, and though I was sure as sure can be of Miss Peckham, a doubt crept into my mind about Bozo as I recalled further details of the shooting scene. Just what had Bozo been doing in Miss Peckham's yard? There had been that strong animal smell around the bush, and then at the very end that scream and the small body landing on the earth a few feet away. I had forgotten that in the excitement of my other discoveries, but now I realized gloomily that Dolores had entered the picture. She was the small object and had uttered the ear-splitting shriek.

So Bozo *had* been chasing Dolores after all, and she had sprained her hock at the same time he got his infection. Father said that Bozo's trouble had been developing for some time. Still, there was something wrong with that argument. Bozo had been following a strong scent, but was it Dolores's scent? I felt somehow it wasn't, but how could I tell? I had smelled what Bozo had smelled, but I had no practice identifying such smells. But—but—.

I sat up and rubbed my head again. Bozo had *not* been tracking Dolores. Goodness knows what he had been after—a rabbit perhaps (I must take a good sniff of the next rabbit to come my way), but certainly not Dolores, for she had at that time an obnoxious, perfumed smell. We noticed it when she came in with her sprained hock. It seems that Miss Peckham had put flea powder on the creature and then had objected to the smell. So she had sprayed Dolores with toilet water, much, she claimed, to Dolores's satisfaction. I closed my eyes and concentrated. Yes, I was sure Bozo had caught a whiff of that perfume when Dolores landed several feet in front of him, and it certainly wasn't anything like the smell he had been investigating.

Then what had happened? Dolores hadn't *run* onto the scene; she had fallen into it, and off the marble bench behind the lilac bush, of course. I ought to know that bench. I had to cut Miss Peckham's lawn once when her odd-job man was sick, and she made me lie on my stomach and trim the grass under the bench by hand for fear I'd nick the marble with the mower. Yes, and she said it was Dolores's favorite outdoor spot; she liked to lie on the bench in the shade of the lilac. She would! Well, that cleared Bozo. He had been tracking something not Dolores, and Miss Peckham had shot him, and he howled and startled Dolores so that she fell off the bench and sprained her hock.

Once more I raged at the infamous Peckham. But what could I do! I could hardly denounce her on the strength of a vision, however convincing the vision was to me. I soon turned my thoughts to the more practical matter of how to protect Bozo from her when he was at large again. Over this project, I fell asleep and dreamed that Bozo, Jones, and Pounce were all singing like birds at each other.

9. Bozo Starts Transmitting

I awoke in the morning to find myself huddled deep in the bedclothes and a cold east wind blowing across the bed from the dormer window. I rolled over and peered groggily around a mound of quilt at the sky. It was so pale a gray that I judged there would be no rain for a while yet. Then, after raising myself enough to look over the foot of the bed at the electric clock on my desk, I burrowed back into the warmth to consider the state of affairs. My mind was on Bozo and the quickest way to find out how he was.

Jane would have found out; she's an early riser. But it was after nine and Mother was sure to be shopping, and Jane would most likely be with her. Jane has the strangest taste for shopping; I can't imagine anything more boring, but she says she likes meeting all the people in the stores. So I'd have to get dressed and go out to the hospital to get any news of Bozo unless—.

I got out of bed, closed the window, and made for the desk, instinctively leaping from island to island of rag rug to keep my bare feet off the cold floor. I hesitated a moment with my hand on the pull of the bottom drawer. Then I yanked it with such resolute vigor that, instead of opening grudgingly little by little as it usually does, it popped out suddenly and the front end fell on the floor. The recorder was in it all right; it was no dream, but could it really do what I thought it did last night? I picked up the metal case and leapt shivering back to bed.

Propped on my pillows, I piped the first four notes of *Silent Night* a couple of times and followed that up with a few random notes as I fumbled around trying to go on with the song. But I soon cut these short as I began to see vague shapes, to smell strong smells, and to hear loud sounds, chief among these last a bloodhound yell. I closed my eyes and found that I was looking up through wire mesh at a huge human figure that was undoubtedly Mike, colorless and indistinct as he appeared. In an unusually resonant voice Mike said, "What's the matter, boy? You want some more milk?" Another melodious bay answered these questions, and as its echoes died away, the scene and smells faded too.

I sighed with relief; Bozo was better, and the magic flute still worked. It had seemed really rather sinister last night, but now I was excited by its possibilities—and its problems. It would appear that with the help of the recorder I could tune in on Bozo whenever I chose. But could he tune in on me? And that reconstruction of Miss Peckham's crime last night, was that just a feverish dream, or could he have been trying to send me a message? If we could only exchange messages like that, I could—why, I could save Still Waters for the Major just by persuading Bozo to stay away from Miss Peckham and Dolores! I reveled in this wonderful possibility for a few moments before I came down to earth and remembered I wasn't even sure that Bozo and I could establish two-way communication. I cast about in my mind for some test to settle the matter. Finally I thought of one I could try right away. It was rather elaborate, but it should work if Bozo was well enough to be hungry.

I dived under the bed for my slippers, but, as usual, I could find only one; so I hopscotched around the bed to my battered old chest of drawers and rummaged till I found a pair of heavy socks. I pulled them on and padded down the stairs. I opened the attic door cautiously and listened to make sure I was alone in the house. Nothing stirred. I lost no time whisking down to the kitchen and back, grabbing a plate of bacon and eggs from the warming-oven and a fork from the table en route.

When I got back to my room, I picked up the recorder from the bed and settled with my breakfast in the old Morris chair by the radiator. Then, to get this scientific experiment started, I began to blow any old notes I could get. As soon as Bozo began to bay, I stuffed a forkful of egg and a piece of bacon into my mouth and closed my eyes. Before I knew what had happened, I had swallowed my mouthful of food without chewing it at all and was reaching ravenously for more. At no other time in my life have I felt so hungry. The smell of bacon and eggs was so overpowering that it made my mouth water; I had to swallow so that I wouldn't start drooling.

Before I could get another forkful, however, vague shapes coming between me and the food reminded me that this was an experiment, and exerting all my will power, I closed my eyes again (as I reached for my breakfast, I had opened them without thinking) and sank back in the chair. The shapes promptly arranged themselves into a clouded television version of me opening the door to Bozo's pen with an echoing, bell-like clang and setting the deliciously-reeking plate of bacon and eggs on the cement floor with a sharp clink which somehow included an incredibly high and delicate tinkle and a couple of quick squeaks rather like the sound of skidding chalk on a blackboard. This simple scene, which had background sound effects of quick, excited panting, faded quickly, leaving me dazzled, but sure of two things: Bozo was able to tune in on me, and he had sent me a very plain message.

I put the recorder down on the desk and hastily pulled on some clothes. Then I sped downstairs, breakfast in hand, on my way to the hospital. As I hurried through the back door onto the porch, an outraged squawk warned me that, though Mother and Jane were still gone, I was not alone. Pounce had apparently parked himself right by the door and had been shoved back as I flung the screen open. I paused to apologize, and Pounce, instead of stomping off with an injured air as I would have expected, purred and rubbed his whiskers on my hand. Then we both ran down the steps and took off in different directions, he toward the stable and I across the park.

Father and Mike were in the operating room, which fortunately I didn't have to pass to reach Bozo. I found him panting and drooling. At sight of me he raised his nose to bay, but I shushed him and put the plate on the floor of his pen, noticing as I did so how complicated the noise it made really was. Bozo gobbled up my breakfast in nothing flat. Then he grinned at me and began to rotate his tail, but with the first bong he whined and lay down again. I went into his pen to console him. "Cheer up, Bozo!" I said as I stroked him. "You're much better already. And you won't be lonesome or bored while you're here. You and I are going to be busy." Bozo licked my hand and closed his eyes with what I took to be a contented sigh.

I had a few words with Father and Mike and then managed to smuggle my plate back into the kitchen, where I drank my orange juice and hunted up some more breakfast. I had just settled down to a large bowl of shredded wheat when Mother and Jane returned, laden with the weekend marketing. Mother looked from me to the rinsed plate on the drainboard and shook her head. "Really, dear," she said, "I can't understand how a boy your size can put away so much food."

"I'm getting ready to change my size," I replied, keeping my eyes studiously directed to the spooning up of the cereal.

Jane gave me a teasing grin and murmured something about young Hippo, the football hero, as she draped her jacket over a chair and started emptying the bags and sorting the items into groups. I always like to watch Jane do a job like that; she's so quick and silent and systematic. By the time Mother was back from hanging up her coat, all the things that needed to be washed were ready for her on the counter by the sink. Jane was stowing other things in the refrigerator, and a couple of moments later I could see her on the step-stool in the pantry, busily packing groceries into the cupboard. Next she gathered up the bags and papers from the table, stuffed them into the old wood stove, struck a match to them, banged down the lid with cheerful finality, and was off upstairs in a flash, not forgetting to take her jacket with her.

Mother turned from the sink as Jane whisked out of the kitchen, and we smiled at each other. "She's like an orderly tornado, isn't she?" I said. "What energy!"

"Well, dear," said Mother, "as far as energy goes, you don't lack it yourself. And you shouldn't," she added, looking meaningly at my cereal.

It seemed best to change the subject. "Bozo is much better," I announced.

"That's good," replied Mother. "I do hope," she added with a worried frown, "that he doesn't cause the poor Major any more trouble when he gets back home."

"Oh, I think I can take care of that," I replied. "I have a scheme for training him not to go near Miss Peckham's property." I felt fairly sure I could do that now, and I hoped that later I could somehow get enough acceptable evidence to expose the wretched Peckham. With the magic flute, anything seemed possible.

My mother regarded me doubtfully. "Well, I hope your scheme works, dear," she said. Luckily she didn't ask for details of my training program. Just then the clock caught her eye and diverted her. "Oh, it's almost ten," she said. "I've missed the news every hour so far. This time I should be able to get it." She turned on the kitchen radio, which, after humming a few moments, treated us to a burst of martial music. While she waited for the program to change, Mother busied herself with the things on the drainboard and left me to my own reflections.

These, of course, were about Bozo. I was eager to begin his training, but he was still feverish, Father had said, and would probably sleep most of the day. It wouldn't do to disturb him; I'd have to postpone my experiments. Meantime I had the lawn to mow, and this afternoon, if it didn't rain—. I paused in the very act of putting the last spoonful of cereal in my mouth. The radio music suddenly sounded as if somebody had turned the tone control to a sort of super treble, and yet above it all I heard some slow, fluty notes not in time or tune with the band. They were unmistakably the first three notes of *Three Blind Mice*. At the same time the shredded wheat, which I had never thought of as having any smell at all, had suddenly a strong, pleasing fragrance. That was quickly overlaid, however, by a stronger meaty smell. In an effort to locate the source of this new scent, I glanced over toward the sink, where Mother was now washing vegetables. Some dim shapes loomed between us, but I could plainly see a juicy red leg of lamb lying on the drainboard where Jane had left it.

I closed my eyes and immediately saw myself again opening the door of Bozo's pen. This time it was not bacon and eggs, but the whole leg of lamb that I was putting on the floor. I opened my eyes in dismay. The lamb was still safely on the drainboard, of course, but a ghostly vision of it on the pen floor still hovered before me. This was carrying things a little too far. I screwed up my eyes tight and with all the force of my will tried to send Bozo an explanatory message. I imagined my father coming upon the scene in Bozo's pen. He scowled ferociously, snatched the lamb from under Bozo's nose, seized me by the scruff of the neck, and marched me down the corridor, across the park, up the porch steps, and into the kitchen. Here he brandished the leg of lamb at my mother and pointed balefully at me. Then he marched me up the stairs to my room, pushed me in, and slammed the door. To make doubly sure that Bozo understood me, I invented another sequence in which I was expelled from the dining room as my family sat down to a bountiful meal. I trudged up to my room and lay on my bed, a victim of dire hunger, which I thought could best be conveyed by vividly recalling my sensations when I wanted to eat the bacon and eggs.

Tired by the unusual effort of the imagination required for these dramatic scenes, I looked across at Mother to make sure I wasn't observed. She was still busy at the sink with her back to me. I noticed that the news was on now and that the notes of the recorder sounded quite loud. They had the same peculiar richness they had had last night, but as the player fumbled around trying to get beyond the first three notes of the song, a dreadfully sour note would be sounded occasionally, and then Bozo would bay.

As a new smell assailed my nose, I seemed to see something moving in front of me and closed my eyes again. An extraordinary and confusing picture presented itself. At first it was like a print from a doubly exposed negative, except that one picture was stationary and very dim and the other more distinct and active. The stationary one was simply a large, standing, human figure (Mike, I guessed) through which the active figures moved unhindered. But Mike vanished abruptly before the scene was finished; so I realized Bozo must have shut his eyes. The actors were myself and what appeared to be an enormous St. Bernard carrying a dish in his mouth. This I took from him as he wagged his tail with a circular motion. Not until the tail began to rotate did I realize that the mysterious St. Bernard was merely Bozo's idea of what Bozo looked like and that he was offering me a meal of dog food. It really smelled good enough to eat.

I couldn't help laughing, but I had the presence of mind to open my eyes, so that when Mother looked at me, I must have appeared normal. Since she was listening to the news, she merely raised her eyebrows in inquiry. I pointed to my head to indicate an idea and stepped briskly into the pantry with my box of shredded wheat, which Jane had not removed with the unopened groceries. While there, I pocketed a molasses cookie from the cookie jar, being careful to replace the lid noiselessly. Not that we're rationed on cookies, but I didn't want to call any more attention to my extraordinary appetite just then. Thus equipped, I dashed out to the hospital unquestioned as the news report droned on.

I found Bozo inhaling the aroma of a real dish of dog food and Mike watching him with a puzzled look. "You said he was hungry," said Mike. "So I brought him some food, and look at him! He just smells it and drools. Once he started to pick up the dish, and he closed his eyes for awhile. Do you suppose he can't eat?"

"Oh, no!" I replied. "I think he's just got his wires crossed."

I went into Bozo's pen, picked up the dish, put it down again, and said, "That's yours, Bozo. You eat it."

Bozo looked at me with as puzzled a face as Mike's. I took the cookie from my pocket, let Bozo sniff it, and then began to eat it slowly so that he would know I wasn't starving. He rotated his tail once, fortunately without hitting the wall, and began wolfing his second breakfast.

"Well," said Mike, still looking puzzled, "I hope that will keep him quiet for awhile. He sure has been noisy this morning—been keeping the whole place in an uproar. He ought to be sleeping." Mike is a conscientious worker and likes to have everything running smoothly at the hospital, so it upsets him when any of the animals do anything unexpected.

I assured him that Bozo would be all right after his meal. The recorder, which had been sounding as if it had laryngitis for the last few minutes, had given a final squeak and stopped, and I was determined to keep it from starting again that day.

Mother had left the kitchen, but I met her on the second floor as I made for my room. "What were you laughing at?" she asked.

"Oh, just a crazy idea," I replied, "but it reminded me of something I had to do in the hospital."

"Your father said you were going to mow the lawn this morning," said Mother. "You haven't forgotten it, have you?"

"No," I replied. "I'm just going to get a sweater before I start." I didn't see any point in adding that I was going to hide a recorder too.

"That's right, dear," said Mother. "It will probably be cold riding the mower. And do comb your hair; it's all on end."

"It's the cowlicks," I replied as I always do when my hair is criticized. They really do make my hair unmanageable, but they are also a handy excuse when I have forgotten to comb it.

"I'm afraid your game will be rained out this afternoon," Mother went on. "I just heard a weather report, and it said rain starting about noon."

"I suppose so," I said gloomily. "I hoped to break the sales record today." The freshman class of our high school always has the right to sell candy bars at football games to help stock its empty treasury, and I've turned out to be an unusually successful salesman because of Jones, whom I ride around the field with the candy box hanging from my neck. Everybody can see and signal me from quite a distance, and I can move about fast. At first some people were afraid of Jones because he makes his way through a crowd like a police horse, but they've learned he's harmless and treat him like a mascot now. I get him to charge Sam Paine when we get a chance, and Sam jumps back and generally falls over. Everybody on our side knows it's just an act and laughs, but it scares some visiting spectators stiff. They think we're a pretty cool bunch in Haunceton.

Jane had appeared in the doorway of her room during this conversation, and now she spoke up. "Game or no game, Hippo, remember it's your turn at the kennel chores today."

"I've reserved time for them," I replied loftily. "And I'll thank you to keep out of my room while I do them or any other chores. I don't like people prowling around up there without my permission."

"I wasn't prowling," said Jane. Then her eyes widened. "How did you know I was there?" she demanded.

"You had to go there to get my recorder," I said, "and you sure played a lot of sour notes on it."

"*Your* recorder!" said Jane. "I like that."

"Well, it's Hilary Birdsong's recorder," I said. "If I have to put up with his name, I ought at least to be entitled to his recorder."

"Children, children!" said Mother. "Stop your quarreling! If you can't be peaceable about that little pipe, neither of you will be allowed to play it. You had better get busy with the mowing, Phil, before it rains. And Jane, you had better help him with the clipping or it will rain before he's done."

"But—" said Jane.

"I was going to ask you to help me with some basting," said Mother, "but Phil really needs some help if he's to finish."

"O.K., O.K.," said Jane, who detests sewing. "I'll get my jeans on."

My first act when I got to my room was to yank the bottom drawer of my desk out completely and dump its miscellaneous contents on the floor. Then, with my knife, I carefully pried up its false bottom, disclosing a hard-covered notebook, which I thumbed through for a moment, feeling rather silly. It contained a secret code and a number of messages, coded and decoded, which Sam Paine and I had exchanged a couple of years ago. I had made the false bottom to protect this precious volume (though its most important messages were such commands as "Meet me at the drugstore at 3:30 P.M."); and since I couldn't think of anything else worthy of the hiding place, I had had to pad it with an old torn pillowcase to keep the notebook from sliding noisily around every time I tugged at the drawer.

This padding provided a good nest for the recorder, which I now took from the desk top and examined carefully before stowing it away. I had been puzzled by the weak way it had squeaked into silence, and now I discovered it was quite moist inside from Jane's prolonged blowing. I thought it probably wouldn't work well till it had dried, and decided it was just as well that the airtight metal case was too thick to fit into the secret compartment. I packed it carefully, making sure that both ends and the front holes were exposed to what air would be available. Then I replaced the false bottom and the contents of the drawer. These include a large folded map which pretty well covers the bottom and hides any telltale roughness in construction. As a final touch I tossed in the empty metal case before I pushed the drawer firmly to.

I caught up with Jane on the stairs a few moments later. "I don't believe you know a sour note when you hear it, the way *you* sing," she hissed in my ear. "And anyhow, I'd like to know how you heard any notes at all when Mother didn't hear anything in the sewing room last night."

"Oh, I have wonderful ears," I replied with what I hoped was a superior smile, but I was shaken. I would have to be more careful in the future.

10. A Little Light On A Dark Subject

As soon as we were out of the house, Jane began complaining, as usual, because she couldn't do the mowing. I'm the only one who hears these complaints now, because Father has laid down the law that she can't drive the mower until she's twelve at least, and he won't put up with what he calls nagging. At first when he said she was too young, I offered to build up a pair of her shoes like the ones I use for mowing, only thicker, so that she could reach the pedal and the footrest; but Father said that even if I extended her legs a foot, she'd still be too young, and that was that. So I ride the mower, and she often has to help me with the clipping around the tree trunks and the buildings. I don't blame her for complaining, because clipping is miserable work; but once the motor starts, I can't hear her, and she settles down and does a good job.

A driving mist, the beginning of the rain, started before we were quite through, and by the time we put the tools in the stable, the little tendrils that always spring up from Jane's curly hair in damp weather were covered with tiny drops. As we were calling the ponies in from the paddock, a sudden wild gust of wind sent heavy drops splattering against the stable windows. "Wow, look at it come down!" said Jane. "There goes your game, Phil. What'll you do instead?"

"I guess I might as well clean the stable," I said uncertainly. We sweep out the stalls every morning, of course; usually Jane does Evans's and I do Jones's, though sometimes one of us does both, as Jane had this morning because I was sleeping late. But on the big weekend cleanup we take turns, and it was my turn this time. There was a chance, however, that I might inveigle Jane into helping me; so I asked, "What are you going to do?"

"I'm going to Ellen's," replied Jane. "She's asked Mary and Linda, too." I might have known! Jane has so many friends and there is such a constant going and coming among them that I can't keep track of them all, but I know Ellen. Jane seems to be the leader of the gang and Ellen, who is also very active and enterprising, her lieutenant.

"Well, enjoy yourself while you're young," I said gloomily, as I looked around at the hay-strewn floor.

Jane giggled at this and replied that she'd help me water the ponies and give them some hay now, though she wasn't obliged to since she'd taken care of them both before breakfast. By the time we had finished, it was pouring so hard that the raindrops seemed to be bouncing up from the driveway as we stood in the big doorway and looked out. We turned up our jacket collars and made a dash for the house.

We arrived pretty wet about the head and shoulders, but otherwise merely damp, and with only the customary repairs to head and hands, were able to sit down hungrily to a lunch of fragrantly-steaming beef stew. I was so happily occupied trying to analyze the smell (a new hobby inspired by my recent experiences with Bozo) and anticipating the flavor, that it was an unpleasant shock to have Father say, as he passed me my helping, "Where's that recorder? Have you got it, Phil?"

"Well, yes, I have," I replied, feeling both guilty and mystified. I didn't see how Jane could know yet that I'd hidden it, and it wasn't like her to complain to Father about it anyhow.

"What's the matter?" asked Father. "You haven't broken it, have you?"

"Oh, no," I replied, "it's perfectly O.K."

"Well, I want it," said Father. "I'm going to take it to Charley Duane."

"Take it to Charley Duane?" I asked, aghast. Father has no office hours Saturday; so he often does odd errands in the afternoon, but why on earth he should want to take the recorder to Charley Duane, who is a radio,

my experiments with Bozo till he was better, made me grumpy and restless. I decided to leave the cleaning of the stable till tomorrow and, despite the storm, to ride over to Still Waters. A ride is always soothing, and perhaps the Major and I could have a game of chess, which he had recently taught me to play. There's no time for mooning when a game's on between us.

That decision made, I completed the chores quite briskly and was ready to leave the hospital when I thought I heard the phone ring. On the chance that it might be for me, I went into the office. The bell wasn't ringing when I got there, but I lifted the receiver cautiously to find out if a call which might be for me had been taken in the house. I heard Jane say genially, "Sure, come right along. He'll be glad to see you. He's only cleaning the stable."

Sam Paine's voice replied, "Thanks! I'll be right over."

They both hung up, and I plunked down the receiver, hurried to the kennel entry, shrugged on my raincoat, and ran across the park to give Jane a piece of my mind, for I was in no mood to clown with Sam. We almost collided in the kitchen entry; she had been on her way to summon me by striking the gong on the back porch.

"Sam Paine's coming," she said. "And where's the recorder?"

"I heard you inviting him on the phone, and you had no business to," I replied. "I was going to Still Waters."

"In this weather!" said Jane. "You said you were going to clean the stable."

"I didn't say so for sure," I answered, "and I'd changed my mind. Jones and I don't mind a little rain."

"Well, you can't go," said Jane. "Mother's gone with Father, first downtown and then to the Bradburys', and I can answer the phone, but I'm to call you if it's an emergency or anything to do with the hospital. So you and Sam had better stay nearby."

"But I thought you were going to Ellen's," I said.

"Her mother thinks she has chicken pox," said Jane. "So Mary and Linda are coming here instead."

"Oh, gosh, what a day!" I groaned.

"I knew you'd be glad to see Sam," said Jane. "But meanwhile where's that recorder? It's not in your desk."

"Not in my desk!" I exclaimed. "How would *you* know? I didn't give you permission to go in my room, much less to rummage around in my desk."

"Well, I did," said Jane unconcernedly, "and I found the metal tube, but I didn't find the recorder. Where is it?"

I looked at Jane severely. "I've put it in a safe place," I said. "It's a valuable antique and not something for little girls to play with."

"Huh!" said Jane. "How would *you* know? Anyhow," she added, "if it's not for little girls, it's not for little boys either. I'd better tell Mother so she can take care of it."

"For Pete's sake, don't do that, Jane!" I said, shaken. "I really think it may be valuable and she might want to sell it for our education or something."

Jane looked alarmed for a moment, but then smiled smugly. "Then hadn't you better tell me where it is?" she asked.

"But Jane," I protested, "you mustn't play it today. It makes Bozo bay every time he hears it, and he needs rest today."

"But how can he hear it way out in the hospital?" asked Jane. "It's not very loud."

"It carries farther than you think," I said, "and you

know dogs can hear more than we can—especially high notes. He howled last night when I was playing and he howled his head off this morning while you were at it. Mike didn't know what had come over him."

"Then why didn't you say so before?" demanded Jane.

"I'm sort of muddled today," I said weakly. "So much has been happening."

"Like what?" asked Jane.

I ignored this question, but went on, suddenly inspired, "If Bozo is better in the morning, I'll give you the flute and you can play it while I go down to the hospital and shush him when he starts to bay. I think I can train him to be quiet when he hears it. If he isn't, Father will soon find out what's the matter and keep us from playing at all when Bozo's around."

"O.K., O.K.," said Jane. "Here are Mary and Linda, anyhow."

Two bedraggled little girls in streaming raincoats were removing their rubbers on the back porch.

I paused long enough to say "Hi!" to the girls and escaped to the stable, where I was soon joined by Sam and his dog Nifty, both dripping as if they'd been in the river. At my suggestion Sam hung his raincoat on a nail beside mine, and Nifty solved his problem by a series of noisy shakes that liberally sprinkled everything within a radius of four feet. Nifty is a bumptious young Irish setter whom we are trying to train to behave himself—at least I'm still trying, but I don't think Sam tries very hard. The trouble is that he and Nifty are too much alike, and when the dog starts clowning, Sam can't resist joining him.

Today Nifty started by chasing Pounce, who jumped onto the open door of Jones's stall and then onto Jones's back, where he immediately became absorbed in washing himself.

"Cool customer, that Pounce," said Sam.

"A lot of cats are," I replied, "but Pounce always feels safe with the ponies anyhow—especially with Jones. They seem to have some sort of understanding. Pounce'll come whooshing in here as if he were late for an appointment, and then all he does is jump into Jones's manger and tuck his paws under him, and then the two of them stare and blink at each other like a couple of old gossips."

"Perhaps he brings the hospital news," said Sam. "Who's come, who's gone, who's had an operation. By the way, how's Bozo? Is he here?"

I explained about the BB shot. "Some careless kid," said Sam disgustedly.

"Maybe," I replied.

Sam whistled. "You suspect a villain?" he said.

I nodded mysteriously and said, "But I'm forbidden to talk about it because I have no proof."

"Ha! the plot thickens," said Sam.

"I'll say it does," I replied. "If you only knew all the dark doings!"

"But your lips are sealed?" asked Sam regretfully.

"They'd better be," I said, thinking not only of Miss Peckham's dark doings, but also of my own. Then, as Nifty was still scrabbling around at the door of Jones's stall, I grabbed him and started drilling him on *Down!*, *Stay!*, *Come!*, and *Sit!*, and he didn't do too badly; but when I turned him over to Sam for the same routine, on the second *Down!* he rolled over on his back with his legs up in the air and wiggled his tail on the floor. Sam then called *Up!* and Nifty bounded up to him and stood on his hind legs with his paws on Sam's chest. It was hopeless after that; so we finished cleaning the stable and Sam helped me get a bale of hay down from the loft. Then we sat on the bale and, through the open double door, watched the rain sweeping across the park and battering the leaves down.

The afternoon was so dark I had turned on the light to clean the stable. It's a naked bulb that dangles on a long cord and seldom stays absolutely still. Today I suppose drafts made it uneasier than usual so that the queer, distorted shadows of Sam and me that it cast on the floor in front of us kept wavering slightly. "It's sort of spooky here, isn't it?" said Sam.

"Spooky?" I said. "How do you mean?"

"Oh, I don't know," said Sam. "The whole place is so old-fashioned, and it looks as if nothing had ever been changed."

"Your ESP's been polluted by that horror movie we saw last month," I said. "Any Victorian building looks haunted to you, I bet. Say," I added as I remembered my surprise at Sam's knowledge yesterday, "how did you happen to know about ESP anyhow?"

"Oh, I have an aunt that's nuts about it," said Sam. "She's always sending us prophecies and revelations in her letters."

"Do they ever come true?" I asked.

"Well, sort of, sometimes," said Sam, "but she has her best luck with her cat."

"Oh?" I asked as casually as possible. "What does her cat do?"

"She tries to hide her newborn kittens, but Aunt Mabel always knows where they are anyhow. She says she just closes her eyes and 'sees' them clear as day. And she 'sees' the cat when it wants to come in, sitting on the doorstep too, though the door doesn't have any glass in it. Oh, she's as balmy as a June morning, but she's a nice old duck; we all like her."

"Does she live around here?" I asked, thinking that was one old lady I'd like to meet.

"No, in Connecticut," replied Sam. "Why? You specialize in aunts or something?" Sam grinned, and I knew he was remembering Aunt Serena's inscription.

"Not exactly," I said, "but they keep popping up. My great-aunt died recently and left us, among other things, a family history; it was ancestors *she* was nuts about. And you know what? My name *is* a family name after all—just by accident, of course." And I told him about my namesake.

Sam was properly impressed. "Gosh!" he said. "That's class, that is. A wizard in the family tree rates way above a cannibal's escaped dinner. Hilary is a name you should be proud to bear. You should let people know about it."

"No I shouldn't," I said, "and you be careful, Sam S. Paine III, or I'll put a spell on you so you'll always sign your name complete."

"You're a hard guy, Hippo," said Sam. "I always thought you were too dark and glinty-eyed for an ordinary garden variety of Englishman, but I never suspected the danger I was in. Say," he added in a different tone, "aren't you cold? It's not very balmy in here when you're not moving around."

"Well," I said doubtfully, "we can go in the house, but it's full of girls."

"Really?" said Sam. "What are they doing there?"

"Oh, they're just Jane's friends," I said. "They're all about eleven years old."

"Oh!" said Sam. Then after a pause he added, "Even so, we might be able to pep up the party some. I suppose they're just playing with dolls or crayons or something?"

"You don't know Jane," I said. "But come on. We can always dive through them and get up to my room." So Sam and I put on our raincoats and dashed for the house as Jane and I had done earlier, only this time a joyous red setter led the way.

While we were stocking up on cookies and apples in the pantry, Sam was startled by thumps and thuds overhead. "What's that?" he asked.

"Oh, just dolls and crayons," I replied. "Come on."

We found Jane instructing her friends in the art of turning cartwheels up and down the second-floor hall, and Sam did not offer to pep things up, but followed me quickly upstairs. Even Nifty, who is usually a joiner, looked startled and scuttled up the attic stairs as if he were escaping some danger.

Sam and I made the bed (which I had neglected to do in the morning) and then sat on it cross-legged and played chess. Though I was the one who had taught him how to play, he beat me every game and finally went off home in high fettle, chiding me jocularly for my absent-mindedness as he left. If he had known that my absent thoughts were principally on his Aunt Mabel, goodness knows what he'd have said.

11. The Plot Thickens

That evening before dinner I went out to the hospital with Father to check on the postoperative patients and Bozo. They were all doing well, and Bozo's tail was rotating more freely all the time. Before leaving the building, Father stopped in the office to tidy up his desk and he handed me the batch of new magazines that had collected on it. "Try to get these checked this weekend so I can put them in the waiting room on Monday," he said. "And don't let them get wet," he added. So I trudged back across the park with the magazines under my raincoat and after dinner settled down in my Morris chair to skim through them.

I had some difficulty concentrating on them, just as I had had playing chess, but practice has made spotting items of possible interest to Father more or less automatic; so I got through a dog and a cat magazine fairly quickly, skipping the show and breed club notes and listing a couple of things as I skimmed the articles and the questions and answers in the veterinary columns. The wildlife magazine is heavier going because it's almost all articles, but I usually skip the *Letters to the Editor* page, and was just turning it over tonight when the heavy print caption above one of the letters caught my eye. It read *Plea for Further Research in Animal ESP*. Eagerly I read the following letter:

> Dear Sir:
>
> In his article *ESP in Animals* in your September issue, Colin Lapwing made a very convincing case for the existence of ESP among beavers and herd animals and even between individuals of the more solitary species, but I was disappointed that he did not extend his acute powers of observation and analysis to the neglected subject of ESP between animals and human beings.
>
> I think there can be no doubt in the mind of anybody who has carefully observed animals and human beings together that communication of this sort does exist between them in some cases. I have been con-

vinced of this ever since, as a boy in Central Europe, I witnessed an uncanny demonstration of it when my father bought a handsome and very tame white stallion from a gypsy. A peasant who worked for us warned my father against the purchase on the ground that the stallion was "bewitched" and would return to the gypsies at the first opportunity; he had done so when sold before. My father took this to mean that the gypsies would try to steal back their horse; so he kept the stallion under lock and key for several weeks until he knew that their band had moved on to an encampment over fifty miles away. But as soon as he relaxed his vigilance, the stallion did escape by jumping a high pasture fence. My father and I with some difficulty traced him cross-country to the distant encampment, where his gypsy master claimed that there had been no theft; the horse had returned of his own accord. We knew that the stallion had made his remarkable journey alone because the people who had seen him (they were surprisingly few) always described him as riderless; but we could not understand how he knew where to go. When the gypsy was questioned on this point, he replied, "What men know, the white stallion knows also." This explanation was hardly satisfactory to my father, but to his astonishment the gypsy offered to refund the price of the stallion, declaring that he would never sell him again. We never knew for sure whether he kept his word, but I did see the gypsy and the white stallion at a fair three years later. There was a large crowd collected around them, and the stallion was doing all manner of tricks requested by the spectators, only waiting after each request for a nod from his master.

Such striking evidence of the existence of this curious affinity between man and beast has not since come my way, but once the mind is alerted to the phenomenon, signs of it are abundant in everyday life. Who does not know someone who "has a way" with animals, and perhaps an especially strong rapport with some particular animal? History and mythology, the twin mirrors of mankind, certainly abound in such cases. Bellerophon and Pegasus, Alexander and Bucephalus, Androcles and the lion, St. Roch and the dog—are not all these cases in point? Even the old belief that witches had as familiars animals with whom they conversed could be classed as an expression of the ancient recognition of human-animal ESP.

Mythology and legend have lately been receiving respectful attention from archaeologists, historians, and psychologists, and I wonder that the latter have neglected the significant body of lore about animal-human relationships. I myself have done some modest research in this field and am fascinated by its possibilities. Being an amateur musician, I have been particularly struck by the recurring association of music with the communication between man and beast. Pan, the companion and protector of animals, played his reed flute to them; Orpheus tamed them with his lyre; and the Pied Piper called forth the rats with his pipe. Anybody who has observed the sometimes strange responses of animals to music and recalls these legends cannot but wonder what obscure influences may be at work; and I don't doubt that other equally interesting characteristics of these tales may be traced by alert and open minds. Let us hope that Colin Lapwing and his colleagues will not long neglect them and their implications.

Yours sincerely,
Ernest Poring

I remembered the article now; that was where I had first met the term ESP. The subject was not one to attract Father, but I had found it interesting. But how much more interesting was this letter! Something about the style of it reminded me of the Major—another amateur musician, I reflected with rising excitement, and an open-minded one interested in science. The very one to consult about my strange experiences now that I had this letter to back me up! I would take both the letter and the recorder and lay the matter before him tomorrow. Meanwhile I had better look up a couple of those legendary names, for I hadn't recognized them all.

Accordingly, I went down to the dining room to consult the big dictionary. Father was using it, but not the proper-names volume, which I took from the shelf and spread on the table.

When Father closed his volume and put it back, he came and looked over my shoulder and inquired what I was looking up. I put my forefinger under *St. Roch.* "You know him?" I asked.

"Isn't he the one who protects dogs?" asked Father.

"He ought to," I replied. "He was saved from starvation by a dog who supplied him with bread."

"Do you think Bozo'd do the same for you?" asked

Father. "It might solve the problem of your perpetual starvation."

"Sure," I replied, "only it might be dog food he'd bring." With that I went back upstairs and to bed, my mind busy with my schedule for tomorrow. The morning promised to be rather congested, what with training Bozo not to bay when he heard the recorder, and finishing up the magazines and probably having to go to church besides; but the afternoon should be free for my private conference with the Major.

These plans were still uppermost in my mind when I awoke Sunday morning, and I noted from my bathroom window that the day had started favorably for them. It was still very wet outside, and more rain threatened; but at the moment none was falling, and Father and Jane were coming back from the stable, Father sauntering along whistling. This meant that both the stalls had been cleaned (Father often helps with the ponies on Sundays, chiefly because he likes to be with them, I think) and that Father was in a relaxed mood; his whistling is a sure sign of that, even though it's a jumbled, disjointed sort of whistling. Actually he whistles very well, but seldom any whole tune—mostly just bits and pieces from old songs he heard in his childhood.

The morning schedule did work out as planned, though I felt pretty silly at breakfast when I had to decline Father's invitation to accompany him on an emergency call some miles out in the country. I said that I had to finish the magazines and go to church; and he gave me a funny look and replied he wouldn't want to interfere with such a worthy program. Jane giggled, of course.

I had time before church to work on Bozo. Jane had

instructions to pause occasionally in her playing, and each time she started up, I was ready and shushed Bozo so that, instead of baying when he first heard the flute, he merely closed his eyes with a blissful expression, all ready to resume what might be called our interrupted conversation. I noticed, too, that there was now no time lag in starting up as there had been at first; we tuned in on the first note, though the connection lasted for a few moments after the music stopped. Toward the end of the session, however, Jane's playing became quite wild (she had mastered the second group of three notes in *Three Blind Mice,* but went to pieces on the more difficult part that follows) and Bozo bayed most dismally when she blew a succession of sour notes. Several boarders, including Houdini and the baying cairn, joined in, but luckily I got them quieted down before Mother complained.

All the time Jane played, I concentrated on conveying to Bozo the need for avoiding Miss Peckham's property. I repeatedly visualized a huge St. Bernard trotting down the road and making a discreet detour behind some bushes opposite her house. Bozo finally replied with a dim vision of the St. Bernard pausing to look doubtfully from the bushes to Miss Peckham's house, as if torn between them. I brought Miss Peckham on the scene aiming her BB gun, and that did the trick; the St. Bernard vanished into the bushes. I was very much pleased with these results. They were due largely, I thought, to my improving style of communication. I now added appropriate sound effects and I even tried to recapture in imagination some outdoor smells, but I was glad to rest from these efforts when Jane finally stopped playing.

I was surprised to have Pounce greet me as I opened

the door to leave the hospital, especially as he was all wet and bedraggled. He hates rain, but it looked as if he'd been out in the downpour that had been pelting the roof of the hospital all the time I was in it. "What's making you so sociable all of a sudden?" I asked as I bent down to scratch his head. "You'd better get into the stable and dry yourself off." Pounce stared at me a moment, his yellow eyes enormous, and then headed for the stable. He kept pausing to shake the wet off his feet at first, but then he gained speed, and as I crossed the soggy park, I saw him bounding across the stable floor in the direction of the stalls.

I managed to get back to my room without having attracted Mother's attention to my absence, and even found time to make some notes for Father on the magazines before I was borne off to church in the Volkswagen with Mother and Jane. And I sandwiched in a little more time on them after church so that when Father asked me at dinner if I'd finished the magazines, I was able to say yes. I also was able to tell him what the morning's sermon was about; I'd expected to be asked. I was silently congratulating myself on this foresight, when Father asked, "Having spent the morning in such an exemplary manner, how do you propose to spend the afternoon?"

"I was thinking of exercising the ponies," I said cautiously. Jane is supposed to keep her own pony exercised, but she has such a busy social life that I occasionally do it for her, sometimes leading one pony while I ride the other.

"Oh, I'll come too," said Jane. "Let's go to Still Waters."

"I thought you were busy," I said.

"Not now," said Jane. "We were going to Janet's to learn to play badminton—she's got a new set—but the weather finished that. It'll be O.K. for riding, though, if we wear our ponchos. The showers aren't very heavy now."

"It seems to me," said Father, "that you're always going to Still Waters. See that you don't wear out your welcome."

"The Major says we're always welcome," said Jane.

"The Major is polite," said Father.

"It's all right, dear," said Mother. "The Major has solemnly promised me that if it is ever inconvenient to have them, he will tell them so. He really does enjoy them, you know."

I said nothing to all this. I certainly didn't want Jane with me when I told the Major about the flute, but I knew better than to object to her company. I'd have to think up some way of evading her.

I had reckoned without Father, though. As we rose from the dinner table, he said, "Phil, come into the den. I want to speak to you." I followed him in and closed the door, wondering nervously what I was in for. "Is there any good reason," he asked, "why Jane shouldn't go with you to Still Waters?"

"N-no, I guess not," I replied.

"Well, then, please oblige me and take her along. She's safe riding with you. The more I think of that trouble with the glass chariot, the less I like it; but I don't want to forbid her to ride alone. She's done nothing to forfeit the right, and besides she was a little frightened when Evans tried to bolt, and I don't want to frighten her more. Do you think she might be safer on Jones?"

"Maybe," I said. "Jones is friskier than Evans, but he's not afraid of anything. He didn't like the glass chariot the first time it sneaked up on him, but he pays no attention to it now."

"That's what I supposed," said Father. "And he might not be so playful with Jane as he is with you. Try her on him if you think it's a good idea, and if she objects, say it's my orders."

"O.K.," I said.

We grinned at each other, and as I turned toward the door, he added, "And Phil, some day when you're by yourself and have time, you might try getting Evans used to the glass chariot, but don't annoy Miss Peckham. You know what I mean."

Again I said, "O.K.," and again we exchanged grins.

"I told Jane I'd train Evans myself, but it's hard to find the time," Father concluded as I opened the door. I left the den much more reconciled to Jane's company than I would have thought possible a few minutes before. I would have to postpone my conference with the Major, but perhaps, I reflected, it might be better to wait till Bozo was home and thoroughly trained to avoid Miss Peckham; then I could prove my claims.

I went to do the kennel chores while Jane helped with the dishes. She finished first and helped me in the kennels so that we could get off to Still Waters in good time. As we were saddling up, I said to her casually, "How would you like to swap ponies today?"

"I'd like it fine," said Jane, "if Jones hasn't had too many oats. Then I wouldn't have to worry about that old chariot. But how come you're willing to give up your precious Jones? You never are."

"I've changed my mind," I said, trying not to smile.

Jane made no immediate reply to this, but I held Jones's bridle as she mounted, and when she was astride him, she gave me a puzzled look and asked, "Is this by any chance Father's idea?"

"Yes," I admitted, "but not exactly his orders."

"Well, thanks," said Jane. "Sometimes it's really handy to have an older brother."

It rained most of the way to Still Waters and it was sloppy underfoot, but we were prepared for this and enjoyed the splashing. "Doesn't it smell good!" I said between showers as we were walking the ponies down a little hill.

"Doesn't *what* smell good?" asked Jane.

"Why the ground and the grass and that bush we just passed," I said. "They smell so strong when they're wet."

"Do they?" said Jane. "I never noticed." She sniffed and then conceded, "Well, there is a sort of damp smell, but you must have a nose like a fox if you can sort smells out that way. I don't know what's come over you," she added. "Yesterday you claimed you could hear me playing the recorder way up in your room. I suppose next you'll be saying you can see people crossing the road in Appledore from our paddock."

"No," I said. "My sight's just ordinary and I don't expect it will improve any." Since we were down the hill, I put Evans into a canter to end the conversation there.

We both had mud on our faces when we drew up at the Major's barn, and having had an argument as to who had the most, we appealed to Caleb, who opened the door to the harness room and called to us to bring the ponies in. He said that Jane's face was decidedly the dirtiest.

"Evans kicked it up on me with those fancy steps he's doing; he's acting like Jones today and Jones is as sober as a parson." She handed me Jones's reins and began cleaning her face with a handkerchief and a handful of water she scooped out of a nearby pail. I left my mud on; I'd just get more going home.

"I noticed you'd swapped horses," said Caleb. "You can't race today, you know," he went on. "The track's too wet and the Major's not here anyhow. He walked into town to pick up the paper and play chess with a friend. But put the ponies in the empty box stall and come visit me for a while. I've a little fire in the harness room."

Jane and I looked at each other in surpise. Caleb was so unusually talkative, and he had never invited either of us to "visit" him before. But of course we accepted his invitation. He and Jane went into the harness room together and I followed when I had put the ponies up and walked around to all the stalls and pens to return the noisy greetings of the Major's stock. It was cozy in the harness room with the warmth of the old pot-bellied stove and the pleasant smell of leather and saddle soap. Caleb sat by the table, stitching some leather straps together with an awl-like device he has for such work, and Jane leaned on the table watching him. "Caleb's making a harness for Starbuck to use next year," she said. Starbuck is the male kid of the Nubian goat's twins.

"He'll be a big husky fellow then," said Caleb, "and can take over plowing the garden from old Betsy. I hope it will be the same garden," he concluded solemnly.

"Oh, don't say that, Caleb," said Jane. "Do you really think you're going to have to move? It just seems like a bad dream."

"Miss Peckham's no dream," said Caleb grimly.

"I know she isn't," said Jane. "But can't she be stopped somehow?"

"I have a plan for training Bozo not to go near her place," I said. "That ought to pacify her."

"If it works," said Jane. "And it will have to work pretty quick—quicker than your training of Nifty by a long shot."

"Bozo's quite a different proposition," I said. "I think I can train him quite quickly."

"How?" asked Jane.

Caleb, who had dropped his work to gaze steadily at me, turned for a moment to her and said, "Never ask a master how he does his work." Then he turned back to me and said, "How quickly?"

"In a day or two, I think," I replied. "I've already begun—I mean," I amended in some confusion, "I've got it all planned and Bozo's coming home tomorrow, you know."

Caleb nodded. "Good!" he said. "Be as quick as you can. It would be a great blow to the Major if we had to leave here. There was a time after Mrs. Featherstone died when I thought we would never settle anywhere again. We went here, there, and everywhere. But when he got this place and began to collect his stock, he stood in the dooryard one evening and looked all about him, at the barn and the house and the pond and the pasture and you two riding your ponies over the brow of the hill, and he said to me, 'Cale, we're home at last. We'll never move again.' "

A heavy silence followed this speech, which was all the more overwhelming coming from the usually silent Caleb.

Then Jane said gently, "Have you always been with the Major, Caleb?"

"Ever since the war," said Caleb. "I was a driver, you know, and I was driving him and another officer the day I lost my leg. He came to see me in the hospital, and when he found out I had no folks left and no job waiting for me, he said, 'When they send you home, get in touch with Mrs. Featherstone. We live in the country and she needs help about the place, if you'd like that kind of work.' Of course I was the one who needed the help, but nobody ever mentioned that. Mrs. Featherstone was a lovely lady," he ended with a sigh.

"I'm sure she must have been," said Jane.

Caleb resumed his work and another silence fell upon us. I broke it this time by saying, "It's hard to imagine the Major as a soldier."

Caleb smiled faintly. "He didn't fight," he said. "He was an interpreter. He was brought up in Germany and can talk like any German. That's where he got his taste for walking, too. He says he used to walk three miles to school and back every day when he was six years old, and he's been walking ever since. No, he's not a fighter, but he's a very brave man, and don't you forget it."

"Oh, I know," I said. "The day the Vickerys' bull chased Jane, he wanted to jump into the field to distract its attention. I had to hold onto his jacket tails to prevent him while I yelled to Jane to lie down and roll under the gate instead of trying to open it."

This incident was so typical of the Major and suggested such an amusing scene, he being so lanky and I so small, that we all had to smile over it, and our conversation then turned to more cheerful subjects, with Caleb falling back into his habit of contributing only a word now and then.

As we were getting ready to leave, Caleb inspected the ponies' hoofs and said they'd soon need shoeing. He's an excellent blacksmith, but has only what you might call a small private practice, including our ponies, because he will not go to the horses; they have to come to him and then only by appointment so as not to interfere with his work for the Major. Even so, there are people who will have no other blacksmith and bring their horses by truck or trailer many miles to be shod.

Jane and I splashed home in a thoughtful mood. Jane wanted to know what Caleb meant when he said, "Never ask a master how he does his work."

"Does he mean there are tricks in all trades that other people aren't supposed to know?" she asked.

"Maybe," I said, "but maybe he means that when you do something extra-well, you can't tell how you do it because you don't know yourself. What would you say if somebody asked you how you manage to draw so well?" Jane is always winning prizes for posters and other drawings.

"Well, I've had a lot of practice," said Jane.

"I had to practice too," I said, "and look what *I* produce." Nobody knows how I ever passed drawing in grammar school.

Jane giggled. "I see what you mean," she said, "but does that make me a master at drawing? I never knew you were a master at training dogs, but I suppose Caleb knows."

I was just as much surprised as Jane was at Caleb's confidence in me, but it gave me a pleasant feeling. "Don't take him too literally," I said. "He just meant I'm better at it than some other people."

"Well, I sure hope you're good enough," said Jane. "Something's got to be done for the Major—and Caleb," she added.

"—and Bozo and the stock," I finished for her.

We had reached the Appledore road by now, and as we turned south on it, Jane suddenly exclaimed, "Oh, *look!*" She was pointing at the western mountains which had been at our backs, and I saw that they were crowned by a strip of pure gold sky into which the setting sun had just started to sink, casting a strange yellow light over the soaked valley. One low, wraithlike, dark cloud was silhouetted against this radiant background, and I knew that Jane's attention was centered on it, for we have always been cloudwatchers.

"It's a bear on his hind legs with one arm raised," I said.

"Oh, *no!*" said Jane, who usually sees something quite different from what I see in clouds. "It's not fat enough, especially the arm, and that's stretching out all the time. It's a woman with a closed umbrella, or maybe a stick."

Whatever it was, the bear-woman soon dissolved into nothingness as the sun came out in its full glory, and no trace of it remained as we turned into our lane and headed for our dripping and glistening stable.

Before supper I shut myself up in my room and had a successful session with Bozo and the recorder. He didn't bay when I started, and I was careful to blow true notes to prevent accidental baying. I cautiously stuck to Jane's theme song, blowing the first three notes of *Three Blind Mice* slowly over and over again. Bozo dutifully repeated my vision of a vanishing St. Bernard several times and then tried one of his own, apparently hopeful that I was teachable too. It was the old one of me putting a plate of bacon and eggs on the floor of his pen. I recognized the contents of the dish immediately, more by their smell than by their look. I merely shook my head in reply and said, "Not now." Then, before I signed off, I sent him as consolation a vision of Caleb and a St. Bernard riding home in the Still Waters pickup truck in the morning. This truck is the only motor vehicle the Major owns. He never drives it and very seldom rides in it, since he prefers to walk or to ride Moonlight most places he goes. Jane says he keeps it to provide transportation for Caleb, who, being lame, is the only person associated with the Major who isn't urged from time to time to take up long-distance walking. But the truck's handy for odd jobs, and Bozo loves to ride in it.

After supper I did my homework (while I was cleaning the stable Saturday, I found my books beside the sugar, where I had left them Friday afternoon) and went to bed early; but just as I was going to sleep, I came to with a jerk. I had been happily rehearsing how I would demonstrate to the Major that Bozo could be trusted to avoid Miss Peckham's premises in the future, when it occurred to me that both the Major and I would have to be present at the demonstration and that our presence might distract Bozo. What a fiasco if he refused to leave us! I immediately got the flute and put the matter to the test. Alas! I had been only too right. Bozo, faced with a vision of all three of us walking toward Miss Peckham's house, promptly sent back a picture of the St. Bernard pulling, and me pushing, the Major into the bushes.

I worked terribly hard on pictures which demonstrated a most improbable cordiality between the Major and me on one side and Miss Peckham on the other, while she kept a grim eye and a grim BB gun out for Bozo; and somehow or other I got the idea across that though he must detour, we could walk by unharmed.

By this time I was almost exhausted (it is hard to imagine how tiring that sort of communication is till you've tried it), but I had thought of another possible complication and felt I must check it. I introduced Dolores onto the scene—with astonishing results. The St. Bernard got down on his elbows and revolved his tail vigorously. Then Bozo must have opened his eyes because the picture disappeared abruptly and was replaced by the dim atmosphere of the isolation ward, while a high-pitched shriek quivered in the air. I know that shriek—there was no mistaking Dolores's voice—but it startled me terribly. It almost seemed for a moment as if I had conjured her out of thin air. Then suddenly Bozo reappeared in the position in which I had last seen him, but this time I viewed him from the front, and he was no St. Bernard; the picture wasn't very clear, but it was undoubtedly Bozo as he really looks. Dolores had tuned in on Bozo's message and, doubtless recognizing him by the peculiar motion of his tail, was broadcasting her own excited version of the scene. She must be somewhere near.

I had stopped tootling in my surprise; so the picture faded quickly. But the shrieking, though considerably reduced in intensity, continued and bore out my theory of Dolores's nearness. I hurried barefoot into the bathroom. From its window I could see the glass chariot rolling majestically toward the stable through the golden strip cast by the back porch light on the drive, and inside the chariot I glimpsed Dolores's head jerking up and down at every shriek. As this tableau moved on into darkness, I noticed the hospital lights shining between the trees in the park. Of course Miss Peckham would have warned Father by phone of her impending arrival.

Though Dolores was screaming enough to have swallowed a whole box of thumbtacks, I suspected her screams had quite a different source. Nevertheless I was curious to know what ailed her and would have liked to go over to the hospital and find out, but I knew I'd just be sent back to bed. So I returned to my room, turned out the lights, and crept back between the sheets with my head in a whirl. Two facts, both probably disastrous, were clear: Bozo thought Dolores delightful, and Dolores could tune in on the recorder just as Bozo could. Of all the animals in the kennels it would be Dolores! The possibilities suggested by these discoveries were so staggering that after a few minutes I refused to consider them and comforted myself with the reflection that tomorrow Bozo would be home where I could communicate with him and continue his all-important training without interruption from Dolores.

12. An Encounter With Miss Peckham

At breakfast on Monday I learned from Father that X-rays had revealed no thumbtack in Dolores. "It's just the same old story," said Father, "—indigestion brought on by overfeeding."

"I'm glad it's no worse," I said.

"So am I," replied Father. "The way she screamed coming in, I thought it might be a real emergency."

"She did make an awful racket," I agreed thoughtfully. Then, since Father checks his patients before breakfast, I asked, "Is Bozo O.K.? Is he going home on schedule?"

"Yes," said Father. "He gets one more penicillin shot for good measure, and Caleb's to pick him up before noon."

"Good!" I said and resolutely kept my thoughts from straying back to Dolores by laying plans for the continuation of Bozo's training. The first and probably most important consideration was how to get enough time at Still Waters. I always have to do the kennel chores on Mondays, since Jane goes to Girl Scouts from school and doesn't get back till after four. Speed seemed the only answer.

Accordingly I was the first pupil out of the Emerson Street door of the high school that afternoon and, in company with a border collie who joined me as I passed the first house on my route, was making such good time up the tarred sidewalk that the trashman on his rounds yelled to me to run faster or the dog would win. I raised my hand in greeting, but didn't waste any breath on an answer. The collie and I were both panting when I gave him a pat and dived into our house. As I turned to shut the door, I could see him through the glass trotting slowly back to Emerson Street. He never leaves his home for long.

I stopped briefly at the house to change into jeans and to slip the recorder in its case into the game pocket of my poplin jacket. Game pockets don't come in clothing my size, but they're so handy for a lot of things besides game that I had persuaded Mother to make me one by firmly attaching a lining across the back of my jacket with a slit opening in it at the side seam. Mother wasn't home that afternoon, but she'd left a sandwich and a glass of milk on the kitchen table for me. I gulped down the milk, stuffed the sandwich, which was wrapped in a plastic bag, into a front jacket pocket, and sneaked across the park so the ponies wouldn't notice me and start calling for sugar.

I whizzed through the chores in record time for me and was just making my escape when Father called me in to hold a nervous cocker spaniel who was having an infected paw treated. It really was provoking to be delayed, and I couldn't see why he picked on me when Mike was right there doing nothing more important than unpacking some supplies; but you don't argue with Father about things like that. I scratched the trembling little creature gently with one finger as I held him, and when he began to relax, I became fascinated despite myself with Father's quick, sure movements. As he wound the last strip of adhesive tape around the bandage, I said enviously, "I don't think I could ever learn to do a bandage like that; it's more in Jane's line."

"It's just a matter of practice," said Father. "Jane would probably get the knack a little quicker than you—if the patient was unconscious." I didn't quite get what he meant by that, but I didn't have time to ask. He nodded toward the waiting room and added, "Carry him in to Mrs. Thorpe and tell her I'll be right out. She couldn't bear to watch the operation." I followed instructions, getting my chin licked on the way. Then, before Father could think up another job for me, I took the opportunity to vanish out the clients' door.

I had been planning to ride Evans instead of Jones to Still Waters on the chance that I might encounter the glass chariot on my way there or back and work in a little training on the side, but the delay changed my mind; I decided I'd better reserve all my time for Bozo. So I slipped Jones's bridle on him in the paddock and was off up the lane bareback before Evans realized he'd been deserted. I heard his whinny as we reached the Appledore road.

We cantered along at a good clip more than half the way to Still Waters and then slowed down to a walk for Jones to cool off and for me to eat my sandwich and an apple I picked from a roadside tree as we passed. In this relaxed state I suddenly noticed again how good everything smelled—first the food and then the vegetation. It had been sunny and clear all day so that the road was dry, but from deep grass and damp thickets delicate odors kept rising and mingling. I tried to isolate them and identify them and even would have liked to get down and do some sniffing near the ground, so keen had my interest in smells become, but I had no time for such research today and pressed on to Still Waters.

There were no signs of life in the dooryard, but when I reached the barn I could see Caleb and old Betsy plowing the vegetable garden and rode over to them just as they finished a row. Caleb nodded to me and, taking an apple from his pocket, split it in two with his strong fingers and divided it between Jones and Betsy. "Betsy's last job?" I asked, remembering the harness for Starbuck to use next year. Plowing in the fall and harrowing in the spring are the only two jobs Betsy has ever been called upon to do at Still Waters.

Caleb nodded again. "The Major says it's not much use if we're not going to be here in the spring, but Betsy and I know that plowing's got to be done, no matter what. It doesn't pay to meet trouble halfway anyhow. You want Bozo?" he added. "I've put him in the back pasture where he'll be safe. The Major's gone to town, but I thought you'd be stopping by, so I told him Bozo shouldn't go on long walks for a few days." And to my astonishment Caleb winked at me as if we shared some amusing secret. I replied to the wink with what I hoped was an appropriately mysterious smile and went off to join Bozo.

He was waiting at the gate, and most of the stock, alerted by the noisy geese, converged on us from all directions. I slid to the ground and opened the gate a crack, through which Jones and I managed to edge without letting anybody escape. When we had all greeted each other, I slipped off Jones's bridle and we walked in a group to a sheltered spot beside the racetrack where there must have been a house once, for there's a huge old lilac clump there and an ancient apple tree that still bears delicious fruit. Here I hung the bridle on a lopped branch and, sitting down on a sun-warmed rock, pulled the recorder out of my game pocket.

As I began to play, I kept my eyes open, curious to see how the animals would react. They were all interested; there was no doubt about that. Even the ducks waddled up from a nearby puddle to investigate the new sound, and the goats tried to find a foothold on my rock. One of the kids leapt into my lap and sniffed the top of the recorder, while his mother on the ground rubbed the top of her head on the other end. Then suddenly all three went capering off across the track into a still fairly lush patch of grass and clover, where they began to graze.

Bozo sat a few feet to one side of me, watching me expectantly. I knew we must be tuned in because the autumn smells had become sharper, the crickets seemed to be shrieking, and there were vague shapes hovering before my eyes. On the other side Jones was nuzzling the recorder and breathing heavily. Suddenly he kicked up his heels and dashed out onto the track, but quickly returned, lay down, and rolled luxuriously. This was unusual behavior; could I be tuned in on him too? We never had tuned in on each other at home, but I wasn't sure whether a pony could hear as far as a dog. Perhaps I had never played near enough to him. I shut my eyes hopefully, but all I saw was a view of myself from Bozo's vantage point; so I went ahead with his training without further delay. Now and then I'd peek at Jones, who stayed near us. He loitered around nibbling grass, but still watching me as if he thought I might disappear. This was odd; Jones is not a nervous pony, and when he's turned loose in the Major's pasture he generally grazes with the horses. I was puzzled and thought it might be a good idea to experiment further with Jones, but this afternoon I had to keep my mind on Bozo.

I went carefully over his former lessons about avoiding Miss Peckham and her property. All was in order even when the Major was on the scene; Bozo had remembered. Then I went one step further and tried to make him understand that he must also avoid Dolores, no matter how charming he found her. This was harder work, and we had an unexpected interruption. A picture Bozo was sending me suddenly turned to a meaningless blur. I broke off playing and opened my eyes just in time to see Bozo vanishing behind the far end of the lilac clump.

This clump is a real barrier; it's at least five feet wide at its narrowest and more than twice that long, and it's too high for even a tall person to see over. So I had no way of knowing what was going on on the other side of it, though that something was going on was plain enough from the way that Jones sidled up to the bushes and peered snorting around the end near the track. The geese were honking, too, and all the other animals that I could see were staring in the same direction as Jones. I stole up behind Jones and then on past him around the end of the clump, where I suddenly found myself face to face with Miss Peckham, who was approaching as cautiously from the other direction. She gave a little scream and dropped the empty basket she was carrying. As I picked it up and returned it to her, she said, "Oh, Philip, how you frightened me! Does the Major know you're here?"

"No," I replied, "but Caleb does."

"Oh—Caleb!" she said, dismissing him as if I had said that old Betsy or the goats knew I was there. I would have liked to ask her if the Major knew *she* was there; but I only took a step or two out toward the track to get a better view of the lilac bushes beside her. I knew I had seen her drop something into them a split second before she dropped her basket from the other hand, and now I could see what it was—a long bamboo pole lying slantwise among the sturdy lilac branches. I stepped behind her and retrieved it, offering it to her politely.

Miss Peckham did not seem pleased to see it, and I thought she was going to deny it was hers, but since bamboo poles don't grow on lilac bushes, she had to acknowledge it. "Oh, my *walking stick!*" she exclaimed. "I wouldn't want to lose *that*; it's such a comfort on my country rambles. I suppose young legs like yours never feel the need of such support."

"It might be handy for vaulting fences if it's strong enough," I said.

At this Miss Peckham gave me a nasty look and leaned heavily on her "walking stick," which towered above her. Then her manner changed abruptly. She simpered at me and said, "I heard some sweet, sweet strains of music and thought I might surprise some woodland spirit playing in this glade."

"It was only me," I said, feeling my face getting red. "I was practicing on this flute. It belonged to an ancestor of mine, but I've just got it and can't play it very well yet."

"An ancestor—how interesting!" gushed Miss Peckham. "What belonged to our ancestors is doubly dear to us, isn't it? It was remembrance of my grandparents that brought me here today. Dear Grandpa always loved the apples from this tree, and dear Grandma always made him a pie of the first ones that were ripe. So I always pick up a few little windfalls every year before the animals get them and I make a pie in memory of them both."

I wondered why she needed a long pole to pick up windfalls, but I just looked around the ground and said, "I'm afraid the animals have beaten you to them this time, except for a couple stuck in the bushes," and I pulled out three or four from between the lilac stalks and handed them to her. Then I couldn't resist adding, "Would you like me to climb up and shake some more down?"

Of course I didn't really want to oblige that dreadful woman; I was being sarcastic and wanted to see just how far she would go in helping herself to other people's property. After I had asked the question, I was afraid she might complain to the Major that I had been rude; but she took it at its face value and replied virtuously, "No, indeed; that would be robbing the Major. I'll just make a teeny little pie out of these." And with that she finally departed, mincing back down the track toward the pasture's rear gate, which opens on a lane leading back to Foothill Road. I noticed that she was doing her best to use the pole as a walking stick, but it was awkward work. Jones, who had been restlessly pawing the ground all this time and jerking his ears back as he eyed Miss Peckham, now started off after her. I quickly called him back; he has a way of poking people in the back sometimes, and if he doesn't like them, he will even playfully nip them.

13. Light Through A Burning Glass

As soon as Miss Peckham was out of sight, Bozo came out of hiding, and I praised him for his discreet withdrawal. We had resumed the Dolores-avoidance lesson and were making good progress when I got another of those double exposures from Bozo and realized that somebody else was approaching. This time Bozo was looking in the opposite direction from which Miss Peck-

the old race that came before the English never quite died out," said Caleb. "There's always been a lot of the Power there. I wasn't born in Cornwall myself, but all my ancestors were."

"You mean you have the Power, too?" I asked excitedly.

"Not like you, Philip—just a little," replied Caleb, "enough to recognize it in somebody else. I thought you knew that," he added almost reproachfully.

"But how could I?" I asked. "I've only had it myself since I got this flute, and that wasn't till last Friday night."

This seemed to tickle Caleb; he stopped his work with his stick and grinned at me, slowly shaking his head. "You really don't know a thing about it, do you?" he asked. "Well, I suppose it's the way you've been brought up, but it's like not knowing you can wiggle your ears."

"But I can't," I replied.

"You'd know if you could," said Caleb.

"Well, sure—me and anybody who saw me wiggle them," I answered. "But this Power business is different. Of course I knew when I got it—I just didn't know what you called it—but what gets me is how you knew I had it. And how could I know *you* had it?"

"You don't *get* the Power, Philip," replied Caleb, still amused. "It's something you're born with. That little pipe wouldn't work for you if you hadn't been. But the way things are, I guess you couldn't know about me. Now in my granddaddy's time, it was different. He was a blacksmith and he had the Horseman's Word, and everybody for miles around knew it. But even then," he added, "it was considered sort of private. Nobody talked about it much, my dad said, and never to strangers. And nowadays, when most folks don't believe in such things, you can even have the Power strong and not know it, judging from you. I shouldn't wonder if even your dad didn't know about it."

"Oh no," I said, "I haven't told him; he doesn't believe in such things at all."

Caleb chuckled. "I don't mean about *your* Power, Philip; I mean about his own."

"His *own!*" I exclaimed. "You mean he's got it, too? He can't tune in on Bozo and me."

"Maybe not, but he's got his own kind of Power. Your dad has the Horseman's Word if ever a man had it," said Caleb. "Haven't you ever seen the way he can quieten a skittish horse?"

"Yes, of course," I replied. "But what is this Horseman's Word you keep talking about?"

Caleb began poking at the crack again. "Well," he said, "I guess you'd call it a superstition, and it is in a way, and yet it's real, too. Folks used to think that anybody who could manage horses real well knew a special word to whisper in their ears to make them tame and clever. Of course no word could do that; when you have the Power with horses, you just know how they feel, and they know how you feel, and you trust each other."

"Well, my Power is just for dogs, I guess," I said, "and only two so far—Bozo and, of all dogs, Dolores. I can't seem to tune in on Jones at all. I wish I knew the Horseman's Word."

"Oh, you got some Power with horses, Philip; there's no doubt about that," Caleb replied. "When the Power's as strong as yours, you'll have it with all animals, but with some more than others, and perhaps your pipe works better with some than with others, too. Let me see it. It looks real old."

I handed Caleb the recorder and told him its story as he examined it. "I might have known it was a family piece," he said, tapping the five-pointed star with the singing bird on it.

"The Power runs in families then?" I asked.

"Yes," said Caleb, "like other traits, good and bad."

"What about Jane?" I asked. "Has she got it?"

"No, no, not Jane," he replied. "Jane's a golden-haired princess. She has the Power with people."

"She has?" I said in surprise. "It doesn't seem to work with Miss Peckham. I wish it would."

"It doesn't work on everybody the same," said Caleb, "but Jane'll get more and more as she grows. You'll see."

"Would this flute help her?" I asked as Caleb gave it back to me.

"No," he replied, "it's only for animals. I've heard tell of others with your Power that had some such thing. I knew a gypsy once with a fiddle that I'm pretty sure gave him more Power. It works something like a burning glass."

"A burning glass?" I said, puzzled.

"Yes," said Caleb, "one of those rounded magnifying glasses. Don't you know that if you hold one in strong sunlight, you can set fire to a piece of paper with it?"

"Yes," I said. "We did that in science class last year. The glass focuses the light and concentrates it till it's strong enough to burn."

"Well," said Caleb, "that's what your pipe does for your Power. It doesn't make the Power any more than the glass makes the sun; they work together."

"Oh!" I said, interested but bewildered by the scientific turn the conversation had taken. It was hard to tell the science from the magic, or were they the same thing? I tried for further enlightenment.

"Do you—uh—see things with your Power?" I asked.

Caleb shook his head. "Mine's not that strong," he said. "I just *know* things about animals sometimes. I knew Bozo was a dog that felt the Power strong the first time I saw him, and just last week, before I could really point to anything, I knew he was going to be real sick."

"Couldn't you have told the Major? He'd have believed you."

"Ye-es, he'd have believed me," said Caleb, "but it wouldn't have done any good. When the time came, I knew Bozo would get to the hospital, and I didn't want to get the Major excited about the Power, and I don't want you to, either."

"But he'd take such a scientific interest in it," I protested.

Caleb looked at me sternly. "The Major is the finest man I know," he said, "but if he has a fault, it's that he's *too* scientific. If he learned about the Power, he'd never get it out of his mind. He'd want to make tests and write to the papers, and even if he tried to keep it secret, he'd be so excited he couldn't, and people would say he was crazy—to say nothing of you and me."

To tell the truth, after my first inspiration to confide in the Major, I had had a few misgivings myself about the results of his enthusiasm, but Mr. Poring's letter had given me confidence, and I told Caleb about it now.

"Just because that letter came out in a magazine doesn't mean many people will believe it, however true it may be," said Caleb. "And besides, there'll be folks that might believe such things of a gypsy in Europe long ago, but they'd sing a different tune if a boy like you, who they see every day, claimed he could do the same. And what would your dad say when he won't even believe in his own Power? No, the Power's always been a secret thing and it should stay that way."

"O.K., I guess you're right," I said, regretfully. "But the Major will have to know something about the flute, because Jane is bound to mention it."

"That's all right," said Caleb. "Show it to him and tell him as much as Jane knows, and no more. He's coming," he added, pointing to Bozo, who was sniffing the air and rotating his tail.

As Caleb rose awkwardly from his seat on the rock, I put the recorder back into my game pocket and jumped down to get the bridle from the apple tree. I slipped it onto Jones, and we all set forth down the track to meet the Major.

He was still near the gate, hemmed in by his clamorous stock, who were protesting that feeding time had come. I had been leading Jones, but now I scrambled onto his back to help herd the whole gang down the lane and into the barn. "What on earth makes you rattle so, Phil?" asked the Major as Jones and I came trotting up driving Starbuck, the last straggler, before us.

Caleb grabbed Starbuck, and I pulled the recorder and its metal case out of my game pocket. "I guess I should have put this in its case, but I was planning to show it to you before I left," I said, and launched once more into the recorder's history.

The Major seemed to be fascinated. He examined the

instrument carefully, and I could tell by the way he rubbed his long, bony thumb on the wood that he enjoyed the feel of it as much as I did. "It's very old, worn ebony," he said. "There's nothing like it. This is probably quite a valuable antique; you shouldn't let it bang about like that, Phil. Can you play it?"

"Not much," I replied, but blew a few notes so he could hear its tone. I felt Bozo start to respond, as usual, but shook my head at him.

"Very mellow and delicate," the Major said. "We must work out some scales on it some time. Meantime, take good care of it." As I wrapped the flute carefully in its oiled rag and fitted it into its case, I thought how much more sensible than most adults the Major was; it never even occurred to him that I shouldn't use it because it was valuable.

As I slid the case back into my pocket, I tried to think how best to spring the news of Bozo's speedy training. Finally I said, as casually as possible, "I really came to see Bozo today. I've spent quite a lot of time training him to steer clear of Miss Peckham's place and I'm pretty sure he won't go there again. I don't think you'll even need to put him on a leash if you walk past there with him; he'll just disappear and join you farther up the road."

"You mean you've trained him already? Just this afternoon?" asked the Major. He looked incredulous.

"He's a very remarkable dog," I replied. "He's even easier to teach than I ever thought he'd be. Let's try him out now. Dolores is in the hospital again—it's just overeating this time; so he can't do any harm even if he isn't fully trained yet."

"You must be what you'd call a 'speed artist' if you've managed to train Bozo since three o'clock this afternoon," said Father.

"Caleb says he's a master," said Jane solemnly.

"He must be," said Father, grinning at me.

I felt my face getting red. "Caleb didn't say exactly that," I protested. "He just meant I was sort of good at training dogs."

"And so you are," said Father. "I just didn't realize you were *that* good."

"Bozo's special," I replied.

"Yes, he is," agreed Father. "There's something about him . . . It's not that he's especially intelligent either. Of course he's very willing to oblige, and that's half the battle in training."

"I shouldn't think it would take much intelligence—or much willingness to oblige either—to learn to keep out of Miss Peckham's way," said Jane.

This was so true we all laughed, and the subject of my ability to train dogs was dropped, much to my relief; but Father's comments on Dolores's condition did nothing to cheer me up. "I'll take a look at that hock right after dinner," he said, "but I know what I'll find. As long as that little dog stays so fat, Miss Peckham can expect trouble of that sort. When Dolores went home last time, her hock was all right. She's just gained more weight again; so we'll have to keep her here longer than usual. And you will be excused from exercising her for a few days, Phil. I know that will grieve you."

"It will at that," I replied, "because we've got to get her back to Miss Peckham in good shape pretty quick, or the Major won't have a chance with his option. Isn't there anything else we can do that would hurry up her treatment?"

Father shook his head. "Not unless you can think of some way of taking the weight off her feet before she reduces. It's a vicious circle: the excess weight makes the hock weak so she can't run off the weight. We'll have to depend on a rigid diet and vitamins for a while."

This was depressing news indeed, though ordinarily I'd have rejoiced at not having to exercise Dolores. The job had become entirely mine, since Jane showed no talent for it. With an ordinary leash attached to her harness, Dolores would dig her toes in and be pulled onto her nose rather than budge. And Jane could not, or would not, get the knack of using what I called the 'bull staff'—a little device I had made with a rod and a snap. Using this to replace the limp leash, I could propel Dolores in front of me briskly and with ease, if not with pleasure, but Jane said she couldn't move her without lifting her right off the ground. Now that the bull staff was out, I wondered if the recorder couldn't be put to some use. I'd have to try it, of course, but I didn't expect much cooperation from Dolores, and the idea of conversation with her certainly lacked charm.

As Mother and I were doing the dishes after dinner, Father came in from inspecting Dolores. "Nothing new—just what I supposed," he replied to my questioning look, and he went on into the living room where I heard him rustling the evening paper.

Shortly after, a series of squeaks and bleats from the second floor announced that Jane was struggling with the recorder. Mother paused to listen. "Really, that noise—your father—" she said.

"She's blowing too hard," I replied. "If you breathe softly into it, you get mellow and delicate notes," I added, proudly recalling the Major's description of the notes I blew for him.

A loud voice interrupted from the living room. "For heaven's sake, Phil, stop that noise!"

I hurried into the living room, towel in hand. "I'm not making a noise," I said, "I'm wiping the dishes."

"Oh, I beg your pardon," said Father. "I forgot." Father complains about my absentmindedness sometimes, but Mother says I get it from him. "Jane's upstairs, I suppose?" he asked.

I nodded and offered, "She probably can't hear you with all that noise." *All that noise* included for me, but obviously for me alone, the shrill yapping of Dolores. As he started up the stairs, I closed my eyes for a moment to focus a dim vision that had been floating before me for the last couple of minutes. I saw myself depositing on the floor of the isolation pen a clanking and tinkling burden consisting of a tray and three dishes. One dish reeked lusciously of liver, another of chicken broth, and the third principally of vanilla, apparently from a serving of ice cream.

Father's sharp tones aroused me from a stupefied contemplation of Dolores's idea of a good meal. He had turned at the landing and was looking down at me. "Phil!" he said. "What the dickens is the matter with you? Are you sick?"

I opened my eyes, dazed. "No," I replied, "I'm hungry."

"*Hungry!*" repeated Father. "Even *you* can't be hungry after all the dinner you ate. And if you were, why should you stand with your eyes closed, shaking your head? Your mother has pointed out to me that you're in your teens now, but I had no reason to suppose that it would take you this way. For heaven's sake, keep your eyes open and get back to your job."

Very shortly after that the noise, the vision, and my hunger ceased. As I hung up my towel, however, the whole business began again. Since neither of my parents paid any attention, I concluded that Jane was now playing in my room. Muttering something about the ponies, I fled out the back door and across the park to the hospital intent on quieting Dolores. Her yapping, unlike Bozo's baying, had not produced a general riot in the kennel, but already I could hear one more voice. A chorus would arouse Father to investigation.

My sharp "Hush!" as I looked into Dolores's pen produced surprising results. She stopped screeching immediately and looked over her shoulder. Then she hobbled around in a small circle, looking back all the time; this maneuver looked like tail-chasing in slow motion. Finally she lay down, and after staring for a moment at her outstretched paws and then at me with a more than normally popeyed stare, she suddenly closed her eyes and simpered.

I was puzzled by this conduct, but since she seemed to be in a receptive state, I lost no time sending her what I hoped would be an improving message. I pictured the tray of food she had demanded still on the floor of the pen, but with the dishes empty and Dolores, gorged and swollen, staggering painfully away from them. I had been feeling twinges in my leg as Dolores moved about, but now, to drive my point home, I tried to recall the agonizing pain that poor Bozo had felt. This vision produced such a piercing yelp that I opened my eyes in alarm. But Dolores didn't seem to be suffering much physical pain; she was sitting up glaring at me. I had barely time to observe this, however, when she again closed her eyes and simpered. I tried sending her a more cheerful vision, in which, after consuming a very small portion of dog food and some water, she airily tripped about and even danced on her hind legs, but the result was exactly the same as before, except that this time the angry yelp ended in a growl.

It seemed hopeless to pursue the subject of diet further; so I kept my eyes closed and waited to see what message Dolores might choose to send me. She snarled a bit before she sent one, but when it came, a great light burst upon me. I merely saw rather dimly the same things I would have seen if my eyes had been open, but Dolores herself, the center of the picture, appeared in color. It didn't really do justice to the shiny red gold of her coat—it was rather a washed-out shade—but it was the first color that had appeared in any of the visions. Both dogs had communicated in black and white, and I, being used to ordinary television, had done the same; but of course when I looked at Dolores in the flesh, I saw her in color. And when she closed her eyes and saw herself in color, the experience was obviously pleasing. Bozo must also have had a human-eye view of himself, but as far as I could recall, it had made no particular impression on him; at any rate he was evidently still willing to appear as a colorless St. Bernard.

The discovery of Dolores's vanity gave me new hope. I sat down on the floor with my back to the wall and gazed at her raptly till she began to sway and seemed about to swoon with pleasure. Then I repeated the diet lessons. This time I gave a brief glimpse of a faintly colored, fat Dolores approaching the dinner she had ordered, and followed this closely by a gorged, swollen, and muddy-colored Dolores staggering away from the empty dishes. There were shrieks, of course, but I promptly switched to the other picture where, slim and golden, she cavorted with grace and ease.

Since Dolores remained silent through this picture, I dwelt on it for some time and then waited for a reply. She merely indicated, as before, that she wanted me to look at her.

This wasn't exactly encouraging, but by that time I was finding colored pictures even more of a strain than plain ones and I had to keep Dolores quiet somehow; so I obliged again by just staring at her. The sight became tiresome to me, but apparently not to her; her enjoyment was so great that even at Jane's sourest notes she merely twitched her ears, though I felt like howling myself. I could tell from these sounds that the recorder had gotten wet from long blowing and looked forward hopefully to the moment when it would give out altogether. When it finally did, I stood up and stretched. Dolores opened her eyes and sighed, but she wiggled her tail at me, and when I stuck a finger through the mesh of her pen, she even hobbled over and licked it.

On this happy note, I stole out of isolation and snapped off its light in the corridor. All was quiet, and I was allowed to leave the building without further disturbance. I found Pounce crouched on the doorstep again. He accepted one stroke of my hand from his head to the tip of his tail and then ran off toward the stable. There's a cat hole in it so that he can come and go as he pleases even when the doors are closed.

As I walked back across the park by the tranquil light of an already waning moon, I decided it would be best not to expose Dolores to recorder music again until I had done some deep thinking.

15. Thwarted Efforts

My deep thinking about Dolores had one encouraging result: as a first step toward further communication with her, I trained her remarkably quickly not to be noisy when she heard the recorder. Her problem was more complicated than Bozo's had been, because she not only screamed whenever the music started, but also whenever she didn't see herself in color. I was firm with her, however, and she was so much smarter than I had ever given her credit for being, that, in the course of one short recorder session when Father and Mike were out the next afternoon, she learned that the only way to get a good human-eye view of herself was to keep quiet at all times —and she wanted a human-eye view of herself whenever she could get it. Pleasing as this accomplishment was, it seemed to be a dead end, for I just couldn't figure out a way the recorder could be used to speed her recovery.

I did, however, have what seemed at the time a good idea for a more conventional kind of treatment. Miss Peckham had ordered a bath with Castile shampoo for Dolores, and Father, with an exasperating grin, had detailed me to do the job. I had to hunt up the shampoo in the medicine cabinet of the second-floor bathroom; so, since Dolores was very small even for a Peke, I decided to take her along and wash her right there in the basin.

When we entered the bathroom, I was surprised, and Dolores was wildly excited, to find that the bathtub was filled with water. It looked as if somebody had drawn a bath and then gone off and left it. Dolores squirmed so at the sight of it that I thought she was afraid I'd drop her in. But when I put her on the floor while I rummaged for the shampoo, she scratched at the tub and, balancing as best she could on her good hind leg, tried to climb into it. I felt the water and found it only lukewarm. The temptation was irresistible. I picked up Dolores and put her in the water, holding onto her harness in case she should sink; but she struggled to be free, and I let her go. She didn't swim quietly like most dogs; she gasped and splashed about most ungracefully, but she went round and round the tub without trying to get out, and I sensed that she was enjoying herself. It was as I stood watching this odd spectacle that the idea burst upon me. Buoyed up by water, disabled people can often take beneficial exercise, so why not Dolores?

Elated by this new hope, I let Dolores continue her exercise undisturbed till Jane marched into the bathroom and made a grab at her. I intercepted the grab, and in reply to Jane's protest, "She's drowning!" I replied, "Oh no, she's not. She's taking the water cure and having the time of her life. Swimming takes the weight off her feet while she reduces," I ended triumphantly.

"Well, I don't see why she has to reduce in *my* bath," protested Jane, once she was assured of Dolores's safety.

"Oh, is it yours?" I asked, noticing for the first time that Jane had her bathrobe on. "Why the dickens do you want to take a bath this time of day?"

"I don't want to," replied Jane, "but I have to. I fell into Coulter's brook, and Mother said to take one so I wouldn't get pneumonia."

"Well, this one wouldn't save you," I said. "It's almost cold."

"I know," replied Jane. "I forgot it."

I looked at her in surprise; Jane is seldom absent-minded. She was scowling fiercely, apparently at Dolores; but then she looked out into the hall, edged closer to me, and hissed in my ear, "I know who shot Bozo. It was that awful Elvira Peckham."

"What?" I exclaimed as if *I* had been shot. Then, to cover my confusion, I snatched Dolores from the bath and began soaping her in the basin. With my back to Jane, I managed to ask, quite casually, I thought, "How do you know?"

Jane made a long story of it, though all in a confidential undertone. The gist of her account was that she and two of her friends had been exploring Coulter's brook and had hopped happily along from rock to rock in the brook's bed until they were tired. When they realized that they had no idea of their whereabouts because the banks were so high they couldn't see any landmarks above them, Jane had climbed a bank to reconnoiter and had found herself face to face with Miss Peckham target-shooting in her back yard.

"I nearly fainted," said Jane. "She was pointing the BB gun right at me, though I guess she didn't know I was there because I was behind the target and some bushes too. Anyhow, I was in such a hurry to get away, I slid down the bank right into the water. It's lucky the brook's so noisy after the storm, or she'd have heard me and shot me for a spy." The girls had then retreated back down the brook and climbed to the surface at the crossroad bridge, which Jane had failed to recognize from below on the way up. Shortly afterward they had gotten a ride home in the truck with Caleb.

"Did you tell Mother all this?" I asked.

"Of course not," replied Jane. "She was upset because I got home so late. I told her I'd dropped my pen over the Allen Street bridge and we went down to get it and got playing. That's just what happened, too; but I didn't say we'd gone as far up as Miss Peckham's. It's quite a long way up there. We'd no idea we'd gone so far or taken so long. I didn't tell Caleb either—not about Miss Peckham," she added. "I told him we'd come up the brook from town, and he thought that was crazy enough, especially since I'd gotten so wet."

"It's lucky you didn't say anything about Peckham," I said. "Father gave me the dickens when I told him she'd shot Bozo. He lectured me about jumping to conclusions and making unfounded accusations. And he said Miss Peckham was *Miss* Peckham; I'd called her 'that ghastly Peckham woman.' If he heard you call her 'that awful Elvira Peckham,' he'd hit the ceiling—and so would Mother."

"That's who she is just the same," said Jane. "But how did *you* know she shot Bozo? You seemed awfully surprised when I told you."

"I saw her once with a BB gun too," I replied. "I was surprised that *you* knew."

"Why didn't you tell me?" asked Jane in an aggrieved tone.

"I didn't think I'd better after Father blew up. I knew you'd jump to the same conclusion."

"I didn't jump," said Jane. "Its just the sort of thing she would do, and she oughtn't to be allowed to get away with it. She ought to be paying Bozo's hospital bill instead of the Major paying Dolores's."

"Oh, is he?" I asked. "How do you know?"

"First *she* phoned and said he was paying it, and then *he* phoned and asked to have the bill sent to him. I heard Mother tell Father on the intercom just before he left. Peckham must have been after the Major about Dolores's leg. I was furious, but I'd just been sent upstairs in disgrace; so I didn't dare say anything."

"You'd better not, either," I replied. "If you say a word about Peckham's shooting Bozo, Father will be down on you with all fours. The only thing he'll listen to is absolute proof, and you can't get that." Of course I sympathized with Jane's anger, and I was more disgusted with Miss Peckham than ever; but since Caleb had cautioned me not to reveal my Power even to the Major, I had given up all hope of proof. Proof wouldn't help the Major anyway; it would only infuriate Miss Peckham so she'd never sign the contract.

Jane went on grumbling a bit, but was diverted by the sight of Dolores rinsing herself off with another swim in the tub. "But now what am I going to do about *my* bath?" she demanded as I lifted Dolores from the tub and wrapped her in a towel.

"It's all yours," I said. "Dolores is finished for today. But if you're fussy, you can use my shower. Don't pull the curtain too hard though; it's sort of wobbly."

Jane jumped at this offer and hurried off to the attic. She seldom gets a chance at this invention of mine, because Mother has always been afraid the shower apparatus would fall on her. And, of course, I usually didn't encourage Jane's presence in the attic anyhow.

I had gotten Dolores safely back to the hospital and was adjusting the heater so it would blow warm air into her pen when I heard the jeep come in. Since it was after office hours, Father would have dropped Mike off at his house and might not come into the hospital at all; so I hurried out to tell him about my solution of Dolores's reducing problem. I concluded my outline for her treatment by saying, "My bathtub would be O.K. for her, wouldn't it? I have to keep it scrubbed myself, and besides, Dolores must be cleaner than I am. She doesn't do anything to get herself dirty."

"I daresay you're right about that," replied Father as he leaned against the jeep with a not-unsympathetic grin on his face, "and the idea has merit; but I'm sorry to say we can't use it. Remember Dolores gets eczema now and then, and repeated soaking and drying, especially drying with artificial heat, would probably bring it on. It's tough, I know, but we'll just have to stick to the present treatment—unless," he added as he took the trash box out of the jeep and handed it to me to dispose of, "that fertile brain of yours can devise some way to get the weight off her feet while she's still on dry land."

I didn't return his grin; I was too discouraged at the collapse of my plans. I dumped the rubbish and then slouched over to the house and on up to my room, where I sat brooding in my Morris chair till dinner time, hoping for some new inspiration; but none came.

Even dinner didn't do much to revive my drooping spirits that evening, for during it Father reproved me, though with unusual mildness, for forgetting to go back and turn the heater off when Dolores was dry; and Mother was displeased at the condition of the bathroom. At the end of the meal, Father suggested that I go stimulate my brain with some algebra. Algebra is his favorite brain stimulant. When, after my first week of it, I protested that I couldn't see what good algebra could do a vet—and that's what I want to be—he replied, "It can do anybody good who can think. It's a foundation for all straight thinking." His mention of algebra that evening reminded me uneasily that my algebra homework had fallen into arrears during the last few days and that my teacher had been threatening about it. So I took his advice even though the next day, thanks to a teachers' convention, was a school holiday.

Before settling down at my desk, I picked up the re-

chariot, which we passed with no trouble since it was on Jones's side.

I was glad to find a steady stream of traffic on the state road so that we could appear to be waiting to cross. When the chariot sidled up to us, Evans reared, and being unable to shy because of Jones, he backed up a few steps; but I had shortened the reins and held them firmly in my left hand, while I pressed him forward with my right leg and heel. He was starting forward again, when Jones suddenly blocked the way by turning his head and peering into the chariot. He even took a step toward it so that his nose pressed against the glass. I had been holding his lead loosely in my right hand, but now I jerked on it sharply and cried "Jones!" He drew his head back a couple of inches but, to my horror, lifted his upper lip in a hideous grin that displayed his teeth, and uttered one of his screaming neighs before he got back where he belonged.

From the depths of the chariot I heard another scream that scared me out of my wits, but I couldn't just ride away without explanation; so I edged the ponies back toward the driver's side of the chariot and called, "I'm sorry, Miss Peckham. I was just trying to train Evans."

Miss Peckham opened her door a crack and shrieked, "Train him! Train him to hold up motorists? He'd have bitten me if it hadn't been for the glass. Your father will hear of this, young man."

"Oh, that was Jones," I replied. "You don't have to worry about him; he never bites hard—only in fun. It was Evans—"

At this point Miss Peckham slammed the door and with a parting glare launched her chariot out onto the state road, causing a jaunty Triumph sports car to alter its course with a screeching of brakes. She'd blame me for that, too, I reflected, if she even noticed it.

On the way back to Still Waters we met the Major and Bozo. The Major had been weeding his chrysanthemums when the sound of cantering hoofs passing the house had roused his curiosity. He had reached the road in time to see us overtaking the glass chariot and, knowing that all of us would probably have to stop at the state road, he had followed, hoping to get some light on the mystery; but all he had seen was the chariot nearly colliding with the Triumph. I told him the rest.

"Miss Peckham's very much disturbed about Dolores," said the Major when I had finished. "I'm afraid it makes her a little excitable and irritable just now. But your father is a reasonable man; I feel sure he will understand that it was not your fault when you tell him just what happened."

"That's so," I replied, "and Evans really behaved pretty well; he's getting over his fear of the chariot. But I hate to get her any madder than she is already; I'm afraid she associates me with you and Bozo."

"I hope not, for your sake," said the Major. "Bozo and I are in worse disgrace than ever now that Dolores is limping again."

"I know," I said glumly. "His training came too late."

"I'm afraid so," said the Major with a sigh. "I told her about it and wanted to give her a demonstration, but she wouldn't listen. And the worst of it is that I saw my financial adviser in Boston yesterday, and he told me my only hope of keeping the farm was to butter her up. Legally, he says, I haven't a leg to stand on."

"Oh, you went to Boston yesterday?" I said, surprised. "You must have gotten home early."

"I did," replied the Major, "just a little after four. I rode home with Mrs. Molloy. She was at the airport to get her dog, and she was having a little trouble; I thought she might need my help. So when she offered me a lift, I accepted."

"Her dog?" I asked, mystified. "Has Houdini taken to the airways?"

"No," said the Major. "Houdini was there, but the dog on the plane was a big, black, woolly poodle called Spook. The Molloys have adopted her; she used to belong to friends who have moved to Europe. While Mrs. Molloy was signing some papers, Spook got out of her crate somehow, and she and Houdini were running around greeting everybody at the airport. We rounded them up and got them in the car, but I didn't know what two dogs together for the first time might do on the way home."

"What did they do?" I asked.

"Nothing much," replied the Major. "They sat together on the back seat very sociably; but I noticed when I got out that they both had their collars off. When I told Mrs. Molloy, she just laughed and said, 'It looks as if Houdini has found a kindred spirit.' "

"Oh, boy!" I said. "Wait till I tell Mike!"

The Major had brightened as he told me about Houdini and Spook, and now he said with his usual cheerfulness, "I have a surprise for you, Phil. As soon as I was through with my financial adviser, I went to Schirmer's."

"Schirmer's?" I said, puzzled.

"It's a big music store in Boston," said the Major.

"Oh!" I said, still puzzled but guessing he had brought

me a birthday present from there. It is one of the Major's peculiarities that he never gives Christmas presents on Christmas, or birthday presents on birthdays. He says he prefers to wait and let circumstances inspire him, and I must say his inspirations are excellent when they come.

We had turned into the Still Waters drive by now, and while the Major picked up his hoe and carried his basket of weeds off to the compost pile, I unsaddled Evans and put both ponies in the front pasture with the Major's stock, speculating as I did so on the nature of the surprise awaiting me. By the time we had washed our hands in the kitchen and gone on into the living room I was not surprised to see a booklet entitled *Playing the Recorder* on the top of the spinet piano, but I was surprised to see beside it a small bottle, a goose feather, and a strange, wire-handled object shaped like a cattail on its stalk. The Major explained them all with gusto; he had gone thoroughly into the matter of recorders with the clerk at Schirmer's. The bottle contained oil which you applied to the recorder's inside surface with the goose feather (which came not from Schirmer's, but from one of the Major's own geese) and the synthetic cattail was a swab to dry it with after playing. He had wanted to get me a carrying case too, but they had none that would fit my instrument because it was all in one piece, and the modern ones come apart for storage; so he was planning to make me one of leather. I thanked him sincerely for the gifts, realizing as I did so that nobody else would ever have thought of them. Then, when I had produced the recorder and experimentally applied some oil to it with the goose quill, we settled down with the help of the instruction book to work out scales.

Thwarted Efforts

We spent an hour checking the notes of the recorder with those of the piano, and a trying hour I found it. I'm afraid the Major did, too, but for different reasons. My trouble was that Bozo had settled himself outside under the window next to the piano and at first kept baying every time the two instruments were not in perfect harmony. I stopped that, but then he began sending me messages that he would like to have us all go on an expedition into the woods. We often go looking for butternuts this time of year. I finally persuaded him to take a nap, but then he apparently dreamed of chasing some animal in the woods, and I was subject to a very jerky and odorous series of impressions. I resolutely kept my eyes open so that the pictures were mere vague blobs, but I could not give my full attention to the matter in hand.

This must have annoyed the Major, but I think my insistence on correct pitch, when I could attend, annoyed him even more. "What a perfectionist you are, Phil!" he said. "I had no idea you had such a sensitive ear. That *d* you're blowing sounds all right to *me*."

"It's not quite right," I replied. "I'll swab out the moisture and try again." Bozo had stopped baying at the discords by then, but he could still hear them, even in his sleep, and so, of course, could I. When, at the end of the session, I made a mess of trying to play a simple air in my new book, I decided that this was one day I should have stayed in bed.

16. Balloons For Buoyancy

After our musical struggles, I suggested to the Major that we go look for butternuts. They probably weren't quite ripe yet, but we could inspect the crop. The Major agreed, but when we stepped out and found a breeze had sprung up, he said that first he'd like to test a little invention of his on the pond beside the house. The invention turned out to be a six-inch balsa wood boat with the string of a red gas balloon tied through its tiny hawseholes. It had been designed for use at the annual bazaar given for the benefit of the Haunceton Memorial Hospital. The Major is a sort of perpetual chairman of the children's entertainment division of the bazaar and takes his duties seriously. Last summer he had succeeded in having the site of the affair changed from the old fair grounds to the town park and had personally umpired toy sailboat races on the pond there. These were a great success, but there weren't enough sailboats to go around, and he was casting about for a cheap substitute which could be made in quantity and sold on the spot for the pleasure of more children and the enrichment of the hospital fund. If this little boat he was testing today worked to suit him, he planned to make many more during the winter. Since he had contributed balloons, helium, and even string to last summer's bazaar, he had brought the leftovers home and so was still equipped to produce buoyant gas balloons on demand.

I launched the little craft while the Major waited to receive it at the other side of the pond. It sailed bravely, and as I noted how the red balloon not only towed it along, but also lifted its bow, I suddenly grasped the idea I had been groping for for so long.

"Major!" I shouted, and then remembering Mother's objection to that form of address, I amended it to "Major Featherstone!" and pointed to the balloon. "That's just what Dolores needs. *That* would take the weight off her leg."

The Major looked from me to the boat and then all around the yard in a puzzled way. Then he called back, "What's that, Phil? You say Dolores needs a boat?"

"Balloons!" I shouted. "Lots of gas balloons!" Then I ran around the pond to discuss the matter. My idea, of course, was to fasten enough helium-filled balloons to Dolores so that, relieved of some of her weight, she could exercise briskly and painlessly.

The Major was doubtful at first. "Even a large, freshly-filled balloon will support only a very small weight," he cautioned. "And anyhow, how would you attach them?"

"That's easy," I replied. "She wears a harness, and I could extend it with two straps—one around her just in front of her hind legs and the other along the top of her back. We could tie the balloons mostly to those to hoist up her hind end a bit. Even a little weight off that would help. With all her fat she only weighed eight pounds when she was admitted, and she's already lost a little of that. I know because we keep weighing her, but she's not losing fast enough and we *must* get her in good shape as soon as possible if Miss Peckham's ever to sign that contract."

"But do you think Dolores would stand for it?" asked the Major. "She always seems so nervous."

"Leave that to me," I replied. "I have ways of persuading her. She and I are pals now."

"It would certainly be an interesting experiment," said the Major, and I knew by the gleam in his eye that the idea had taken hold, "but I have an appointment in town this afternoon. I don't know when I'll be through."

I had heard the truck come in while we were in the house; so I said, "Couldn't you come right now? It should only take a few minutes."

The Major looked at his watch. "Well, I guess we could if we hurry," he said. "It's only a little after eleven."

"Oh, good!" I said. "You'll come in the truck, won't you?"

"Yes, to save time," said the Major. "I'll call Caleb and get things together right away."

I patted Bozo apologetically because he was going to miss his jaunt in the woods, and then hastily collected the ponies and made for home with all speed. As we dashed away, I heard the Major call something after me. I thought I heard the word *permission,* but I couldn't stop to explain that Father was not available to give permission, if that was what the Major had in mind. I just looked over my shoulder and waved.

At home, I found the downstairs in that state of noisy chaos which Mother revels in on cleaning days. The furniture was all askew; Mother was taking down curtains, and the cleaning woman was running the vacuum cleaner so fiercely that neither of them could hear me when I spoke. I went up close to Mother and in a bellowed conversation learned that Miss Peckham had already made her daily call on Dolores—and had made it unescorted. "I just happened to look out the window and saw her leaving the hospital," shouted Mother. "Your father won't like it, but if she knocked here first, I didn't hear her."

I nodded and ran on upstairs, quite pleased with the way things were working out. Peckham was out of the way and had so far been unable to report on my crime at the state road, and Mother would take no notice of anything but cleaning for another half-hour.

If there were any light straps in my attic hoard, I was in too much of a hurry to unearth them, but I finally found a roll of carpet binding in Mother's sewing table from which I could make a comfortable and secure harness extension. While I was rummaging about there, I also collected three different-colored ribbons, which proved useful in getting the idea of the balloons over to Dolores. I had selected the rose hedge enclosure (where I had found Houdini sunning himself on my birthday) as the most private and sheltered place for our experiment, and there I carried Dolores and set her down on the big cable spool to receive the news of her impending defiance of gravity. How much she understood of my explanation I'll never know, but it was plain that she approved of being decorated with those gorgeous balloons, which I portrayed in the same colors as the ribbons. She was so thrilled by the sight of the blue ribbon that I draped it over her for a few minutes and would have tied it to her harness as a permanent adornment if I had not foreseen comments and questions about it that might be awkward to answer.

The Major and Caleb soon arrived with their equipment and we promptly got to work, with the Major blowing up the balloons from the helium cylinder and tying strings on them, while Caleb and I fastened them onto Dolores. It took us quite a while to tie all the knots (we agreed that, for the future, some sort of very light wire hooks would be more practical) and Dolores began to get restless. I was prepared for this. I had my recorder ready and, explaining to the Major that music soothed her, I stood where I could get the best view of her in all her glory and tootled *Drink to Me Only with Thine Eyes.* Immediately she gave a rapturous cry and stood stock-still, her head high and her back legs stemmed as if she were being judged in a show, while Caleb fastened on the last few balloons. But as soon as I stopped playing, she craned her neck around to see the balloons and accidentally stepped over the edge of the spool.

Caleb made a grab for her, but then with a smile withdrew his hand. Dolores drifted gracefully to earth, landing on her forefeet, the better-supported back feet gently following. She gave one excited yap and danced down the strip of lawn, her feet hardly touching the ground. At the end of the enclosure she turned and, on her way back to us, leapt upon an old tree stump in her exuberance.

I had intended to control Dolores with the bull staff, which I had brought along from the hospital, but there seemed no need for this; Dolores was doing splendidly on her own. She found a small rubber ball among the roots of the stump and swooped up to me with it.

"Blessed if she isn't having a wonderful time!" said Caleb. "I never thought Dolores had it in her."

"What marvelous buoyancy!" exclaimed the Major. "I congratulate you, Phil, on an entirely successful experiment!"

But even as he spoke, the ball, which I had thrown back down the yard, hit a root of the stump, changed course, and rolled under the rose hedge. Dolores, of course, changed course too, and a moment later there were a couple of loud pops followed by canine screams and more pops. The balloons and Dolores were thoroughly entangled among the thorns.

I dived under the hedge and grabbed Dolores, who continued to scream, trying to hold her still while Caleb cut her free with a pocket knife and the Major rescued what balloons were still unexploded. Suddenly a loud voice dominated the clamor. "What in thunder?" it demanded. I instinctively pulled my feet closer under the hedge, but in vain, for the voice continued, "Phil, come out of there immediately!"

"Just a minute, Doctor," said the Major. "He can't get up till we've freed Dolores. What a vexatious accident, just when everything was going so well!"

"Accident?" said Father. "But what's Dolores doing out, anyhow? She ought to be in her pen."

"Phil," said the Major, peering reproachfully down through the briers at me, "didn't you get permission for this experiment? I reminded you to."

I was spared replying by a horrible shriek, this time undoubtedly human. It was the second time I had heard such a shriek that morning, and it was unnerving. A moment later two strong hands clasped my ankles and yanked me out onto the lawn, and Dolores, whom Caleb had just managed to cut free, was torn from my embrace. I lay for a long moment on my back, gazing up with fascinated horror into Miss Peckham's face, which was bent over mine as she hissed, "Wretched child! Little monster!" As her face receded, I sat up and, avoiding Father's eye, examined my scratched hands and grass-stained jacket.

The Major undertook to explain the experiment, which he described as "most ingenious and effective up to a point." When I finally stole a glance at Father's face, I saw a familiar expression on it; fury was struggling with laughter, and with Miss Peckham present, laughter couldn't win.

Surprisingly it was the usually retiring Caleb who saved the situation—as much as it could be saved. He looked at Miss Peckham with the utmost seriousness and remonstrated mildly, "But Miss Peckham, I never did see Dolores so happy as she was with the balloons. Why, she danced and played like a puppy, and her leg didn't hurt her a bit. It was only that accident with the ball that scared her a little. Look how she brightens up at the sight of this blue balloon now." As Caleb was speaking, he had taken the blue balloon from the Major and was now holding it at Dolores's eye level. Meanwhile I had retreated to the big spool and, turning my back on the assembled company, blew in the recorder one soft, birdlike cheep which went unnoticed, I'm sure, by everybody but Dolores and Caleb.

Dolores's reaction must have been satisfactory, because Miss Peckham's voice replied calmly, "She does love blue. Oh, I know they say dogs can't see color, but Dolores can, and her favorite colors are blue and gold. She can have this balloon tied to her pen; it will just match her pillow."

I had turned around just in time to see Miss Peckham take the balloon, and now I looked at Caleb dumbfounded. He merely raised his eyebrows and nodded toward Miss Peckham who, I noticed for the first time, was cradling Dolores on a brand new baby-blue pillow. It was probably the delivery of this and perhaps the hope of being able to complain to my father about the ponies attacking her chariot that had brought Miss Peckham back to the hospital for a second visit. Later Caleb admitted to knowing that Dolores liked blue and he supposed that Miss Peckham knew it the same way. "Lots of folks can call forth a little Power for their own pets," he said. When I protested that Dolores had never seen color before I showed it to her, he replied, "Don't you be too sure of that, Phil. You never know."

At the time I could only gape with a grudging respect

at Miss Peckham as Father shepherded her and Dolores into the hospital, first telling me to wait for him in the house. As it happened, our interview did not take place till late in the afternoon, because Father had merely stopped off at the hospital to pick up some equipment and had to rejoin Mike immediately at the racing stable. By that time Jane was home, and giggled so uncontrollably when she heard the story of the balloons that Father himself had to laugh, and he couldn't help laughing again when I gave him my version of Jones's behavior with the glass chariot. So the storm was over, and the lecture I received dealt mostly with the importance of getting his explicit permission for any further experiments.

What worried me most was that Miss Peckham might blame the Major; but Father was reassuring about this. "I put all the blame on you, where it belonged," he said, "and pointed out that the Major thought I had authorized the treatment and was only doing his best to help Dolores. Oh, I did all I could for the Major, but it was an uncomfortable interview altogether. You do think up the darndest things, Phil," he added plaintively. It did not seem the proper time to announce that I had already thought up something else.

That afternoon before Father returned and delivered his lecture, I had not been idle. First I had to tend the office for half an hour and then, since a full waiting room allowed no time for the settlement of family troubles, I was sent back to the house. Here Mother, with the cleaning fever still upon her, packed me off to the attic to put my part of it in order. "It looks like a hurrah's nest!" she said. "And for goodness' sake start with that pile of junk under the eaves." These were strong words for Mother, so

I plodded upstairs without argument and settled down to organize and diminish, if possible, what she so unimaginatively called a junk pile. It's a mixture of odd items, of course, but anyone with vision could see that they were almost all bound to come in handy some time.

One of the first of these I came upon was a single roller skate I'd picked up at the dump. While trying to decide whether or not I could part with it, I took an old atlas (retrieved from a trash box behind the town library), laid it across the skate, and sat on it, trying to balance and propel myself along with my feet. I wasn't very successful, but the exercise gave me an idea that I divined at once was one of my best. Why not strap Dolores's hind end onto a roller skate, or something similar, and let her run around on her forefeet? Of course there were things to be ironed out; the platform of the skate would have to be broadened a little even for Dolores, and perhaps two wheels would be better than four.

When my interview with Father about the balloon experiment was safely behind me, my mind was free to consider the possibilities of the roller skate in more detail, and they still seemed promising. After dinner I slipped out to the hospital and phoned the Major, whose help with the project I knew would be invaluable. He showed interest in my plan immediately, but then asked solemnly, "Does your father know about this, Phil?"

"Gosh no, not yet!" I replied. "He'll have to, of course, before we try anything out, because I've got orders not to experiment without his permission; but it would be better to get the thing all ready and then spring it on him. He wouldn't be interested in a plan of Thomas Edison's tonight."

"Yes, I take your point," said the Major. "After Miss Peckham left this morning, I asked him if we couldn't try the balloons again in a safer place, they worked so well, but he said he was afraid they were impractical. He was quite pleasant about it, but I gathered he didn't want to hear any more about balloons."

"No, I wouldn't mention them for a while," I said, "but I think he'll like the skate better. Of course it could only be used on smooth surfaces, but Dolores could get quite a workout in the cellar."

"I'll give the matter some thought, Phil," the Major replied. "Why don't you come over after school tomorrow, and we'll see what we can turn out."

17. A Cat On Horseback, A Dog On Wheels

All the next day, no matter what I was doing, my mind kept reverting to my new idea and my forthcoming date with the Major. I was scheduled for kennel chores again, but I was getting to be a speed artist at them when necessary; and since the waiting room was empty and Father was busy with a drug salesman when I finished, I escaped from the hospital in good time. But before I reached the stable, I heard Jane calling to me from near the house. "Wait for me! I'm coming too." Then she came running up the drive to exact a binding promise from me that I would wait.

"I thought you had a date," I protested. "And you're not even dressed for riding yet."

"I was going to Mary's," said Jane, "but now *she's* got chicken pox. Everybody's getting it. There wasn't anybody to walk home from school with, so I came on the bus. It'll only take me a minute to change." She sounded forlorn.

"Oh, all right," I said. "I'll saddle both ponies; but for Pete's sake hurry up. The Major's expecting me."

As soon as Jane heard "all right," she turned and raced back toward the house, and she didn't keep me waiting. I assigned her Jones again, though I warned her, "You've got to keep *him* away from that blasted chariot now, or he'll make faces at Miss Peckham."

"I'd enjoy that," said Jane with a giggle.

"Father's had about enough of it," I replied. "And I'm scared Peckham might manage to blame the Major somehow. We're always meeting her near his place."

"I won't dash up to the chariot if I see it," said Jane, "but I still think Jones has the right idea." Then she added, "What on earth have you got *that* for?" as I pulled the roller skate out of my game pocket.

We were trotting along the lane now, and the skate kept banging me painfully in the back; so I decided to carry it in my hand. "It may be the thing that will save Still Waters," I replied mysteriously. Jane, of course, didn't let it go at that, and eventually I explained my plan to her and the purpose of my present call on the Major.

"Well, I'd sure like to see Dolores skating," said Jane. "But what will Father say?"

"That's my big trouble," I replied. "I'm going to have to persuade him somehow to let me try it."

Jane gave me a pitying look, but the conversation ended there as we turned into the crossroad and I put Evans into a canter. As we slowed down to cross the bridge across Coulter's brook, Jane said, "Look! There's some kind of animal on the railing. Why," she added a moment later, "it's Pounce! Whatever is he doing way over here?"

"Fishing, perhaps," I said. He seemed, however, to be merely sitting on the railing meditating, and when we stopped and spoke to him, he looked as if he didn't know us. Then without warning he sprang from the railing onto the pommel of Jane's saddle, jolting a startled "Oh!" from her.

"He wants a lift, I guess, and Jones is his favorite," I said. "Just steady him with your hand. He'll be all right." So there were five of us instead of four as we rode into the Major's dooryard and were greeted by Bozo's welcoming bay.

Caleb was busily raking gravel as we turned in, for the Still Waters drive, like most others in the valley, had suffered some damage in the first deluge of fall rains; but he straightened up and stared at Pounce, who was sitting in front of Jane admiring the scenery as if he'd ridden horses all his life. Then Caleb looked at me with a faint smile and said, "So he's *your* cat. We've been wondering about him."

"Has he been here?" I asked.

"Yes," said Caleb, "he's been around a couple of times

this week. We didn't think much about him; he seems to be a friend of Bozo's. But he's been spending some of his time at Miss Peckham's, and last night he nearly scared her out of her wits. The Major was out for a constitutional before he went to bed, and he heard a scream from her yard and rushed in to see what was the matter. Seems she had gone out to get some bundle she'd accidentally left in the chariot, and on the way back a large cat dropped out of that maple tree in the side yard onto her head, scratching and hissing—so she said, anyhow. She carried on something terrible."

"Gosh!" said Jane. "Pounce had better be careful; she's dangerous. Did the Major see him?"

"No," said Caleb, "the cat had gone by the time the Major got there, and there wasn't much light anyhow; the moon's small now and it was cloudy, you know. Miss Peckham asked him if the cat was his, and when he said no, she wanted him to find it and take it to the pound; but you can't find a black cat in the dark—if it *was* a black cat; she couldn't tell really, but she's sure in her mind it was the black cat she'd seen around. And for once I think she's probably right, though the Major said she was just about in hysterics. Of course she'd had a hard day."

Jane giggled, I grinned, sheepishly, I'm afraid, and Caleb's lips twitched as he lowered his eyes discreetly. I had been remembering certain things about Pounce, and as Caleb looked up again I caught his eye. "Pounce is an unusual cat," I said.

It was really a question, and Caleb understood it so. He gave the smallest of nods, and looking at me with that faint, secret smile, said, "He is that." I looked at the impassive Pounce and groaned inwardly as I silently hailed another loyal supporter and sharer in the Power. I wondered if it would do any good to send him a message to stay away from Miss Peckham, but I had little hope of that; he and Jones must have tuned in on Bozo's training in some way or other, but they certainly hadn't profited by it. Apparently they had just enough of the Power to feel my dislike of Miss Peckham and were dealing with her in their own way. If only they had a little more—or a little less!

At Caleb's suggestion I shut Pounce in the harness room, so he couldn't get into any more mischief. Then we unsaddled the ponies, and while Jane and Bozo went to meet the Major, who was strolling over from the workshop, Caleb and I turned them into the front pasture and stepped out the side door to have a brief chat about this new development in the Peckham situation. Caleb, I thought, seemed rather pleased with Pounce's behavior. "Don't worry about *him,* Philip," he said. "He's the one that can hold his own against Miss Peckham. She doesn't know he's yours, and she's not likely to find out. A scare or two will do her good."

"But she's got a BB gun," I said.

Caleb's eyebrows went up and he uttered a very slow, expressive "Ah-h-h!" Then he said, "Well, a cat with mischief in mind won't offer much of a target. He's not like a great big friendly dog, you know." Caleb's voice was quiet, but something about the way he said that last sentence told me he was very angry with Miss Peckham. I might not have noticed if I hadn't been so angry with her myself.

The Major and Jane were standing in front of the barn talking as Caleb and I came back through the side door.

The Major had learned that Pounce was our cat and was alarmed for fear Miss Peckham might discover his identity and make trouble for us.

"Well, she won't see him in the harness room," I said. "And I'll scout around to make sure she's not coming this way before we start home. Once we're on the cross-road, we're safe; she never goes there."

"She might see him at our place some time," said Jane. "She's there often enough."

"It's a chance we'll have to take," I said, "but I don't believe she could tell one black cat from another."

As we left the barn, Caleb returned to his raking, and Bozo and I followed the Major and Jane into the workshop. It's a fascinating room, long and narrow with windows on all four sides. In between the windows there are racks with all kinds of tools and shelves with all kinds of equipment, including odds and ends like mine under the eaves, only they're arranged more systematically. There's a long, heavy table down the center of the room with a vise and a power saw on it, but we followed the Major past these to the clear space at the other end where he does the finer work. Jane was ahead of me, walking beside the Major, and by the time I had reached my place, the Major was already making strange passes with his right hand over the table and smiling a satisfied smile. "How's that?" he asked, withdrawing his hand and revealing a piece of wood mounted on three rubber swivel casters. "A tricycle," he continued, resuming his motions with it. "It can't tip, but what mobility! It ought to do the trick, don't you think? Try it."

I put my hand on the wood, whirled off a figure eight and agreed heartily. Then Jane, on the Major's other side, executed even more complicated figures and observed, "Why Dolores could even play hockey with this!" The Major looked extremely gratified.

"I guess we won't need this skate," I said, holding it up. I had put it down in the barn, but had remembered to pick it up again.

"Not for Dolores," said the Major, examining it thoughtfully, "but I'd like it if you can spare it. It would make a good, heavy base for a trailer truck for the Lions' toys, and the clamps would come in handy." The Major is not a Lion, but he reconditions many of the old toys that the Lions collect for poor children at Christmas, and in addition he makes a lot from scratch. Last year some of these were so remarkable that they were exhibited in a store window and were the envy of all the little kids in town too rich to qualify as candidates for them.

I was pleased that my skate was destined for such a distinguished career, but I couldn't help wondering if the Major would still be in Haunceton by Christmas. I didn't even know how soon he would have to leave Still Waters if Miss Peckham decided to put him out, and I didn't like to ask. I looked dolefully around the room. Everything was in apple-pie order as usual, and the delicious scent of pine sawdust was stronger and richer than ever to me now, but I noticed that the little old cast-iron wood stove that the Major had bought so triumphantly from Tom Vickery a couple of weeks ago was still not connected to the chimney, though there had been plans to install it by October first.

Jane nudged me, and I realized the Major was talking to me. ". . . but zinc might not be so comfortable for Dolores. I have a heavy, flexible plastic dish that I don't need for anything. We can shape it to fit around the back of the tricycle. I think it would hold her all right, though of course it's not so durable as zinc. What do you think?"

We decided on the plastic. The Major cut it out with scissors and fitted it; Jane neatly cut some slots with a sharp knife for the straps that would fasten Dolores's back and hind legs to the platform; and I tacked the plastic support to the wood.

The only thing needed to complete the device was straps, and here we hit a temporary snag. All the Major's straps—and those Caleb had in the harness room—were either too heavy or too narrow. I was wondering if something couldn't be done with carpet binding again, when Jane said, "I've got just the thing. You remember those cotton straps for carrying school books I got last Christmas? You wanted to swap your diary for them. Well, I'll swap now if you like. They're adjustable and soft and strong, and you can fasten and undo them quickly."

"Oh gosh, Jane!" I replied. "I can't swap the diary now. I'm using it for a homework assignment book; it saved buying a notebook. But can't you just donate the straps? You haven't done anything yet to get Miss Peckham in a good humor so she'll sign on the dotted line for the Major."

"How could I?" protested Jane. "You never let me in on anything." This silenced me for a moment, and Jane pursued her advantage. "I'll gladly donate the straps for the Major's sake," she said, "but since they're partly for you, too, I should think you might at least let me play the recorder when you're not using it."

"Doesn't he?" asked the Major, giving me a disapproving look.

"No," said Jane. "He takes it with him when he goes out or else he hides it."

The Major looked quite shocked at this and I daresay I looked very foolish. I certainly felt it. "I like to practice outside," I mumbled. "And anyway she can't play it. She makes awful noises."

The Major's disapproval deepened. "We haven't all got an ear like yours, Phil," he said. "Jane can be taught. You come over Saturday, Jane, and bring the recorder and the music book I gave Phil, and we'll practice the scales." He did not add that I was to let her have the recorder when she needed it for practicing, but that was understood.

I felt so thoroughly squelched that, even though Bozo thrust his cold nose comfortingly into my hand, I could only stare stupidly down at the tricycle till Jane asked the Major what time it was, and finding it was a little after five, said, "Oh dear, I'd hoped we'd have time for a race, but I guess we'll have to go home now."

"Yes," I said. "There's Pounce too, you know. I'll scout around, and if the coast is clear, we'd better go while the going's good."

The Major decided, however, that it would be more practical for him to do the scouting, since he could keep watch in all directions, if necessary, while Jane and I—and Pounce—were actually escaping. He planned a rather elaborate system of signals to indicate whether the chariot was in or out, and if in, whether there was any sign of Miss Peckham herself outside. Since we were to be so thoroughly protected from her, we rode our own ponies, and I had Caleb hand Pounce up to me. We lurked in the dooryard until Caleb, interpreting the Major's signals from the road, reported that the chariot was in and Miss

Peckham invisible. We then set forth at an easy canter and reached the crossroad in safety. Jane waved good-bye for both of us as we cantered on up the hill, while I kept my right hand across Pounce's chest to support him, though he rode like a veteran, sitting with his hind legs astraddle the pommel and the claws of his forepaws hooked over the edge of the leather. The precious tricycle, wrapped in a piece of gunny sacking, thumped a little in my game pocket, but wasn't uncomfortable.

Later when we slowed down to a walk for a while, Jane asked, "What was Caleb so mad about when you came back into the barn?"

"How did you know he was mad?" I asked. "He didn't say anything, and he always looks the same except when he smiles."

"Oh, I don't know," said Jane. "I just knew he was, somehow. What was it about?"

"I told him Miss Peckham has a BB gun," I replied.

"Oh!" said Jane. "And Caleb knew right away that she'd shot Bozo. That's three of us now; we can't be wrong. We mustn't let her get away with it—that awful woman."

"We still haven't any proof," I said gloomily.

"Who needs proof with *her?*" demanded Jane.

"Father," I said. "I told you before."

"Well, it's very unfair," said Jane. She looked defiant and was unusually silent for several minutes till Tom Vickery's truck passed us and then stopped, waiting for us to come up on the driver's side. When we reached him, Tom was grinning with his eyes fixed on Pounce. "Does *everybody* at your place ride?" he asked.

"Sure," I said. "Everybody but the ponies themselves.

But please don't mention around town that you saw Pounce riding this road. He's annoyed Miss Peckham, and we're trying to smuggle him home so she won't know he's ours."

"O.K.," said Tom. "I'll only tell my wife, and she'll keep quiet—probably won't even believe me when I tell her I saw a cat on horseback. But anybody may see you on the Appledore road, and you're liable to cause a traffic accident. Hadn't I better take him along with me and let him off at your lane?"

"I guess it would be a good idea," I said. "I didn't realize he'd attract so much attention. Thanks very much. You'd better keep hold of the back of his neck till you've got your window up," I added, as I handed Pounce over. Jane leaned forward to call her thanks through the window and then sank back in the saddle in one of her fits of helpless giggling.

"What's so funny?" I asked.

"You and Pounce," she said, "but even more the Major and Caleb and me. We're so used to your crazy ideas, none of us thought there was anything out of the way about a cat riding horseback. After all, it's nothing to a Peke on roller skates. I suppose if you came riding along on Bozo some day, we'd hardly notice it."

The best reply to such nonsense was silence, and I maintained it, but secretly I was glad that Jane had stopped brooding about Miss Peckham. Jane seldom gets silently angry, but when she does, nobody knows *what* she may do. She could be a worse problem even than Jones and Pounce.

At Still Waters that afternoon, when Jane had reluctantly suggested that we'd better start home, I had agreed with her promptly not really because of Pounce, but because it was important to my plans to get the tricycle painted as soon as possible. I knew there was part of a can of blue latex paint in the cellar, and I lost no time getting it up to my room and slapping on a priming coat before dinner. Jane came up with the book straps while I was painting.

"Oh, good!" I said, as I examined them. "They're just what we needed. I can thread them through the slots, and they won't have to be sewed or anything—just cut off to fit Dolores." Each strap, when fastened, formed a loop which could easily be adjusted to various sizes by moving a slide along the strap, which took up the slack. One loop could fasten Dolores's legs to the platform and the other could encircle her body. "See, they're ideal for safety belts," I said, as I hooked a loop and demonstrated that no pressure from the inside could change its size; it had to be unhooked. Then I added enthusiastically, "And that blue-gray color will go very nicely with this blue."

"I'd like to know why you're so crazy about blue all of a sudden," said Jane. "I thought your favorite color was red."

"It is," I replied, "but Dolores's happen to be gold and blue."

"Dogs can't see color, silly," said Jane. "Didn't you know that?"

"Miss Peckham says Dolores can, and what's more, she said that those were her favorites."

Jane giggled. "Well, really!" she said and then added, "But she won't see this—Miss Peckham, I mean."

"I'm hoping she will," I replied. "If it works the way it ought to, I'll try to persuade the Major to give it to her, or have Father give it to her with the Major's compliments. That should sweeten her up a bit."

"Don't be too sure of that," said Jane. "It will take a lot to sweeten *her,* and first you'll have to sweeten Father a little."

This was, of course, one of my immediate problems. I didn't quite see how I was going to persuade Father to consider using one of my inventions, even one improved by the Major's skill and foresight. I spent a lot of time that evening trying to think up a good approach.

Jane had spread the news about Pounce, and it came under discussion at dinner. "It seems a queer place for Pounce to be and a queer thing for him to do," said Father. "He never did anything like that before."

"Jones never made faces at people in cars before either," said Mother. "It's odd they picked the same victim."

"Unless," said Father, "Phil has organized a conspiracy against her among the animals."

"Well, I haven't," I said. "If I could organize a conspiracy, it would be to do something to put her in a good humor."

"You know I don't approve of appeasement as a policy," said Father. "Look at the war it caused in Europe. But I suppose when the enemy has all the power, it's inevitable."

I made a mental reservation that the enemy didn't have quite all the power, but I merely asked, "Are you going to do anything about Pounce?"

"No," said Father. "He's never been confined, and I don't see any reason to confine him now. He may never go over that way again. Besides, we don't know for sure it was Pounce; nobody can prove that it was." I was glad to learn that proof could work against as well as for Miss Peckham.

After dinner, while Jane was drying the dishes, I put another coat of paint on the tricycle, tidied up my desk, and put the recorder and the swab on the blotter. Then, with a couple of school books under my arm and the tricycle, held by its casters, in my hand, I went down to Jane's room and sat down at her desk. These preparations were all in accordance with Jane's demand for the use of the recorder—and my room to blow it in—that night.

I had been able to finish only one algebra problem when I heard her running upstairs. She waved at me as she passed her room, but opened the attic door and slammed it behind her without a word. A minute or two later I was communing with Dolores to the tune of *Three Blind Mice*. The subject, of course, was the tricycle, which I kept on the desk in front of me in order to convey its beauties accurately. When I demonstrated how the device worked, I pictured Father strapping her in, in case the balloon episode had made her a little shy of my management. She seemed pleased with the arrangements as nearly as I could tell, and having prepared her as best I could for the hoped-for experiment, I would have closed the interview. But Jane was trying to master the whole of *Three Blind Mice,* and now that she had the swab to keep the flute's inside dry, she could keep blowing indefinitely. As she went on and on, Dolores got fretful and howled at the sour notes, and I got exhausted trying to keep her quiet by visualizing her in color. So finally I was driven out to the hospital, where all I had to do was sit on the floor and gaze at Dolores on her blue pillow. I took the tricycle with me, though, and rolled it around on the floor in front of her for a while before I slumped down and relaxed.

Father, entering the hospital quietly for evening rounds, found me practically asleep, but still fixing Dolores with a hypnotic stare and trying to think of some good way to broach the matter of the tricycle to him. "*Now* what's the matter?" he demanded. "Don't tell me Dolores is sick."

"Oh, no. She's all right," I replied. "She was just a little restless. She likes company, you know. She'll be fine now," I added as I stood up and thankfully heard Jane's practice end.

Father put his hands on his hips and puckered his brows at me. "There's something very strange about you lately, Phil," he said. "Do you feel all right?"

"Oh, sure," I replied. "I'm fine."

"Well," said Father, "you mustn't take this trouble of the Major's too much to heart. It's to be hoped, of course, that he'll be able to stay on his farm; he'd be a great loss to the community, especially to you and Jane. And of course we'd all like to help him, but really there's nothing much we can do that I can see."

I saw my opportunity and seized it. "There's one thing," I said.

"What?" asked Father.

I produced the tricycle from behind my back like a conjurer and explained its intended function. Father laughed when he saw it, but when I had done some figure eights on the floor with it, he got quite interested. He sent me for the bull staff, and when I returned with it, he was holding Dolores all strapped in and ready to go. "I had no trouble at all with her," he announced. "It's strange how docile she's become lately."

I ran Dolores up and down the corridor several times with complete success, though the performance roused the kennel to a furor of barking. For the next few days I was permitted—nay, commanded—to exercise her daily on her tricycle in the cellar. She could soon run around loose and chase a ball, executing rapid turns with no difficulty. And with all this exercise she lost weight rapidly.

18. A Weasel At Miss Peckham's

The next morning when I turned the ponies out into the paddock, I checked their hoofs and found that one of Jones's hind shoes was loose. I didn't have time to do anything about it except to tell Father. He said he'd either fasten it on or remove both hind shoes and he'd call Caleb and see if he could shoe both ponies after school. Since Jane was going to spend the night with a friend who lives way up beyond Appledore, she wouldn't come home from school at all that Friday; so I had another of those busy afternoons cut out for me. I didn't mind, though, for by doing the kennel chores on Friday, I'd be done with them for the rest of the weekend, with my debt all paid to Jane, too, and I knew Father wouldn't detain me for fear of keeping Caleb waiting. As it happened, he sent me off to Still Waters before I was quite through, saying that Mike would finish up for me. He also said for heaven's sake to steer clear of the glass chariot while I had Jones in tow.

That was no problem since we never saw any traffic at all after we left the Appledore road. We didn't, in fact, even see a human being in the fields or at the Vickerys' as we passed by. When we got to Still Waters and found neither Caleb nor the Major there, I began to wonder if the whole neighborhood had been deserted. Since I had an appointment with Caleb, I could only suppose that he had gone somewhere in the truck and had been delayed. The Major, of course, might be walking anywhere, and Bozo was probably with him. The only thing to do was to wait and see what happened.

I put the ponies in the big box stall where they'd be handy, and walked on down the lane to see if Bozo was in the back pasture with the stock. He wasn't, but I greeted the stock and played with the goats for a few minutes. Then I walked back past the barn and out into the road, where I stood looking up and down uncertainly. I wondered if Miss Peckham had vanished, too; and, remembering that I hadn't seen Pounce around home, I thought I'd better check and see if he might be haunting her again.

I noted with satisfaction as I passed her driveway that the glass chariot was out, but I walked on past the house to make sure nobody was there. Then I circled the grounds, inspecting the target by the brook, which Jane had mentioned, and peering around in likely places for a black cat. Finding no cat, I had returned to the front of the house and was about to leave when I saw a small brown animal scurry across the lawn and into the lilac clump by the marble bench. I waited quietly, and a moment later I saw it streak across the lawn again, this time from the other side of the lilacs to the granite doorstep. It paused an instant here and, raising its body, looked shrewdly over the step at me. Then it disappeared into the narrow space between the doorstep and the foundation of the house. It was the first weasel I had ever seen close up, and I was interested.

I went over and examined the crack where it had vanished, but could see nothing unusual. As I knelt there, however, I detected a peculiar smell that seemed somehow familiar. I sniffed at the crack and recalled suddenly the unidentifiable animal smell in Bozo's feverish dream. So *that* was what poor Bozo had been tracking when Peckham had winged him from behind the chariot! A wave of anger swept over me as I remembered that unprovoked attack and the trouble it had brought to Bozo and the Major and even to Dolores—to all of us, really, except Peckham herself. But it was an old anger now and soon gave way to my curiosity about the weasel. I wondered if perhaps he lived under the doorstep and had a regular route through the lilacs. If he had, perhaps I could locate it by its scent. I walked over to the lilacs, got down on my hands and knees, and sniffed at the place where I judged the weasel had emerged. There was only a grassy, leafy smell at first; so I kept moving back and forth, sniffing until I caught it. I was just looking to see if there might be any visible path among the stalks, when a well-known and disapproving voice hailed me. "Philip, what *are* you doing here?"

Too late I realized that my ears had been trying to tell me that gravel was crunching nearby; the creepy, crawly glass chariot had rolled into the drive and stopped opposite me, and Miss Peckham was standing beside it. "There's a weasel," I began, as I started to get to my feet. Then, as the door behind her opened and the gangly form of Sam Paine emerged, I sank back on my heels and exclaimed in astonishment, "Sam! What are *you* doing here?"

Sam regarded me owlishly through his glasses and said curtly, "Hello, Birdsong."

"Oh, do you know him?" asked Miss Peckham. "I thought he was much younger than you."

"Oh, of course," said Sam (for all his height he's barely a year older than I am), "but we attend the same school, and one gets to know everyone's name at school." Then, as I got to my feet, he went on officiously, "Now, Birdsong, what's this about a weasel? Do you think you saw one?"

"I saw a weasel, Paine, and no thinking about it," I replied firmly. "It went behind your doorstep," I added, turning to Miss Peckham. "It may have a hole there."

"Well, what had that to do with your crawling around under my lilac bush?" demanded Miss Peckham. "You must have been here before you saw the weasel," she added suspiciously.

"I was looking for Caleb or the Major," I said. "Neither of them is home, and I have an appointment to have the ponies shod."

"And you expected to find them under the lilac bush?" inquired Miss Peckham.

"N-no," I stammered, feeling my face get red at the smirk Sam gave me. "I saw the weasel come through here and I was looking to see if it had a regular path." This sounded silly, of course, but it was true, and I couldn't think of any other explanation.

"You were smelling," retorted Miss Peckham. "I distinctly saw you sniffing just like—" Here she paused a moment, fixing me with a speculative stare and then concluding with a burst of inspiration, "Why, just like that wretched mongrel of the Major's."

"Well," I said defensively, "all the weasel family have musk glands. They smell stronger than most animals." I wasn't sure this was true at all times, but it seemed likely.

Sam and Miss Peckham exchanged looks, and Sam shook his head in a hopeless sort of way as if, in his opinion, further conversation with me would be useless. Before Miss Peckham could return to the attack, I was inspired to go on with my nature lore. There had been an article on weasels in the nature magazine Father subscribes to.

"Weasels are very fierce," I said. "They will attack animals much larger than themselves just for the love of killing. If one lives here, Dolores had better look out."

As a means of diverting Miss Peckham's mind from my curious behavior, this last remark seemed to me a real brain wave. She did look alarmed, and I think we might have had a cozy conversation about the habits of weasels if Sam had not put in his oar again. "I can't follow your argument, Birdsong," he said. "Why should you assume that this weasel which you have seen and—uh—smelled once, lives here? How do you know it wasn't just a traveling weasel?"

"Oh, it's not the first time I've sm—noticed it," I said incautiously. Then, to cover this slip, I hurried on, "I'm pretty sure it's got a regular path through the lilac clump, too."

"Oh, you did smell it out, did you?" asked Sam.

I had gotten so rattled, I couldn't think of any reply. Sam and Miss Peckham exchanged significant looks at my silence, and Sam went on, "I would hate to think, Birdsong, that a boy your age would try to frighten a lone woman with your fancies. If there really is a weasel, I doubt if it could be as dangerous as you make out. Weasels are very small."

"I know they're small," I protested. "I've just seen one, and it was no fancy. And if you don't believe they're dangerous to other animals, I'll lend you a magazine with an article about them. Sometimes they even hunt in packs and attack human beings."

Sam and Miss Peckham again looked at each other, and this time Sam tapped his forehead. The conversation had become so hopeless that I was immensely relieved to hear a truck come down the crossroad hill. I ran out into the road and saw that it was Caleb.

"I have to go now," I called, "but I'd watch that doorstep if I were you, Miss Peckham." Then I added in as menacing a tone as I could muster, "Good-bye, Paine. I'll see *you* later," and strode briskly off. My feelings as I hurried back to Still Waters were mixed. Of course I felt awfully silly, and exasperation is a mild word to describe my attitude toward Sam, but more than anything else I was curious. What the dickens was Sam doing there anyway? It was hard to imagine two people less likely to be pals than him and Miss Peckham, but they must be; he had taken over the conversation and spoken for her and she had let him. It was incredible.

I found Caleb in the barn, talking to the ponies and shaving up a shingle onto some newspaper to start his fire. He was apologetic about being late; there'd been trouble with the truck's clutch, and he'd had to be towed back to town when he was halfway home. "I couldn't get hold of you, and the Major wasn't home," he said, "but I got your mother on the phone and explained, and she said if I still had time when I got back to go ahead and shoe both ponies and she'd wait dinner for you. You're to call home just before you leave."

I thanked Caleb and took over the fire while he led Jones out of the stall, snapped the cross ties to each side of his halter, and began to work on his hoofs. When I had put on the coal and plugged in the electric blower, I stood by to hand Caleb his tools; but all the time I continued to marvel and wonder about Sam and Miss Peckham. I asked Caleb if he knew Sam, and when he said he didn't, I described Sam and asked if he'd ever seen him at Miss Peckham's or in the chariot or on Foothill Road. Since the answers were again negative, I gave up that subject and told him about the weasel. Caleb was interested in my account of it; he'd seen one at Still Waters the week before and had since taken what precautions he could to protect the feathered part of the stock from it. "I've stopped every crack I could find in the barn," he said, "but a weasel can get through a mighty small space. There haven't been any signs of him about since that once, though. Likely he's the one you saw and hunts in the fields around Miss Peckham's." Caleb agreed that the weasel might be living under Miss Peckham's granite doorstep and that if Dolores went sniffing around there at the wrong time, she might be attacked. Encouraged by this confirmation of what I had read, I asked him if he had ever heard of weasels hunting in packs.

"Yes indeed," he replied. "My dad, he saw a pack once in the old country. It was on a moonlight night, and he said it was a sight to chill your blood. The country folks called them 'dandy dogs'; they thought they were the hounds of the Little People, and they kept out of their way." This was interesting information, but I was glad I hadn't known it during my interview with Sam and Miss Peckham. I had said too much as it was.

Then I reported on the success of the tricycle, and we drifted from this into a discussion of Dolores's preference for blue and gold. Our conversation was by no means continuous because there were intervals of hammering too noisy for talking and other intervals when Caleb was too engrossed in his work to talk about anything but the job in hand. So we really didn't say a great deal; but by the time both ponies were shod, I got up my courage to ask him how soon he and the Major would have to move if Miss Peckham refused to sell Still Waters. "We'll have till the end of the month, as far as we know," replied Caleb. "The Major's gone to Appledore today to look at a farm for sale there, but I know the place. It's a hillside farm with rocky pastures and never a spot for a garden on it. And the barn's falling to pieces, too. He'll not fancy a place like that—nor any other in the whole vàlley—after Still Waters."

The Major and Bozo, both looking tired and discouraged, came home soon after I had received this dismal information, and I was glad at least to be able to give a good account of the tricycle. The Major expressed his satisfaction at this, but I could see he was still disheartened. Less than cheerful myself, I attempted no further conversation as I walked to the house with him to telephone Mother that I was starting for home.

19. Sam's Hereditary Affliction

As I rode home in the gathering dusk, I diverted my mind temporarily from the Major's trouble by pondering once more the mystery of Sam's presence and behavior at Miss Peckham's. I was startled when I topped the first rise on the crossroad to look down the gradual slope before me and see Sam himself draped over the railing of the bridge where Pounce had sat yesterday. As I drew near, it seemed to me that he looked extremely limp, and I remembered that he was not an enthusiastic walker. He heard us coming, of course, and turned and grinned feebly at me. "Hello, Paine," I said. "Nice day for a walk, but won't you be a little late for dinner? Or isn't that of any importance when you're managing Miss Peckham's affairs for her?"

"Elvira's a hereditary affliction," said Sam with a weary sort of sigh.

"A what?" I asked.

"A hereditary affliction," he repeated. "That's what my mother calls her."

"You mean she's related to you?" I asked.

"Alas, yes," said Sam. "She's my second cousin once removed."

"Well, if I were you, I'd try removing her again," I said. "Why didn't you ever tell me so before?"

"Why should I?" asked Sam. "It's not the kind of connection you boast about, and besides, you've never given me a list of *your* second cousins once removed."

"I don't think I have anything of the kind," I said, and then, realizing that Sam was trying to distract me from a just grievance, I went on, "Anyhow, that's not the point. Even if you *are* her second cousin," (here Sam murmured "once removed") "why did you have to treat me like a naughty child—and an idiot one at that? Aren't we supposed to be friends?"

The feeble smile flitted over Sam's face again as he replied, "Oh, sure, but what else could I do? Elvira had just been telling me about some frightful cruelty you had inflicted on Dolores with balloons. I really couldn't follow her very well; I wish you'd explain about it. Anyway, she was so mad at you that I did the decent thing and suggested that perhaps you weren't quite responsible for your eccentric behavior. And then there you were, sniffing about like a dog and babbling about packs of weasels. I couldn't let Elvira think I approve of that sort of thing."

"I don't see why not if she's a hereditary affliction. It might remove her for good."

"You don't understand, Hippo. I admit my heart does not leap up at the sight of Elvira, but it does at the sight of her car."

"That creepy, crawly glass chariot?" I said. "Who's crazy now?"

"Not me, Hippo, my boy," replied Sam. "That chariot is the beauty of the past and the hope of the future."

"Not *my* future," I said.

"Oh yes, it is," said Sam. "Haven't you heard about air pollution from combustion engines? The electric car is the answer to that. The new ones will be different, of course, but this one is fascinating. Did you know it has six speeds forward and three in reverse?"

"No, I didn't," I said coldly, "and I can't stop any longer to listen to you babbling about it. I'm in a hurry to get home if you aren't. I'm hungry and dinner is waiting for me. Have a nice walk, Paine."

A sort of spasm passed over Sam's face when I mentioned dinner. He grasped the railing and staggered along a few steps behind me.

"I always said you were a hard guy, Hippo," he quavered.

"Well," I said, "if you're too tired to walk after dancing attendance on Miss Peckham all afternoon, you've no one to blame but yourself and you'll just have to take the consequences, unless," I added as an idea for revenge came to me, "you'd like to ride Jones. *He* won't pollute your air."

"The only horse I've ever ridden was my grandfather's work horse when he was plowing," said Sam doubtfully.

"Jones should be more comfortable than that," I said; "his back's narrower. And since your experience has all been without a saddle, you won't mind riding bareback. It's a long walk home."

My last remark, I think, decided Sam. He's quite agile, so he didn't have much trouble scrambling onto Jones's back; and, though his long legs looked ludicrous dangling way below Jones's belly, he said he felt quite comfortable. That didn't last long, for I put the ponies into a brisk trot and smiled cheerfully as Sam, clutching Jones's mane, joggled miserably up and down and back and forth. "Hold on with your knees, Paine," I said, "and be careful not to bite your tongue."

"Stop, you fiend!" bawled Sam. "You're murdering me!"

"Oh, no," I replied. "I'm just giving you the healthful kind of exercise growing boys need. But if you think you've had enough, I'll slow down on two conditions: First, from now on you call me Phil—no more of that Birdsong stuff, and no Hippo either. Second, tell me exactly what you were doing at Miss Peckham's."

I thought Sam nodded, but he was jiggling and flapping so all over, I couldn't be sure. "Do you promise on the honor of Samuel Serafino Paine III?" I asked.

Sam managed to gasp out a *yes,* and I slowed the ponies down to a walk. Sam detached one hand from Jones's mane, pushed back his hair and his spectacles with it, and glared at me. "Of all the rotten tricks!" he exploded.

"No rottener than yours," I replied, "—just a little more vigorous."

Sam began to grin. "You should have seen yourself, Hip—I mean Phil, when you tried to explain yourself to Elvira."

"You should have seen *yourself,* Sam, when you were trying to stay on Jones," I retorted.

At this we both laughed and then settled down to mutual explanations. I learned from Sam that Miss Peckham had been orphaned while still quite a young woman and that his grandfather, who was her first cousin once removed and her nearest kin in the state, had become a sort of unofficial guardian to her, advising her when she needed advice and helping her when she needed help. When old Mr. Paine died, Sam's father fell heir to the job, though Miss Peckham was only a few months younger than he and rejected all advice from him. She was strong on demanding help, however, so that he had acquired a real genius for vanishing whenever she came in sight. Sam's mother, being the victim who usually had to receive her, had named her "the hereditary affliction." That afternoon Miss Peckham had made one of her calls, during which Sam had availed himself of the opportunity of inspecting the innards of the glass chariot and of detaching a battery cable. Then, when Miss Peckham could not get the chariot started, he had rushed to her rescue, scraped the terminal with a scientific air, and replaced it, suggesting he had better accompany her home in case she had further trouble. He had wanted to observe just how the chariot was driven and hoped he might get a chance to maneuver it around her driveway himself on the pretext of testing it out. Unfortunately, however, Miss Peckham declared the chariot was functioning perfectly and had set him to work polishing it. She had watched him, too, so that he couldn't stop. "I even had to use an old toothbrush on the wheel spokes," he commented bitterly. "And you know what? I was going down to the state road to hitch-hike home, and she wouldn't let me. She doesn't approve of hitchhiking, even with people you know; so she saw me to the corner of this road and watched me till I got over the hill."

I sympathized with his sufferings and summarized my own recent misfortunes with her. Sam had heard nothing of her treatment of the Major and was suitably indignant about it, but *my* troubles he only laughed at. "Alone you're not so dangerous—uh, Phil," he said, "but when you're teamed up with your animal friends, you're a menace to society. What I'd like to know," he went on, "is whether there really was a weasel in the act this afternoon. And what *were* you doing when we arrived?"

"Of course there was a weasel," I replied, "and I was smelling around for his path. Weasels do have musk glands, and I happen to have an extraordinarily acute sense of smell."

Sam shook his head. "I've seen, heard, and smelled everything now," he said. "You should hire yourself out to a hunter."

The ponies had been walking while we talked, but now I gently broke the news to Sam that we'd have to mend our pace to get home before dark. He started to remonstrate, but I cut him short. "We won't trot this time," I said, "we'll canter. Jones has a canter like a rocking horse. All you have to do is sit still and relax." I started the ponies before he could dismount, and though he gripped Jones's mane for dear life, Sam soon got into the swing of the canter and rode without further complaint until we slowed down for the Appledore road, when a few more trotting steps were unavoidable.

"I'll never be the same again," he groaned when the ponies had slowed to a walk.

"Cheer up!" I said. "We're almost home, and we'll walk them from here on. Even though they have only three speeds ahead, you must admit they're faster than your old chariot."

"You have no feeling for the finer things in life, Hippo," said Sam with a sigh.

"Want to trot, Sammy boy?" I asked.

"No, Phil, no!" replied Sam hastily. "The Hippo habit is going to be hard to break," he added mournfully.

"I'll give you all the reminders you need to keep your word," I said. I further comforted him with the observation that the family hadn't had dinner yet and that Mother was sure to invite him to share it; but even here he was unlucky. Mother greeted us from the back porch with the information that Sam's mother had been trying to locate him and had left a message that if he appeared at our house, he was to go home directly. "She said something about your cousin," Mother concluded.

"Oh, gosh! I forgot," said Sam. "They're all going bowling and I've got to baby-sit her."

"Your second cousin once removed?" I asked sympathetically.

"No," said Sam, "my first cousin on my mother's side. She's five years old and almost as determined as Elvira, but they bring her to our house and she sleeps most of the time, thank goodness! Next to food, rest in a soft spot is what I need most."

"Not too soft," I said. "You mustn't allow your muscles to sag. And you might try a hot bath."

"Thank you for the kind advice," said Sam, though he didn't sound very grateful. Then he added dully, "So long —Phil. See you at the game tomorrow if I can creep there."

"What does Sam means by *creep?*" asked Mother.

"Oh, he tried riding Jones bareback and he *would* keep trotting," I said. "He'll be stiff, I daresay."

At dinner I told my parents about Sam's inherited affliction. They were amused, though Mother had doubts of Sam's discretion in confiding the term to me. "Of course *you* mustn't call Miss Peckham that, dear," she said, and then added, "That reminds me. She came to the office early this afternoon and wanted to know if we had a black cat."

"What did you say?" I asked anxiously.

"Well, when she came right out and said, 'Do you have a black cat here?' I had to tell her the truth."

I looked at Mother reproachfully, but she avoided my eye and went on, "I said, 'Why yes, we have; she had three kittens the night before last and two of them are black. Did you want one?' "

"Mother!" I gasped. "You didn't!"

"Yes, I did," said Mother serenely. "It was the truth."

And it was. The cat belonged to Jane's friend Ellen, and had been brought over to have her kittens and be boarded with us for a few days. Ellen's two younger brothers had come down with chicken pox by now and one of them was quite sick; so her mother was afraid the cat would be neglected at home.

"Phil," said Father, "your mother's duplicity is incredible," and he burst into his deep, contagious laugh. I joined in, of course, but I was checked a little as I automatically looked across the table to catch Jane's eye and faced an empty chair. Mother so seldom does anything like that, that when she does, it always takes us by surprise and delights us. Jane would have loved this particular instance of Mother's bland evasiveness.

Father stopped laughing sooner than I expected, to say, "Now that reminds me that Miss Peckham telephoned a little while ago and asked me if a weasel might attack Dolores. She thinks she may have one living under her doorstep."

"What did you say?" I asked.

"I said a weasel might, especially if Dolores annoyed it. Then she wanted to know how she could get rid of a weasel if there was one."

"What did you say to that?" I asked.

"I told her—" here Father started to laugh again, but managed to pronounce the sentence, "I told her she'd better get a cat!"

In the following explosion of mirth I noticed that both parents looked at Jane's empty chair. I missed her giggle too.

20. Miss Peckham Is Buttered Up

The weekend that followed was so uneventful that life seemed almost normal for a change. I spent most of Saturday morning giving Dolores an extra workout on her tricycle and taking a trip downtown with Mother to exchange some overdue library books and to do some shopping at the dime store. We gave a neighbor a ride home, so I sat alone in the back of the Volkswagen and examined my purchases. They consisted of a tiny bottle of quick-drying gilt enamel (which I planned to give Jane on condition that she paint a gold stripe border around the back of the tricycle), and a small sky-blue ball. The ball Dolores had been using was too big for her to retrieve easily and was, besides, red.

At lunch Jane announced that she was going to Still Waters for her music lesson. Father said she'd better ride Jones; so that left me with Evans for the football game. He didn't like it at first—he wasn't used to crowds like Jones—but I forced him along, and he soon began to enjoy himself. Of course he wasn't trained to charge Sam; but I guess we'd have had to omit that act anyway, because Sam said he'd break in two if he had to jump back, much less fall down. He was hobbling around in an absurd, bowlegged way announcing to everybody who'd listen that he had taken up horseback riding. Haunceton won, and I broke the record for candy sales (though I admit I bought a supply of a dozen bars myself). Altogether it was a satisfactory afternoon.

Jane had apparently had a good time too; but she had had enough of the recorder for a while, so I was not obliged to communicate with Dolores against my will that night, and instead settled down to the luxury of reading an exciting book I'd gotten from the library. By the time I got ready for bed, rain, which had been threatening all day but had obligingly held off till now, was pattering against my east windows.

Sunday morning I awoke to find my quilt on the floor and my arms outside the blanket that still partially covered me. I sniffed the muggy air and thought, "Indian summer." I was right; the wind had veered into the south, we had had a heavy rain, and now everything dripped in still warm air under a gray sky. To my grumbling about the weather at breakfast, Mother replied, "But we're bound to have some lovely warm, sunny days when it clears, dear." That was true, but the weather took its time clearing, and every creature on the place, except Mother and Jane, seemed under its muggy spell. Dolores was so languid that she showed little interest in her blue ball and had to be pushed around with the bull staff, and the ponies just stood around taking turns resting their heads on each other's necks. Pounce spent his time sleeping in Jones's manger.

I would have considered that dreary Sunday a total loss as a holiday, for I spent most of it catching up on schoolwork, if Mother hadn't let me escape to Sam's house while she was giving a supper party for some friends of ours who have two little girls, but no boys. Sam's parents had gone to visit some friends in a neighboring town and his brother was off somewhere, too, so we got ourselves a satisfying meal (enthusiastically shared by Nifty) of hot dogs, scrambled eggs, and apple pie. Sam was apparently still feeling the effects of his ride on Jones, for he lowered himself very gingerly onto a kitchen chair to eat. I made no direct comment on this, but was reminded to inquire for his second cousin once removed. "She telephoned a message to Dad this morning," he replied. "She wants him to move the granite doorstep in front of her house and evict any weasels that might be living under it. Dad says it would take at least three men with crowbars to move the step and that he, for one, doesn't care to evict any weasels. So you see what you started, young Hippo."

"I didn't start it, young Seraph; the weasel did," I replied. A hot debate about names and words of honor followed which was finally settled on these terms: that we could call each other what we liked in private, but that the public use of anything but Sam and Phil was strictly forbidden. It was the same arrangement I have always had with Jane. Sam said it wasn't really fair since other people at school called me Hippo, but I maintained that he was the chief offender and that if he didn't use the name, it would eventually die out.

By the time I got home, the guests were gone, the dishes washed, and Jane had disappeared upstairs. I found her in my room preparing, she said, to practice on the recorder. I got Dolores from the hospital and started to give her her evening workout in the cellar. In the cool of the evening she had perked up enough to chase her ball, but the constant music Jane provided was an annoyance at first. I had gotten the habit of playing to Dolores at intervals while she rested; but the sight of herself cavorting around on the tricycle so entranced her that she'd keep forgetting to chase the ball and then she'd slow down and stop. I finally solved that problem, however, by keeping my eyes on the blue ball till she caught up with it, and then shutting them until she brought it back to me, when I would reward her with a long stare, even walking around her so that she could see herself from all sides. I noticed that Jane wasn't having much luck with her scale and none at all trying to play the first air in the book. She soon reverted to *Three Blind Mice,* but she did not even play that for long.

As I lay in bed that night, I calculated that the Major's lease still had four more days to go, which meant four more days of suspense for us. But things were looking up.

Dolores, limp-free and thinner than I had ever seen her, was due to go home tomorrow, and Father had promised to present the tricycle to Miss Peckham with the Major's compliments, making no mention of my connection with it. As I turned over for the last time before I went to sleep, I sighed the contented sigh of one whose work has been well done.

Monday was one of those sunny, soft, Indian-summer days that Mother had predicted. For the first time since my birthday I went to school with a relaxed and virtuous feeling that my homework was all done. It was a little discouraging to find that my algebra teacher didn't figure it that way; she said I still owed her some from last week. But the windows of the Morgue were open, and in that warm, drowsy air, even she couldn't get too excited about my shortcomings. At the end of the day I had a study period in Miss Norcross's room, which is also in the old building, but upstairs in the front. Three times during that period the baying of a not-too-distant bloodhound drifted through the open windows, interrupting the hum of traffic. Each time I automatically started up in my seat with the idea of rising to get a view of the ground below, but each time I was arrested by Miss Norcross's calm, tortoiseshell gaze directed at me. I detected traces of her peculiar smile in the gaze, but still I had received the sort of warning that isn't overlooked in Miss Norcross's room. When the bell rang and I rose to leave, I had my chance, but I couldn't see Bozo anywhere. I thought perhaps he might be waiting at the Mapes Street door; he had done that a couple of times before—usually when the Major was in Boston—but he hadn't been so noisy about it.

I found I'd guessed wrong when, on reporting to my home room, I was handed a mysterious note that had been sent up from the office. It was written on a sheet torn from a memorandum book and read:

> Dear Phil,
> If it's convenient, will you please get Bozo at Charley Duane's and take him home with you? I had to leave him there.
> H. H. F.

H. H. F. stands for Hugh Henry Featherstone.

I lost no time getting to Charley Duane's, which is almost directly across Main Street from the school. His door was fastened open, and before I even stepped into the shop, I was greeted by a roar from Bozo and a rhythmical bonging as his tail hit the old steam radiator to which he was tied by his leash. I shook his paw and got my front cowlick licked as I stooped and unsnapped the leash from his collar. I heard Charley come in from the back room while I was busy untying the knot, and said to him over my shoulder, "The Major asked me to take Bozo home with me."

"I know," said Charley, "but I'll miss him. When the door's open, the bell in the back room doesn't ring when somebody comes in, and he sure is a good substitute for it."

"But how did the Major happen to leave him here?" I asked.

"Well, it was this way," said Charley. "You know Miss Peckham?" I nodded, gloomily, I guess, because Charley grinned and then went on, "She came in to see if her radio was ready, and it was, but I couldn't deliver it till tomorrow. Well, you know she's the kind that can't wait, so she said she'd take it with her. It's an old Stromberg Carlson —one of those standing models, not terribly heavy, but they take up a lot of space. As I was trying to wedge it into that car of hers, the Major happened to come along and offered to help me. We got it in, but then Miss Peckham says, 'How am I going to get it out when I get home?' So the Major agreed to ride home with her and get it into her house for her. But meanwhile Bozo had come up, and the Major was afraid he'd follow along. I don't really see what harm that would do; Bozo could keep up with *that* car without any trouble, and he seems to have enough sense to keep out of traffic. But of course I was glad to oblige the Major, and as I say, Bozo's been quite a help. I was to turn him loose in half an hour if you didn't show up."

"Miss Peckham doesn't like Bozo," I explained, "and you know how he hoots—especially when he's chasing something."

"Oh!" said Charley, and we both grinned at the idea of Bozo's pursuing the glass chariot noisily through town.

As Bozo and I were leaving the store, Charley called after me, "Oh, Phil, tell your dad that his message-recorder should be in any day now."

"O.K., thanks," I replied, though it took me a moment to recall just what he was talking about. On Charley's advice, Father had arranged to trade in the tape recorder Mother had won for another kind all set up for telephone messages. It had possibilities that ordinarily would have interested me, but I was too absorbed in the Major's problem—and a few of my own—to give it much thought.

I hung Bozo's leash around my neck, and we walked home by the Appledore road. When we reached the stable, I gave the ponies their sugar and then got a snack from the kitchen for Bozo and me. I took it back to the stable, where we shared it, I seated in the old porch rocker, and Bozo lying panting beside me on the floor. When the last crumb was gone, I heaved myself out of the rocker and told Bozo to stay where he was and cool off, while I did the kennel chores, promising to ride home with him afterwards if he'd wait.

But on the very threshold of the stable I froze for a moment at the sight of the glass chariot creeping up the driveway toward the hospital. Bozo became aware of it at the same moment apparently, and I turned to him just in time to stifle an incipient howl. I quickly got us both out of sight and stationed myself where I could see what happened through the front stable window that's right in line with the hospital side of the U-drive.

The chariot stopped, as usual, in the middle of the drive right in front of the hospital. Most people turn into the parking space to leave the drive free, but Miss Peckham never did; she left others to do the backing and filling. She was quite annoyed one day when a man bringing in an emergency case drove in on the house side of the U and, being unable to reach the parking space because of the chariot, parked in front of it so that for once *she* had to back.

Today her stubbornness served me well, however, for it gave me a clear view of all that went on. The seating arrangements of the chariot were one of its weirdest features. The space beside the left hand door, which was located as near the front of the chariot as possible, was occupied by the driving shaft. This was operated by a bar that needed so much room to swing that the driver sat in the rear, practically against the back window. There was room for two passengers facing each other on the right-hand side, one beside the driver and the other on a jump seat which had its back practically against the front window. Today the Major sat beside Miss Peckham, only his narrow head with its thick gray hair showing above the Stromberg Carlson. He almost always wears a hat outdoors, but I suppose he had removed it in honor of his impressive surroundings. He made a convulsive movement as if to get up when the chariot stopped, but Miss Peckham said something to him and he subsided listlessly behind the radio. Then Miss Peckham pulled herself up by a strap provided for the purpose, dismounted, and swept into the hospital.

I took the opportunity of her absence to go to the door of the stable with Bozo and wave. The Major waved back, but he also made a warning gesture which I took to mean that I should keep Bozo quiet and out of sight. I returned to my post at the window and viewed the scene as I awaited further developments.

The first action was from an unexpected quarter. The school bus stopped at our drive, and a couple of moments later I could see Jane stealthily advancing from tree to tree in the park, apparently trying to get as near the chariot as possible without being seen. Her Girl Scout meeting must have been canceled. This was unusual, but I learned from her later that even her bouncy leader had been laid low by chicken pox.

My attention was soon diverted from Jane to a sort of royal procession that emerged from the hospital. First

Mike stepped out and, standing impressively at his full height, held the door open. Then Miss Peckham appeared, holding Dolores before her on the blue pillow. Father followed, carrying the tricycle, now further decorated with a gold border. Mike went back in, but Father followed Miss Peckham to the right side of the chariot and opened the door for her. Apparently Dolores was to ride on the jump seat, which at present was screened off from the back seat by the radio; but something about this arrangement didn't suit Miss Peckham, and Dolores was passed across the radio to the Major and disappeared, pillow and all, presumably into his lap. Father then escorted Miss Peckham back to the driver's door, where he made what was obviously his presentation speech and, at its conclusion, with a graceful gesture and a smile directed toward the depths of the chariot, he handed over the tricycle. Miss Peckham, I was relieved to see, seemed pleased; she was even smiling as she got back into the chariot. In fact, she seemed thoroughly buttered up.

21. A New Plan For Peckham Persuasion

When the chariot turned into Emerson Street, I went back to the doorway and gave a whistle to attract Jane's attention as she walked back across the park toward the house. She turned and came toward me while Bozo and I sauntered out to meet her. "Did you see that?" she demanded before we were even within comfortable speaking distance.

"Yes," I said, "I was watching from the stable window. Miss Peckham seemed quite pleased with the tricycle, I thought."

"Oh, you and your tricycle," spluttered Jane. "Didn't you see the poor Major wedged in behind that big case like a prisoner?"

"Of course I saw him," I replied, "but I wasn't surprised." And I explained to Jane how he happened to be there.

"But it was so—so undignified for him," she protested. "I could see that he was very uncomfortable about it. And then to have to hold Dolores on his lap!"

I had never thought of the Major as especially dignified, but I could see what Jane meant; I had suffered indignities at Miss Peckham's hands myself. "Well, I feel for him," I said, "but his financial adviser told him he'd have to butter Peckham up, and I suppose that's what he's doing. And what's more it seems to be working."

"Oh, the Major'd help her anyhow," said Jane impatiently. "He's always helping everybody, but it's the way she treats him that makes me so mad. And don't be too sure that he's making any progress with her; you can't tell with somebody like Peckham. She may smirk, but it doesn't mean she'll sell him Still Waters. It's perfectly outrageous," Jane went on, working herself up to an even higher pitch of indignation, "the way everybody waits on her hand and foot—even Father. And when she ought to be paying Bozo's bill instead of the Major paying Dolores's."

"Father was just trying to help us," I said, "and you must admit he did it with quite a flourish. Could you hear if the Major said anything?"

"He didn't say a thing," said Jane. "He didn't get a chance; Father and that awful Peckham talked all the time. The poor Major just looked embarrassed."

"Well, that's good," I said. "Peckham will give him all the credit for the tricycle." I had been afraid that the Major, out of a mistaken sense of justice, might try to give *me* some credit for it.

"I don't know that that's so good," Jane. "It's—it's—. What started the war in Europe?"

"Appeasement?" I asked.

"That's it," said Jane. "It's appeasement. Father says he doesn't believe in it, and I don't either. Giving bad people what they want just makes them worse. Peckham needs to be treated rough."

"By the Major?" I was being sarcastic, of course, but that didn't bother Jane.

"Oh, no!" replied Jane, "he's too polite for that—and too honorable. We should do it for him."

"And just how would you suggest that we proceed, Felice Jane?" I asked.

"I told you before, but you wouldn't listen," replied Jane. "We could kidnap Dolores or something—and anybody too polite and honorable needn't know about it."

"But Jane," I remonstrated, "we couldn't get away with anything like that. Father'd smell a rat even if we could find some place to hide her, and besides we'd probably get arrested for stealing or blackmail or something."

"I don't care," said Jane. "Something like that ought to be done to get anywhere with a woman like that. And you and Dolores are such pals now, you ought to be able to think up some scheme she'd cooperate in."

"Well," I said doubtfully, and paused to consider the

matter. Of course Jane's ideas were much too extreme, but ever since Caleb had told me that Jane had the Power with people I'd been noticing that she did seem to know how people felt, and I thought she might be right about strong measures being needed for Miss Peckham. Perhaps we could dream up some modified kidnapping plan—or something. I ran my fingers through my hair to assist thought, but was reminded of the demands of the moment when a car drove in with a dog patient whom Bozo greeted with a howl.

"Look, Jane," I said, "I haven't done the kennel chores yet, and I've promised Bozo to ride home with him. Since you're not busy, why don't you come help me, and then we can both go and get started sooner. We can discuss this rough treatment on the way. I sometimes get ideas when I'm riding."

"O.K.," said Jane, apparently glad at the prospect of any action. "I'll get my clothes changed quick."

As it turned out, Jane did most of the chores because Father grabbed me to hold first a cat and then a monkey. The monkey had to have a shot and the only way she would take it was with her arms clasped about my neck.

So we were late starting, and Jane grumbled because we wouldn't have time for a race at Still Waters, and she was disgusted at me because I said it was too hot anyway. Oppressed by this mild discord and the heaviness of the damp heat, I got no ideas at all about treating Peckham rough.

There was no cheer at Still Waters either. Caleb was looking grim and said that the Major was lying down. "Walking never tires him," he said, "but he had to ride all over town for almost an hour in that chariot while

Miss Peckham shopped, and then he had to hold Dolores. We had trouble getting that old radio out and into the house, too. I think it all made him nervous."

At this Jane gave me an I-told-you-so look, and we decided that now we had delivered Bozo and his leash, we wouldn't even dismount. "I would if I had my bathing suit, though," said Jane. "The pond looks so nice and cool."

"I'm glad you're willing to admit it *is* hot," I said automatically as I looked over at the pond. I knew it was shallow and muddy, but it did look inviting.

Suddenly I turned to Jane with more energy than I had felt all day. "Let's get going," I said and, bidding Caleb good-bye, started Evans on his homeward way.

Jones followed, though Jane protested, "What's the hurry all of a sudden? I thought you were wilted."

"I've just thought of something," I replied. "Come on!"

We started, as usual, at a canter, but the ponies, hotter than we were, slowed down going uphill and settled into a walk of their own accord. When Jane, bursting with curiosity, had asked me at the foot of the hill if I really had had a brain wave about Peckham, I had nodded, but had hushed her with a finger to my lips. Now that we were up the hill, I looked carefully around and then said in a conspiratorial tone, "How would it be if we dunked Dolores in the Major's pond?"

Jane looked puzzled. "You mean to scare Peckham?"

"Partly," I replied, "but think. What would Dolores do?"

"She'd swim in that flapping, panting way of hers, I guess," said Jane.

"Exactly," I replied. "And what would the Major do?"

"Oh!" said Jane as the light burst upon her. "He'd think she was drowning and he'd jump in and rescue her."

"Exactly," I repeated. "And he'd return her, snatched from a watery grave, to Peckham; and when he'd saved her darling Dolores, Peckham could refuse him nothing."

"Well-l-l," said Jane, "it'll still be appeasement, in a way, I guess, but at least there'll be lots of excitement and Peckham will get a scare. It may even be dangerous," she added eagerly.

"For me it will," I said not quite so eagerly, "because I'll have to kidnap Dolores and do the dunking while you keep the Major on the scene."

As we ambled home, we laid our plans in detail. I thought at first we should wait till the day after tomorrow, which was Columbus Day and a school holiday, to carry them out, but Jane vetoed that. "We've got to move as quickly as we can," she said. "This weather can't last long, and we shouldn't dunk Dolores when it's cold. We'll be lucky if it's as hot as this even tomorrow."

So zero hour was set for the following afternoon. Jane displayed an indiscreet mania for weather broadcasts on television that evening, but she was excellent on organization and detail. I sat beside her on Father's bed while she phoned the Major and asked, with a perfect blend of enthusiasm and wistfulness, if they couldn't have one more croquet tournament tomorrow afternoon before the stakes and wickets were taken in for the winter. She explained incidentally that I would be busy. Fortunately the Major had no engagements and agreed cordially to the tournament.

At breakfast on Tuesday, Jane was fidgety and expressed her concern that today would not be as warm as yesterday. "Why should anybody want it to be?" asked Father. "Are you planning on going swimming?"

"Oh, no!" said Jane. "The river water'd be too cold by now." After that, to my relief, she kept quiet.

As it turned out, today was an even finer day than yesterday. The heat was no longer oppressive because the air was dryer and there were light breezes; but anybody who had to sprint up Emerson Street at top speed in the early afternoon, as I did, would have agreed that it was hot—quite hot enough for a Peke to go swimming in a sun-warmed pond.

I had strict instructions from Jane to keep my mind on the kennel chores and get through them and out of the building as quickly as possible. Above all, I was not to let Father nab me for any extra jobs. When I asked how I could help that, she had said impatiently, "When you hear him on the prowl, hide—behind a door or in the storeroom closet or anywhere else you can. Then go out through the convalescent yard and climb the fence. If you have to leave anything really important undone, I'll go do it when I get home, but try not to. We want to get going as fast as we can."

The idea of such a program rather scandalized me, but it proved to be efficient. Just as I was completing the chores by sweeping the alley between the pens, I heard Father call to Mike, "If Phil's still here, get him for me, please." I dived, broom and all, into the last dog pen in the line—it was luckily vacant—and sat down on the floor in the back. Mike paused in the doorway and went on his way. The door to the convalescent yard was right at the end of that alley, so I left the broom in the pen and made my escape. The three occupants of the yard, which is back of the hospital and adjoining some of the boarders' runs, seemed glad to see me, but they didn't bark; and since I had already greeted the boarders that afternoon, I managed to keep them quiet, too, without having to whistle, as I scrambled over the fence into our neighbor's field and ran along beside their runs till I came to the paddock fence. Here I crawled between the boards and darted behind the protecting bulk of the stable. As soon as I could get my breath, I went into the stable by the back door and removed both saddles and both bridles. If Father or Mike should just happen to look in, I figured things had better look deserted.

I had no trouble keeping the ponies with me behind the stable, and had just saddled Evans when I heard light footsteps on the boards inside. They sounded like Jane's, so I cautiously opened the door a crack and peeked in. It was Jane, and I hurried her out the back door. "Father was after me," I said in an undertone. "I'm glad you got here so soon."

Jane was businesslike as usual. "Hadn't we better hook this door open?" she said. "That means both ponies have gone in case anybody looks into the stable."

"O.K.," I said, "but lead Evans up there beside the wall where neither of you can be seen through the doorway." By this time I had Jones's saddle on, and as I hooked the door back I beckoned him up beside Evans. I had just slipped on his bridle when I heard something that made me pause and nudge Jane sharply. Father was whistling and the whistle, accompanied by footsteps on the gravel, was coming nearer. I dug hastily into my pocket and pulled out two sugar lumps and passed one to Jane, whispering, "Don't let him whinny." She nodded comprehension—the ponies usually do whinny when Father comes near—and we stood still side by side, each with the fingers of one hand curled loosely around a sugar lump to keep the ponies busy nibbling with their lips, but not quite able to reach the sugar.

But suddenly Jones jerked his head up, attentive to something besides the sugar. I automatically clamped my arms across his nose and under his jaw and whispered urgently, "Hush!" The moment passed; Jones relaxed and I released my grip and again offered him the hand with the sugar in it. But it was a hand that shook a little, not from fright, but from a kind of shock, for I knew what had excited Jones. Among the miscellaneous snatches of melody that Father whistled, Jones and I had heard and recognized that joyous cascade of notes that had formed part of the strange music I had heard so faint and far away on my birthday night. Jones had whinnied then, I remembered.

Jane shot me a questioning glance, which I returned with a warning frown just as the whistling stopped and Father's voice called, "Kate, have you seen Phil?"

Mother's voice called back, "No!" and Father's footsteps sounded on the stable floor. They paused after a few steps and then seemed to start back out, but stopped again near the doorway, as he said, "The bird's flown. Both saddles are gone and the back door's open. I don't see how he got through the chores and off so quickly."

"But Mike's there, isn't he, dear?" asked Mother's voice, accompanied by more footsteps on the gravel.

"Yes," said Father, "but it's Phil I really need. I've got to worm a fifteen-pound tomcat that might as well be a wildcat when it comes to dosing him—if Mike holds him.

With Phil he'd be meek enough. I wish Phil wouldn't go gallivanting off just when I need him."

"I don't think you're quite fair to Phil, dear," said Mother. "You know he doesn't go gallivanting much for a boy his age. Both he and Jane do much more work than most children. You can't expect them to stay home and work *all* the time."

"No, I suppose not," said Father. "Perhaps I do impose on Phil. The trouble is, he's getting almost indispensable around the hospital."

"Jane's a big help, too," said Mother.

"Oh, of course," said Father. "Jane's so quick and neat, she'd be an asset to any business; but when it comes to handling the animals, it's Phil I want every time. What he can do with animals is extraordinary. It's positively uncanny sometimes, as if he had some mysterious way of communicating with them. Why, he's even making headway with Dolores, and that requires some real sorcery."

"He's like you in many ways, dear," said Mother.

"Like *me?*" exclaimed Father. "There's nothing uncanny about *my* ability with animals; it all comes from training and experience."

"Well, it's common talk around that you can 'charm' horses," said Mother. I could tell from her voice that she was smiling.

"Oh—that!" said Father. "That's just more training and experience. I was brought up on a pony, you know, and they say I could ride before I could walk. Most Birdsongs are riders, and Phil's no exception. He can ride like an Indian."

"And Jane does very well, too. Remember she won a prize at the show."

"Oh, she rides correctly, of course," said Father, "and she's a pretty picture on horseback, and she has the better pony, too, from a judge's point of view; but Phil can really *ride*. Can't you see the difference? It always tickles me when Jane beats him in a race. She never would if they changed ponies; but the way things are, she has just the handicap she needs to make things interesting, and Phil doesn't get a swelled head."

"I'm sure neither of them is liable to get a swelled head with you around to take them down a bit now and then, dear," said Mother.

"I'm glad my methods are effective," said Father in an amused tone. "I can't go around singing Phil's praises, though he really is very unusual. He's said for years that he wants to be a vet, and I don't know where you could find better material for one. Even those blasted inventions of his work sometimes. Dolores's tricycle was a first-class inspiration."

"All the more reason why he deserves a rest now and then," said Mother. "Your tomcat can wait a while, can't he?"

"I suppose so," replied Father. "It just seemed a good opportunity when there were no patients waiting. Here comes a patient, though. So long, as Phil says."

"So long," said Mother. "I think I'll go enjoy a little of this lovely day in a deck chair in the clothes yard."

Footsteps receded and we could hear Father's voice greeting the incoming patient. My face felt hot, and I couldn't look at Jane. I let Jones have his sugar lump at last and stroked his nose in painful silence.

But Jane gave me a poke and said in an undertone, "Come on, sorcerer, we've got to get going, unless you can transport us through the air." I looked at her then and was met with a sympathetic grin with no trace of resentment in it. As I grinned gratefully back, I suddenly remembered, and for the first time understood, what Mother meant when I once heard her tell a friend that Jane had a very generous nature. Jane's kind of generosity, it occurred to me now, was really something to boast about.

We exchanged ponies, mounted, and rode down the lane as quietly as possible. "I hope Mother didn't hear us," I said as we reached the Appledore road.

"It wouldn't really matter," said Jane. "She'd never let on if she did."

I was preoccupied for most of that ride to Still Waters. I had a lot to think about, both gratifying and puzzling, but what engaged my attention the most was a fruitless effort to recall exactly that birdlike whistle of Father's. I could recognize it immediately; that was plain. But for the life of me I could not recall it. Even if I had had the whole range of a piano keyboard before me, I would have had no idea how to start trying to pick it out. I kept wondering, too, how soon it would be safe to question Father casually about it without betraying our presence behind the stable today.

But gradually an insistent tide of well-being, compounded of Father's praise, Jane's goodwill, and the glories of a perfect Indian-summer afternoon, flooded over me, and I gave myself up to its enjoyment. As we walked the ponies after a canter, I basked in the sun that slanted down on my face and arms; I looked across the rolling fields to the mountains, now brilliant with autumn color; I inhaled the delicate smells that rose from the vegetation around me; I listened to the chirping of the crickets and the occasional call of a bird and to the rhythmic accompaniment of the ponies' hoofs clop-clopping on the dirt road. Then, in order to miss nothing of this world, for once so perfect, I kicked off my stirrups and stretched out along Evans's back to look up at the sky. Right above us was a white cloud, oddly angular at the top but puffy at its bottom corners. "Look!" I said, pointing upwards.

Jane tipped her head way back, and we called out in perfect unison, "The glass chariot!" and then laughed because for once we saw the same thing.

"It looks," said Jane, "as if somebody was reaching out trying to grab it from that cloud behind. Do you suppose it's a cop?"

"More likely Sam Paine," I replied, as I sat up and settled into the saddle again. "He's nuts about it."

22. *A Soggy But Successful Rescue*

We were now approaching the Vickerys', where we'd agreed I'd better park Evans in the enclosure where the cows air themselves in winter, and then approach Miss Peckham's cautiously on foot. I had once parked Jones there when I was helping Tom hunt for a lost calf, and he had invited me to use it whenever I wanted to go up into his woods.

Accordingly, when we reached his driveway, we pulled up to exchange a few words before we parted. Jane's were cautionary. "Do keep your mind on what you're doing, Phil," she said. "You've been absentminded ever since we left home. You didn't say a single word till you saw that cloud."

"O.K.," I said. "I'll concentrate on Dolores from now on. So long," I added, as I turned Evans into the Vickerys' dooryard. "I'll see you later, but you won't see me—I hope. And remember, if I get caught, you're to point out to Father that this is not an *experiment;* it's just a defense measure. I did the experimenting in the bathtub last week." Jane nodded agreement and waved as she and Jones went on toward the bridge.

Nobody seemed to be at home at the Vickerys'; so I parked Evans and made off stealthily across the field toward Miss Peckham's. When I reached the seclusion of the trees by the brook, I pulled up the left leg of my jeans, gritted my teeth, and ripped off the two pieces of sticky plastic tape that bound the recorder to the outside of my leg below the knee. It was too warm for a jacket that day, but I had to carry the recorder somehow, preferably without Jane's knowledge, and had borrowed this idea from a book I'd been reading. As I walked across the field I had begun to realize that the arrangement, though successful, was hardly comfortable in the long run and wondered fleetingly how my ancestor had concealed the recorder "on his body" in his flight from Dorset to Shropshire.

My leg felt better now, but I had only one hand free to help me climb the fence and to grab bushes and tree roots as I slid down to the brook and scrambled up the opposite bank behind Miss Peckham's house. I reached the top of the bank near the target just as Jane had, but there was nobody in sight today. I edged along the bank toward the crossroad and then stole through a copse of spruces bordering Miss Peckham's side lawn. Peering between these I was first pleased to see Dolores lying on her blue pillow on the marble bench, and then horrified to see Miss Peckham in a deck chair beside her, the BB gun across her knees.

A long inspection revealed that both of them were asleep. This, I decided, was not so bad. I blew a few cautious notes and paused to observe their effect. I thought I had seen some shapes and supposed Dolores would be looking toward me, but she and Miss Peckham both seemed to be still asleep. I was about to try again when I became simultaneously aware that the strong smell of spruce was mixed with another stronger odor and that there was a slight pressure on my toes. I looked down and, much to my surprise, saw there was a weasel sitting on my foot and staring up at me. I returned his stare for a long moment while I tried desperately to think what to do next. Then, closing my eyes, I played low, soft notes, and with all my strength I concentrated on a scene where Pounce, very large and ferocious-looking, sneaked up to the granite doorstep and crouched by the crack between it and the house. I did it in color, just in case. By the time I opened my eyes, the weasel was hurrying away toward the brook.

Dolores had awakened by now and was staring pop-eyed in my direction. I promptly played *Drink to Me Only with Thine Eyes* (a favorite of hers) and suggested that she join me and be borne off for a swim at Still Waters. I opened my eyes in time to see her jump down from the marble bench and start toward me. I also saw Miss Peckham give an all-over jerk and grasp the BB gun. She didn't raise it, though, and immediately sank back in her chair. With a sigh of relief, I put the recorder under my arm and picked up Dolores.

Our flight to Still Waters was uneventful except for finding Bozo sitting in the middle of Foothill Road near the crossroad and looking inquiringly toward Miss Peckham's. When he saw us, he put his nose in the air to greet us with a howl which I stopped with a loud "Sh-h!" He then looked at Dolores and started halfheartedly toward the bushes, as he had been taught to do in her presence, but stopped halfway and hopefully rotated his tail. I told him to come with us and skimmed on down the road to the Still Waters dooryard, where I flitted from cover to cover till I reached the front pasture gate. Apparently the stock, and Jones with them, were in the back pasture today; so I had no trouble opening the gate and urging Bozo inside. It seemed a mean trick as I closed the gate on him, but I had no choice, since on the loose he would be bound to reveal my presence. I said in an undertone, "Go have a swim in the stock pond, Bozo." And then, from force of habit and a confused state of mind, I closed my eyes and visualized the pond and a St. Bernard wading into it. But Bozo just sat down and looked at me sadly.

I had to leave him there and do some more flitting till I reached the big hemlock on the house side of the pond. Here I shoved the recorder under the drooping lower branches and then stood still and peered through a chink in the needles at the croquet ground to make sure that Jane was in view. Then I gave a chickadee's call twice and saw her quickly nod her head. At that I knelt down on the carefully laid but uncemented stones of the retaining wall that edges the pond at ground level and lowered Dolores, who by this time was squirming eagerly, into the water. With my mission accomplished, I tunneled quickly under the hemlock branches, picking up the recorder as I went, till I came to a cool, damp hollow, excavated by Bozo between the trunk of the tree and a smooth, slablike rock that rose from the ground on the inside end just enough to hide me from the house side and the drive if I lay still. On the pond side I relied on the low boughs, the trunk, and the impossibility of close inspection to keep me invisible.

My view was limited, but I could see Dolores puffing and splashing happily as she struck off across the pond. In the middle she changed course and began swimming in circles. At this point I heard an excited cry from Jane, then running footsteps and a splash. Shortly after that the Major came into view wading toward Dolores. The water only came to his hips, but the soft mud at the bottom slowed his progress. Finally, however, he managed to reach Dolores and grab her and stagger on across the pond with his shrieking, struggling burden. Jane ran around and received Dolores while the Major sat down on the stone wall and pulled his feet out of the mud and splashed them about near the surface to clean them off. He and Jane were talking to each other, but even with my new keenness of hearing, I couldn't hear what they said above Dolores's yapping. I was anxious to hear, too, because the next move was important. It seemed best to me that the Major, still dripping from his heroic plunge, should rush Dolores home personally. But being very neat and rather particular about his appearance, he might spoil the effect by delegating Jane or Caleb to do the job. I particularly dreaded what might happen if Jane was the messenger, and it looked as if she might be, since I hadn't seen Caleb anywhere.

I needn't have worried, though, for while the Major was still splashing, Dolores's screams were answered by even lustier ones as Miss Peckham came charging into the dooryard. She snatched Dolores from Jane's grasp (Jane was kneeling on the grass, holding Dolores by her harness so that she couldn't jump back into the pond) and shrieked, "Dolores, I've been looking for you everywhere! What have they been doing to you?"

From this point on I could see very little of the action, because my view extended only to about knee-height, but Jane later confirmed my impression that the Major, even in these trying circumstances, made a bow in her direction as he swiveled around on the stones and got to his feet. "My dear Miss Peckham," he said (I could hear now since Dolores, apparently clasped in Miss Peckham's arms, had quieted down), "I assure you we have done nothing but rescue Dolores from drowning. Jane and I were playing croquet when we noticed her in trouble in the water. I have no idea how she got there."

"She'd never jump off the stones by herself," said Miss Peckham. "Somebody must have put her in." I could see Miss Peckham's feet turn a little, and I had a horrible feeling that she was staring across the pond right at my hiding place. But then there were footsteps on the gravel which I knew from the slight inequality of their fall must be Caleb's, and I felt she had shifted her gaze. "Where's that bloodhound or whatever you call him?" she demanded. "He may have chased her and made her fall into the water."

"No, ma'am," said Caleb's voice politely but firmly. "Bozo's been in the front pasture with me. I've been some time mending the east gate, and when I came back just now, he was swimming in the stock pond. Good day for a swim," he added. "The dogs are smarter than we are."

"Dolores does like the water," admitted Miss Peckham, "but I don't see how she could have got into it by herself. She's never come here before of her own accord, and she wouldn't jump off the rocks."

"Ah!" said Caleb in his wisest tones, "Dolores knows where to find what she wants and a little jump like that wouldn't stop her now she's feeling so good."

This masterly sentence with its implication of Dolores's superior intelligence and spirit, and its reminder of her recent recovery so speeded by the Major's tricycle, calmed Miss Peckham completely and she thanked the Major rather effusively for his rescue. "Dolores can swim beautifully, of course," she said, "but she couldn't have pulled herself up over the rocks. I *knew* she was in some terrible danger because I had such a dreadful dream. I was sitting out in the yard with her—I don't dare let her out alone any more with that cat around and now that weasel—and I must have dozed off. I thought I heard some strange bird singing over in the spruce—a most unusual song it was. And then I saw that horrible black cat skulking around my doorstep. He looked so ferocious and evil that I was paralyzed with fear. For a moment I just couldn't move. Then I heard Dolores fall off the bench, and that broke the spell. I seized my—that is, I jumped up and chased the cat away and when I came back,

Dolores was gone and that really woke me up. I was terribly startled to find that I was still in my chair, but that Dolores really was gone. Some instinct led me here immediately, though. It was almost as if I *saw* Dolores in the pond even when I was still at my own house. These intuitions are very strange, aren't they?"

My scalp tingled and I felt the hair rise on my head as I listened to Miss Peckham. Somehow she had managed to tune in on my message to the weasel. Thank goodness she had been so horrified at my version of Pounce that she had worked him into a dream of her own and had got no more than the vaguest impression of my message to Dolores! Still the whole business was decidedly creepy, not to say alarming. Was Miss Peckham's Power limited to receiving messages in her sleep? She hadn't seemed to notice anything that day she found me communing with Bozo in the pasture, nor the night she brought Dolores to the hospital; but I remembered her knowledge of Dolores's preference for blue and gold and decided that in the future I had better be very careful playing the recorder when she was near.

While I was occupied with these disturbing thoughts, the Major had earnestly been agreeing with Miss Peckham on the strangeness of intuitions and had started to recount an intuitive experience of his own, but Miss Peckham soon switched the conversation by inquiring how his chrysanthemums were doing this year. It was arranged that Caleb should show them to her while the Major changed his clothes, and they went off down the drive in a body with Jane, who hadn't said a word since Miss Peckham's appearance, trailing behind. When they had passed the hemlock, I turned over and even ventured to sit up to get a better view. At the back door, the Major and Caleb went in, but Caleb promptly returned with Bozo's leash, which he snapped onto Dolores's harness. Miss Peckham, who must have been rather damp about the chest from holding her, lowered Dolores to the ground, and the group, minus the Major, moved on. As they rounded the corner of the house, Jane lingered a moment to give me the all-clear signal. After a quick pause to re-strap the recorder to my leg, I lost no time taking off for the Vickerys' to pick up Evans, happily reviewing on my way the successful outcome of our afternoon's enterprise.

23. More Well-Laid Plans

The Vickerys were home when I got there, and Tom said as he greeted me near the barn, "I guess you've been looking for your cat; he hitchhiked home with us. I saw this black cat that looked like yours beside the road just by our property bound; so I stopped the truck and Emma opened her door, and he jumped in and sat between us as cool as you please. When we got to your lane, I stopped and she opened the door again, and he looked up at both of us, swished his tail politely, and got out. What a cat!"

Mrs. Vickery called from the kitchen door for me to come in and have some milk and cookies if they wouldn't spoil my supper. I gratefully accepted, assuring her that nothing ever spoiled my supper. They both assumed that I had been lurking around Miss Peckham's hunting for Pounce; so I didn't deny it and explained, to their obvious enjoyment, how Pounce had landed on Miss Peckham's head.

"She claimed that one of my cows had stolen some jelly she'd left to cool on her back porch," said Tom. "Imagine! No cow could get up and down the banks of the brook—I have to fence them in so they won't fall over the edge and break their legs—much less climb onto her porch, steal jelly, and toss the empty jars into her garden. I told her it must be a bear," Tom ended with a wink at me.

"It probably really was," said Mrs. Vickery calmly. "I know it sounds like boys, but boys don't go roaming around here much—except you, Phil—and Tom did see a bear up in the woods a while ago."

"Really?" I said, and we continued to chat about the local wildlife till I left.

Jane and I had agreed that I had better get out of the neighborhood as quickly as possible, but there seemed to be no danger now. So around the next bend after the Vickerys', Evans and I drew up in the shade of a wild apple tree and waited. I knew Jane hadn't passed yet; I'd have heard Jones's hoofbeats from the field, and I had kept my eye on the road from the Vickerys' kitchen. I shared with Evans an extra cookie Mrs. Vickery had given me, and sat placidly considering the success of my recent adventure.

Soon I heard the sound of trotting hoofs, Evans whinnied, Jones replied, and finally Jane and Jones came into view around the bend. Jones whinnied again as he saw us, and as they appoached the first thing I said was, "Let's swap ponies. You're safe from the chariot for now, and I miss Jones."

"Even though Evans is the better pony?" asked Jane.

"Even though Evans is the better pony," I replied, "Jones will always be my first choice."

"O.K.," said Jane and then added when she had dismounted, "You might as well take this now. The Major sent it to you." It was a narrow buckskin envelope, which she had secured between her belt and her riding breeches and now handed to me.

"Oh, good, the recorder case!" I said. "It will be much more comfortable to carry than that tin tube."

"It beats me why you want to carry that flute around so much," said Jane. "Why can't you practice at home?"

"Oh, well, you know how it is," I replied. "There are always interruptions at home, and I like the great outdoors anyway."

"You must look cute sitting on a rock piping like Pan in the staircase window," said Jane. "Do the animals all come and listen?"

I replied to her giggle with a grin—a feeble one, I'm afraid—and changed the subject. "Tell me what happened after I left Still Waters," I said as we both remounted and started home.

It seemed that Miss Peckham's visit had ended quite cozily; she stayed to tea, which they took on the porch.

"She kept talking about dear Grandma and dear Grandpa, who used to own the place," said Jane. "Dear Grandpa liked to have his meals on that porch, and dear Grandma was a wonderful cook. She said *that* when the Major passed her a plate of store cookies. Then she smiled in the silliest way and said, 'They say good cooks run in families.' It was sickening."

"I suppose so," I replied, "but the main thing is that Miss Peckham *is* getting friendly with the Major, and that's what we want."

"Well, I don't like her friendliness," said Jane. "She's bad enough when she's normal, but when she's friendly, she's ghastly; she gives me the creeps."

"Cheer up!" I said. "She'll never be friendly with you."

"Nor with you either, Hippo the Little Monster," replied Jane with a giggle.

"That's O.K. with me," I replied, "as long as she's friendly with the Major till the day after tomorrow. I do wish she'd be more friendly to Bozo, though. She tries to blame him for everything."

"Well, the Major's been a hero and rescued Dolores. Why don't you give Bozo a chance to be a hero, too?" asked Jane. "You could kidnap her and lose her in the woods tomorrow, and Bozo could track her down. He's mostly bloodhound, isn't he?"

"Gosh, Jane, that's a brilliant idea!" I replied. "Why didn't we think of something like that before? It's really just as important to get Miss Peckham to like Bozo as to like the Major, now I come to think of it."

Jane looked at me in astonishment. "You really mean it?" she asked. "You'll really kidnap Dolores?"

"Well," I said, "I kidnapped her this afternoon, but

I admit it wasn't so easy now that she's under guard. If Miss Peckham hadn't been asleep, I don't know what I'd have done."

"Asleep and dreaming," said Jane with a giggle. "Poor old Pounce! Imagine him looking ferocious and evil!"

"There must be some way to do it, though," I mused. "I'll have to think about it."

"Good," said Jane. "It should be even more exciting than this afternoon, which was fun until Peckham got so friendly. And I suppose I can stand her friendliness for another day, since we'll be working for a worthwhile cause." Appeasement wasn't worrying Jane just then.

That evening after dinner as I sat brooding in my Morris chair, I was aroused by the vigorous clanging of the cowbell. Jane was at the bottom of the stairwell, and when my head appeared over the edge, she demanded hopefully, "Have you thought up anything yet?"

"I'm stuck," I said. "You'd better come up."

Jane bounded up promptly. "What's the trouble?" she asked as she came in and perched on the foot of the bed as I returned to the Morris chair.

"We're going to need an accomplice," I replied, "and I don't know where we can get one."

"An accomplice?" said Jane. "You mean someone to do the dirty work?"

"Well, yes—part of it," I said. "It's not that I don't want to do it myself; I just don't see how I can—or you either. We were awfully lucky today and Peckham's not going to fall asleep outdoors again to oblige us; so the only way to get Dolores out of the house is to have somebody Peckham trusts bring her out and hand her over." (I hadn't told Jane about the BB gun; the mere thought of it excited her so, I was afraid she'd start denouncing appeasement again.)

"I don't suppose Caleb would do," said Jane.

"No," I said. "Caleb does seem to be able to say the right things to her; but I'm not sure she'd go as far as to trust him with Dolores. And besides, we can't have anybody close to the Major. It would look too suspicious."

"Father's about the only one she'd entrust Dolores to," said Jane, "and he's too honorable."

"I'm afraid so," I replied glumly.

"Well, how about Sam Paine?" said Jane. "You said he's some kind of a cousin of Peckham's and polishes the chariot for her."

"I'd thought of him," I said. "But he's such a clown that something's bound to go screwy if he gets into the plot."

"It's a sort of screwy plot anyhow," said Jane. "And what if Bozo isn't bloodhound enough to track Dolores?"

"You don't have to worry about Bozo," I said. "He'll do his job O.K. The only real problem is getting Dolores out from under Peckham's guard."

"Well, then, Sam's your man," said Jane. "Who else would—and could—do it?"

"I suppose you're right," I said with a sigh. "I'd better go get hold of him now. It's going to take a lot of explaining and persuading to get him to cooperate."

It was only half-past seven and the night before a holiday; so downstairs I boldly announced my intention of going to Sam's for a little while. "Be sure and be back by nine-thirty, dear, " said Mother. I agreed and set determinedly forth on my errand.

Luckily Sam was home and out in the garage by himself, taking a battered old electric mower to pieces. "Where'd you get that—the dump?" I asked.

"The dump!" exclaimed Sam with an outraged snort. "I'm no dump rat like some I could name. This fine machine came with one of Father's houses." Sam's father is in the real estate business, and in addition to buying and selling and renting for other people, he himself occasionally buys a good house in need of repairs, fixes it up, and rents it or resells it. Even when these houses are unfurnished, there are usually a few odd items to be cleared out of the barn or the attic—sometimes, happily for Sam, even things with motors in them.

"But does anybody use electric mowers nowadays?" I asked.

"You live in the horse and buggy age, Hippo," replied Sam. "Electric mowers are *in*—no trouble starting them, no noise to speak of, no fuel to fuss with, and no air pollution."

"Modern like the glass chariot, huh?" I asked.

"That's a painful subject, Hippo. You shouldn't mention it."

"Why, what's happened?" I asked.

"I just missed getting to drive the chariot yesterday," said Sam, "and it was all your fault that I didn't. I nobly volunteered to deliver Father's message that he wouldn't be able to tend to Elvira's doorstep for a couple of weeks (he thought she'd have gotten over her "doorstepitis" by then) and he gave me a lift out to Foothill Road. When I got to her place, I found the Major and his man wrestling one of those big old standing radios out of the chariot for her; so I held doors open and made myself as useful as possible. I finished by carrying in tons of bundles that had been temporarily left on the lawn. The Major had left by then, and she was in quite a good humor from all this service; so I suggested, as I tottered in with the last lot, that I put the chariot in the garage for her. And I know she was going to let me, when she saw that confounded weasel of yours run across the lawn and into the field. She just about had a fit and wanted to know when my father was going to move her doorstep. So I had to deliver his message, and was she ever mad! She referred to him twice as 'a strong man with two strong sons' and glared at me as if I were both. So I left before she could put me to work with a crowbar. Anyhow, I was able to hitchhike that time," he concluded more cheerfully.

"You could have her eating out of your hand if you only used the right approach," I said.

"What approach is that?" demanded Sam.

"The way to her heart is through Dolores," I said. "Do you ever ask for Dolores's health? Do you bring her little presents? Do you offer to take her for walks?"

"The answers are no, no, and no. One has to draw the line somewhere when it comes to groveling," replied Sam with dignity.

"But that's the way to butter her up," I protested. "Look at the tricycle; look at the dunking in the pond."

"What the dickens are you babbling about, Hippo?" demanded Sam. "Pull yourself together."

This reminded me that I had not yet told Sam about these triumphs, and I recounted them in detail. He laughed about them, but I could see he was impressed, and I continued artfully, "And now Jane and I are planning one knockout blow that will decide her in the Major's favor if she's still wavering, but we need your help."

"*My* help?" asked Sam suspiciously. "How's that?"

"Yes," I said. "All you have to do is bring Dolores around the bend in the road and hand her to me."

"Oh, that's all, is it?" said Sam. "Then what?"

"I take her up into that patch of woods that Tom Vickery bought last year. There used to be a house there, I guess; there's an apple tree and an old well that was filled in but has sunk again about three feet. I helped a baby skunk out of it once. I'll put Dolores in it and climb up into a big oak that's nearby. I'll have to take a good long rope for that, I guess. The lowest branch is pretty high. And you go back and tell Miss Peckham that Dolores has got away from you and is lost in the woods. Then tell her you're on your way to get Bozo to track her darling down, and go get him—and the Major, too, if possible. Bozo will do the rest."

"Oh, he will, will he?" said Sam. "And where will I be? In the soup, and I'll never get out of it after losing Dolores. Why should I sacrifice all my chances of getting at that marvelous chariot just for one of your loony schemes?"

"But you won't," I replied. "You're the one who'll have the brain wave of getting Bozo on Dolores's track, and he'll find her. And you could lose her under blameless circumstances—even heroic ones. You could be fending off a ferocious black cat when she escapes."

Sam grinned at this, but still objected. "How are you sure he will find her? What if he isn't home?"

"I give you my word of honor he'll find her if he's home," I said, "and if he isn't we'll find out in time to call the whole thing off—unless *you'd* like to find her," I suggested.

"No, thanks," said Sam. "The whole thing's too risky, though it does have some interesting features."

"But what about the honor of Samuel S. Paine III?" I asked. "Would he let an old friend down? Would he stand by and see a good guy like the Major done in and never lift a finger? And done in, too, by Samuel S. Paine III's own second cousin once removed," I added indignantly.

Sam's resistance collapsed under this attack, and we laid our plans for the next day. I was pleased to learn that the program Sam had mapped out for the holiday dovetailed neatly with Dolores's rescue. His brother Bill was going to spend the day working on a tree farm he owns on Foothill Road, and Sam, after some persuasion, had agreed to help him. "I could go down to Elvira's after lunch and fill our water jug," he said. "We'll drink a lot in this weather, and I could manage to spill some too. I only hope she doesn't have that doorstep on her mind just then."

"If she has, it will be all the more appropriate for you to offer to walk Dolores and guard her with your life," I replied. "She needs plenty of exercise." By the time I left Sam, his nervousness had given way to elation at the scope he would have for his dramatic powers in the Dolores affair. This was good in a way, of course, but Sam needs so little scope anyway that it made me rather uneasy as I dogtrotted the half-mile home.

On my way upstairs, I paused on the second floor. Jane's room was dark, but her voice hailed me in a conspiratorial undertone. I tiptoed in and told her in a whisper that Sam had agreed to do his part. "We can make our final plans in the stable before breakfast," I added.

"O.K. Goodnight," Jane replied sleepily, and I went on upstairs to bed myself.

At our early morning conference it was decided that I would ride to Still Waters after breakfast and reconnoiter the neighborhood. It would be easy enough to find out if the Major and Bozo were likely to be home in the afternoon. Unless the Major had definite plans to be elsewhere, I could insure their presence by saying Jane was coming over to finish the interrupted croquet tournament. Miss Peckham I couldn't be so sure about, but Jane and I agreed she'd probably be home on a holiday; she had to save her batteries and wouldn't be likely to go gallivanting around when she couldn't shop. Anyhow, I said I'd lurk about her place and see what I could find out. I was to take my lunch and, if all was well, to go eat it with Sam and Bill. That way I could keep an eye on Sam and get him started on time. Jane would do the required chores at home and leave for Still Waters by one-thirty. If Bozo wasn't there, she was to ride around the bend on Foothill Road, on some pretext or other, and warn Sam and me, who would be waiting there to start Operation Bloodhound.

This arrangement seemed reasonably foolproof to me, but Jane was rather doubtful about it, even though the original idea had been hers. "Won't Dolores yell bloody murder when you put her in the pit?" she asked. "It's not very far from Peckham's, and if she yells we won't need a bloodhound."

"I'll keep her quiet," I said.

"I'm glad that's not my job," said Jane. "If you can do it, I guess I'll have to agree with Father that you're a sorcerer."

"Oh, I think she'll be all right," I said. "Dolores isn't so bad when you get to know her."

"I wish I had more of a part in this, though," Jane went on. "All I get to do is warn you if something goes wrong."

"Well, that's important," I said. "And with Sam in this, you're likely to be needed. And you'll have the fun of running with a bloodhound."

"I just hope Bozo remembers he *is* a bloodhound today," said Jane darkly. She'd have been really worried if she'd known that he imagined himself to be a St. Bernard.

"Don't worry about Bozo," I said. "He's the least of our troubles as long as he's home."

At breakfast I announced that I had an appointment with Sam and would be gone most of the day. "That's nice, dear," said Mother. "You might as well enjoy this weather while you can. It's wonderful how it lasts."

"It can't last much longer," said Father, who dislikes heat. "And when the weather changes, it'll be good-bye, summer, for this year. You can get out your snowshoes. Meanwhile gather ye rosebuds while ye may. By the way, what's Jane doing with her holiday?"

Jane was accounted for, and the conversation rambled on unattended by me; my mind was on the rosebuds to be gathered that day.

24. Operation Bloodhound

Things started out comfortably enough. Since it wasn't too hot to wear my jacket, I was able to carry my supplies, including the recorder wrapped in its new soft case, in my game pocket. Everything went according to schedule at Still Waters, too, both with the Major and Bozo; but I had a nerve-racking time at Miss Peckham's. It started when I was lurking below the bank of the brook with only my head above the edge to spy out the land. First I saw her come out the back door with Dolores, who was on a leash and balking at it; and then, as they progressed jerkily around the edge of the back lawn, I heard Miss Peckham say, "No, no, my naughty little Dodo! If I let you loose that horrid cat might get you, or you might go and frighten the poor, dear Major again. Naughty girl!" She concluded with a horrible titter that somehow chilled my blood. I recalled Jane's description of her in a friendly mood: ghastly, sickening, creepy. She was all of that, though I couldn't have said exactly why, and I was too worried about my mission there to probe the matter; for as they returned to the house, Miss Peckham spoke again. "I think we'll have a little nap now," she said. "I hardly slept at all last night worrying about my little Dodo at the mercy of that horrible cat and the weasel. And I even thought I heard a bear once."

I was so anxious to deliver my message to Dolores before Miss Peckham got to sleep that I just crouched down where I was and recklessly began playing *Drink to Me Only with Thine Eyes* the minute the back door closed behind them. Luckily Dolores responded immediately and seemed to grasp promptly and approve my plans for her dramatic rescue; but I must have played too loudly, for Miss Peckham heard me and sneaked out to the bank and caught me still tootling with my eyes closed. She inquired acidly what I was doing, and though that was obvious enough, it was not easy to explain why I was doing it. At least it was a relief to note that she had no suspicion of the real reason. I'm afraid I left her with the impression that I habitually played the flute with closed eyes and roamed the countryside serenading people in this unusual manner, but in any case I had accomplished the first part of my mission successfully.

Then, in the afternoon, I had my troubles with Sam. My forebodings about him as a partner in crime rose sharply when he insisted on wearing for our enterprise an antique checked cap he'd found in the attic. It was terribly conspicuous and he looked perfectly idiotic in it. Anybody would have, but Sam's spectacles, which seemed to support the big visor, gave it a particularly weird effect. He claimed, however, that it made him feel like Sherlock Holmes and gave him confidence. So off he pranced in it to get Dolores—and didn't return. After what seemed hours of agonized waiting, I crept through Bozo's detour to investigate, if possible, the cause of the delay and discovered that Sam was maneuvering the glass chariot up and down Miss Peckham's driveway, apparently trying it out in all speeds forward and back. I guessed that he had completely forgotten Dolores, and I finally managed to bring him to his senses by rising menacingly from behind the bushes for a moment while he was facing me. And then, when at last he appeared at the appointed place with Dolores, and I was reaching for her leash, Nifty, who was supposed to be back at the tree farm with Bill, came charging down the road at us full tilt. Dolores nipped him and then, as he ran yelping into the woods, she pursued him hotly. When I got that business straightened out, I clutched Dolores firmly in my arms and sent Sam and Nifty off to Still Waters, with instructions to get Jane to arrange for Nifty's detention there till our mission had been accomplished. Sam helplessly complained that he needed a leash, but I told him tartly to use his belt and watched him attach it to Nifty's collar and start stealthily on his way, that confounded cap bobbing up and down, now above the bushes, now only partially concealed by their thinning leaves. If Miss Peckham had happened to look out of her front windows, she would surely have seen it, but apparently she didn't, for from then on everything went as planned for Dolores and me, except that as I sat in my oak tree tootling softly to Dolores in her pit, it seemed to take an interminable time for the rescue party to appear. Finally, however, I heard Bozo baying exuberantly on Dolores's trail and lay down flat on the leafiest part of my branch to observe the results of all my painful preparation.

They fully justified it, I felt, as I thrilled to the sight of the Major and Bozo hurtling toward us on the opposite ends of a leash. Bozo was whooping his loudest, and the Major and Jane, who despite her short legs was following closely, were shouting encouragement. Miss Peckham, supported by Sam in his awful cap, lumbered along tardily in the rear. The rescue proceeded in style very much as we had planned, except that Miss Peckham unexpectedly added to the drama by fainting away when the Major raised Dolores from the pit. Upon reviving, she expressed a wish to hug "that great big clever bloodhound" that had found her dear little Dodo; but Bozo, upon being unleashed, had wisely disappeared.

The rest of the rescuers departed more slowly, Miss Peckham supported this time by Sam on one side and the Major on the other, while Jane, honored with the custody of Dolores on the blue pillow, brought up the rear. Just before she vanished among the trees, she turned toward me and made a perfectly hideous face, indicative of deep disgust.

When I was finally alone in the wood, I dropped my rope over my branch and swung down from the oak, still exulting in the success of our venture and, giving the Peckham property a wide berth, sneaked back across the brook to the Vickerys', where I had left Evans. I was very hungry, I found, after all the excitement; and since I saw nobody around the Vickerys' and didn't know how long it might take Jane to turn up, I saddled Evans and rode directly home.

I was in the kitchen enjoying a large, diversified sandwich made of odds and ends from the refrigerator, when Father stomped in the back door, gave me a sour look, and said, "When you're finished with that three-course dinner, come into the den," and strode on past me. My triumph instantly evaporated, and I finished my hard-earned refreshment fearfully trying to guess just which of my recent activities he had discovered.

When I got to the den, Father was sitting on the couch looking at the paper. He said, "Close the door!" and then pointed to a straight-backed, hard-seated chair that Jane and I privately call "the inquisition chair," and said, "Sit down." I sat and waited. Father always prefaces the more serious sessions in the den with an invitation to sit down, followed by a demoralizing pause. Finally he put the paper down and said, "Miss Peckham phoned me this morning," and paused again, looking at me intently. I tried to register nothing more than a polite interest, but then he went on, "She said Dolores was breathing peculiarly and might have water in her lungs. It seems Dolores jumped into the Major's pond and went swimming yesterday." Here Father paused again.

"Her condition wasn't really serious, was it?" I asked.

"No," said Father. "I had Miss Peckham weigh her and I found she'd been gaining again; that makes her a little wheezy. But it was odd that Dolores would go jump in the Major's pond all on her own."

"Dolores likes to swim, and it was quite a hot day," I replied.

"Yes," said Father, "but I doubt if many people know about Dolores's taste for sport and it sounds as if someone might have given her a helping hand." This time I remained silent. Finally Father resumed, "Furthermore, Miss Peckham complained that you were playing a flute on her property this morning—hiding behind some bushes down by the brook to be exact. Were you?"

"Well, yes, I was," I replied, almost relieved to be asked a direct question. "It was all part of a plot to get her friendly with the Major so she'd sell him Still Waters. It's worked well, too," I added not without a little pride even under these dangerous circumstances.

Of course after that I had to give an outline of our adventures of the last two days. Father listened impassively. At one point he interrupted me to ask, "I suppose Jane was your accomplice?"

"Well, yes, so to speak," I admitted. "She knew about what was going on, but she didn't really do anything. I mean," I added hastily for fear Father'd think I was trying to take all the credit, "she didn't do anything punishable. And Sam was an accomplice too, but he didn't want to be."

"But I still don't understand," said Father, when I had concluded my account, "why in thunder you should play your flute at Miss Peckham. It just doesn't make sense; you weren't trying to annoy her."

"Oh, no," I said. "I didn't think she could hear me."

"Well, then?" asked Father.

It was I who paused this time. At last I said, "Well, it just happens that Dolores likes music; it puts her in a good humor. I discovered that when she was here."

"As I've remarked before," said Father, "there's something very strange about you lately—ever since—" here he paused again, but this time apparently to do some reckoning, and then concluded, "ever since your birthday. That was the day you got that flute, wasn't it?"

"Yes, sir," I replied, looking down at the carpet. But I felt his eyes boring into me and had to look up. I don't know how long we had been staring into each other's eyes, when I heard myself saying, "Can you whistle bird calls?" It was a question I'd been planning to ask for some time, and under this additional provocation it just slipped out unawares.

I was horrified at the result. Father's face flushed and his eyes flashed, and I knew that he thought I was flippantly trying to change the subject. But I continued to look him seriously in the eye, and his look changed to one of perplexity. "I could do some as a boy," he said. "But why do you ask?"

"I heard you one day whistling something like a thrush's song," I said. "It was—uh—beautiful—happy—." My voice trailed off, and I could feel my face growing red; but I kept on looking at him.

Father's perplexity seemed to deepen, but he replied, "It might have been an English blackbird's song. Let's see." He pursed his lips and whistled a succession of clear, flutelike notes, very pleasing to hear; but I shook my head.

"It was something like that, but not quite the same," I said.

Father began to look impatient. "But why—" he said, and then, as footsteps sounded on the kitchen linoleum, he interrupted himself to go open the door and call, "Jane, come in here please."

Jane appeared in the doorway with a guileless look on her face. Behind Father's back I hastily mouthed the words, "I had to tell," and held my hands, palms upward, in a helpless gesture. Jane's expression didn't change. She came in and sat on the couch, her feet demurely crossed as if she were waiting for a party to begin. She's always more lighthearted about the interviews in the den than I can ever be.

Father took up a stand where he could watch both of us. "Phil has been telling me about his recent enterprises, in which I understand you played a minor and blameless part," he said.

"It wasn't so minor," said Jane, straightening up and looking at me rather indignantly. "*I* thought up the plan of kidnapping Dolores."

"Oh, you did?" said Father suavely. "And what else did you do?"

"Well, I arranged to play croquet with the Major yesterday, and I rescued Sam today," said Jane, "and that wasn't so easy," she added with a barely suppressed giggle.

"No?" said Father. "Tell me exactly what you did."

"Well," said Jane, "I was playing croquet with the Major and wondering why nothing happened. Then I heard Bozo baying and looked up and saw the Major standing very stiff and straight, staring at the hemlock beside the pond and gripping his mallet like a hammer. I turned and looked at the hemlock, too, but I couldn't see anything unusual; so I said, 'What's the matter?'

"The Major replied in a very low voice, 'It's the strangest thing, but I'm sure I saw a head in a deerstalker stick out behind that tree a moment ago.' "

"A head in a *deerstalker?*" demanded Father.

"That's exactly what I said to the Major," replied Jane. "I'd never heard of such a thing. He said it was the kind of cap Sherlock Holmes wore."

Father looked at me, puzzled. "Sam found it in the Paines' attic and thought it was appropriate to our adventure," I filled him in. "I couldn't get him to take it off. It was in a horrible big black-and-white check that was visible for miles."

Father all but grinned at this, but managed to look solemn again as Jane continued, "I knew it must be Sam, and I thought I'd better get to him before the Major did; so I started to run toward the hemlock, but I was rocked right back on my heels when the Major snapped 'Halt!' at me. It's the first time he'd ever seemed like a soldier to me. He strode up to me very quietly and whispered, 'Get out of sight, Jane. It may be a dangerous lunatic.' Of course I knew it wasn't, but I couldn't very well say so; so I got behind the corner of the house and peeked out to see all I could.

"The Major sneaked very quietly around the hemlock and then stopped suddenly with his mallet raised. 'Now, young man,' he said, 'what can I do for *you?*' Then he added, 'I wouldn't back up any further if I were you; you'll be in the pond.'

"I had to laugh—just quietly to myself, of course—

when I heard Sam's voice; he sounded so sort of put-upon. 'I came here to see Jane Birdsong,' he said.

"The Major turned and looked uneasily back at the croquet ground, and I had to jerk my head back quickly behind the house. Then he said, 'You'd better do your business with me. What are you doing with that setter? He looks like a valuable dog to me.'

" 'He's mine,' said Sam, 'and I want to hide him.'

"I knew what the trouble was then, of course, but the Major said very suspiciously, 'We'll see about that. Remove your headpiece, please!' "

Here Jane giggled openly at the recollection. I realized that I was grinning, and I could see out of the corner of my eye that Father's lips were twitching, but he said tonelessly, "Go on."

"That was the last of his orders," said Jane. "The next time he spoke, he sounded awfully surprised. 'Why, you're Mr. Paine's son, aren't you?' he said.

"I thought it was all right to come out of hiding then, so I ran over and lined up beside Bozo; he'd stopped baying when he saw the Major and had been standing beside him, swinging his tail around sort of doubtfully every once in a while. 'Sam's a friend of Phil's, Major Featherstone,' I said. 'He's not really dangerous. I know him well.'

" 'But why is he behaving so peculiarly?' asked the Major.

" 'I think he's upset,' I replied.

"Sam answered eagerly, 'Yes, that's just it,' and then he turned to the Major and fell all over himself trying to explain everything. For once he didn't mean to be funny, but he gabbled something like this: 'I was walking

Dolores for Elvira; she's my second cousin once removed—Elvira, I mean. And Nifty got away from my brother and she chased him—I mean Nifty—and then she got lost—Dolores, that is. And now I'll have to tell Elvira, but she doesn't like Nifty, and I don't want her to know he was mixed up in it. And please would you bring your bloodhound and track her down—Dolores, I mean?'

"I almost laughed, but the Major understood him and was very sympathetic. 'Certainly, certainly,' he said. 'We'd be glad to help. You should have told us your trouble sooner. But did you say that Dolores chased your setter?'

"Sam looked sillier than ever, if possible, but he said, 'Yes, she did. She makes Nifty nervous. I don't blame him.'

" 'No, no,' said the Major. 'It's quite understandable. Jane, will you please put Nifty in the harness room while I get Bozo's leash?'

"So I did and we all set off for the place Dolores had last been seen. When we reached Miss Peckham's, Sam went in and broke the news to her and she came out with Dolores's blue pillow for Bozo to sniff so he could get her scent. Then Miss Peckham and Sam followed the hunt. Bozo soon picked up Dolores's track and bayed like mad, and—."

"Phil's told me the rest," said Father. Then there was another of those pauses I find so disconcerting; but somehow the atmosphere had lightened since Jane had joined us, and I could tell from a side-glance at Father's face that he was trying not to grin. Finally he said, "I thought I had juvenile delinquency licked, but with a pair like you two, there's no knowing. Two kidnappings perpetrated in two days is a poor record, to put it mildly."

"But we were resourceful, weren't we?" said Jane. "You encourage us to be resourceful."

"There's such a thing as being *too* resourceful," said Father. "Dolores's tricycle was a good idea. But haven't you ever heard of letting well enough alone?"

For some reason Jane looked crestfallen, even worried, at this and did not reply. After another pause, Father said, "Tomorrow's the fatal day when Miss Peckham finally has to make up her mind about Still Waters, isn't it?" We both nodded, and he went on, "Then I suppose the matter is closed as far as you are concerned; you haven't time to do anything more. And since your intentions were good and you don't seem to have done any real harm, I'll let you off with a reprimand. But I want you to remember this: meddlers are a nuisance and meddling is dangerous. You're lucky not to have gotten into some sort of trouble over this affair and learned that for yourselves the hard way. Now repeat what I have said, both of you."

Jane and I both said, "Meddlers are a nuisance and meddling is dangerous," in subdued tones, and were dismissed with a further caution not to forget it. I was greatly relieved, but Jane seemed downcast. When I asked her why, she merely said, "Oh, I don't know." Then she added thoughtfully, "We really *were* lucky not to get into trouble—I guess."

Later in the evening I telephoned Sam to clear up a few puzzling details of the afternoon's activity. First I asked him why on earth he had hidden behind the hemlock.

"Why, you were the one who told me to hide," replied Sam, "and a fine mess you got me into."

"I never told you any such thing," I said. "I just said to get hold of Jane. Since the Major doesn't know you very well, I thought she'd better introduce you and explain about Nifty."

"You told me to hide behind the bushes, and it nearly broke my back," complained Sam. "I supposed I was to keep on hiding till I got in touch with Jane; it seemed appropriate."

"Those bushes beside the road were to hide you and Nifty from Miss Peckham," I said. "Your wits weren't working—or your ESP. But you'd have been all right anyhow if it hadn't been for that blasted cap."

"I'll have you know," said Sam, "that 'that blasted cap' saved the day for you. Elvira admired it tremendously. She said it was just like one dear Grandpa used to wear. She even thought it might be the same one, though I don't see how it could have gotten into our attic. She was so melted by the sight of it, she let me drive the chariot, and she said not many young people today would have appreciated it."

"She never said a truer word," I retorted. "But I'd like to know how driving that chariot around saved the day when it nearly wrecked all our plans."

"Oh, that was later," replied Sam. "Elvira seemed awfully upset when I told her that Bill and I had seen a bear up in the woods, but even so, she had such confidence in me that I had no trouble taking Dolores for a walk. And even when I had to report that Dolores was missing, she took it better than I had hoped. She said I had great presence of mind to summon the Major and Bozo—just like dear Grandpa. So you see how my cap paid off."

I'd had enough of the deerstalker, so in reply to this I merely asked, "What did you tell her about losing Dolores?"

"Why, the truth, of course," replied Sam loftily. "I said that Dolores detected a large animal nearby and snatched the leash from my hand and took off after it with the courage of a lion. I told her I had never seen such spirit in man or beast and assured her that the animal had fled before the onslaught—I could hear it crashing through the underbrush—and so was no threat to her rash darling. I really put it very neatly," he concluded smugly.

I complimented him on this achievement, tactfully omitting any further reference to his performance at Still Waters. He thanked me, but begged to be excused from participating in any more of what he called my "loony schemes." I didn't say so, because after all Sam had been quite useful, but I had no intention of seeking his help in any such delicate matters again.

25. Miss Peckham Gets Her Goose Cooked

On the morning of Thursday, October thirteenth, just as I came in from the stable, the phone rang. "Will you take it, dear?" said Mother, who was busy with breakfast at the stove.

Since it was most likely a business call at that time of day, I started to say "Dr. Birdsong's office" as soon as I lifted the phone; but the Major's deep voice cut me short.

"I have good news, Phil," he boomed exuberantly. "Miss Peckham has agreed to sell me Still Waters. We're to sign the contract at her lawyer's this afternoon at four. She came to see me about it last night after dinner, and she stayed and played several games of cribbage with me. It was so late by the time she left that I couldn't call you then. She was in a very pleasant mood, and she seems to realize at last what a fine dog Bozo is."

I congratulated the Major joyfully and, as soon as I hung up, burst into the kitchen and relayed these glad tidings to Mother. "That's splendid, dear!" she said. "I'm so glad. But before we go in to breakfast, would you just take this orange juice up to Jane? She's not feeling well this morning, but I think she might be able to drink this."

"You mean she's not going to school?" I asked in surprise. Jane is so small and slim that she has a delicate look; but she's so healthy that she gets a perfect attendance certificate at school almost every year.

"No," said Mother. "I think she had better stay home. There's a lot of chicken pox about, you know."

I went upstairs with the orange juice and surveyed Jane critically as she sat up in bed to receive it. "You haven't any spots," I said, "and you don't look sick at all. What's the matter with you?" Something in the way she looked at me made me vaguely suspicious.

"Mother thinks it's chicken pox," replied Jane, "but I think it's more likely to be Peckham pox. Goodness knows I've been exposed to her enough lately to have caught a bad case."

"Well, it's all in a good cause," I said. "She's promised to sign that contract this afternoon at four o'clock."

"Oh, she has, has she? Um-m-m."

"What do you mean, *um-m-m?*" I demanded. "Don't you want her to sign, for Pete's sake?"

"Of course I do," said Jane. "She's *got* to sign, but there's something wrong somewhere; I feel it in my bones."

"There's no satisfying some people," I said. "You must be really sick—in the head."

"Never you mind about my head, Hippo," replied Jane. "It works better than yours some ways, but right now I think I'll rest it." With that she handed me her glass and sank back on the pillow with her eyes closed, the very picture of a little angel, even to a faint, smug smile on her face.

I gazed down at her perplexedly, my suspicions, though still vague, deepening. "Something wrong somewhere"—it seemed to me as if some time recently I had had the same feeling, but when? I couldn't remember, but the idea haunted me all during breakfast and dampened my joy in the Major's good news. I revived, however, as always after a good meal, and by the time I got to school I was feeling thankful that if Jane was coming down with chicken pox, she had waited till our projects at Still Waters had been completed.

As I was on my way down to the school lunchroom that noon, Miss Norcross stopped me in the hall. There's always a certain suspense in being stopped by her, because she's so many things at school that you never know in what capacity she's acting. This time it was as freshman-class adviser. "Oh, Philip," she said. "They tell me in the office that the candy money from last Saturday's football game is still there in the safe, since your class treasurer has been absent all week. It ought to be deposited in the class account in the bank. Would you take it over when you've finished lunch? I'll tell them in the office to give you a pass if you're late to your next class." Of course I was pleased to do this errand; everybody likes a good excuse for being out of bounds during school hours. Bank business occasionally offers one to class treasurers and teachers, because the bank's not open after school.

I got my little bag of money safely to its destination and, with the deposit receipt in my hand, strolled comfortably along Main Street, pausing to look in a store window now and then and greeting people I knew. By the time I had waved to Charley Duane, I had exhausted the possibilities of that strip of pavement and turned resignedly to the curb to cross back to the school. But even before I had finished turning, I was stopped dead in my tracks by the sight before me. While I had been looking in Charley Duane's window, the glass chariot had glided into an empty parking space at the curb, and now the Major was standing with his back to me on the sidewalk, holding a leash with Dolores on the end of it in one hand, and with the other handing Miss Peckham out past the folded-up jump seat. This circumstance was surprising in itself, because I knew they were due in town at four o'clock, and Miss Peckham was not in the habit of wasting her batteries on more than one such trip a day; but what really startled me was the way they looked. The Major is always neat, but today he was positively natty; a flower in his buttonhole wouldn't have been amiss. And Miss Peckham was resplendent too. I don't know what she wore for a dress, but I noticed a lot of bangles and a crazy-looking hat covered with red poppies. Mother had always maintained that Miss Peckham was handsome in a dark, massive sort of way. She had never looked handsome to me and she didn't look handsome now, but for the first time I had an inkling of what Mother meant. The word that occurred to me, however, was not "handsome" but "dangerous."

She saw me before the Major did and gave me a toothy smile. "Why, Philip," she said, "what are you doing out of school this time of day? Are you playing hooky, you naughty boy?"

Then and there I silently agreed with Jane that I did not like Miss Peckham's friendliness; there really was something ghastly about it. I mumbled that I had been sent on an errand to the bank at the end of my lunch period and indicated my receipt as proof. I was answering Miss Peckham, but I was looking at the Major, who smiled an embarrassed smile at me and said nothing.

"Oh, you've had your lunch?" said Miss Peckham. "Lucky you! Dolores has had hers, too, but we're just famished and can't wait to get to the Tavern for *our* lunch, can we, Hugh?"

As she whisked the Major off toward Haunce's Tavern, an ancient inn that serves the best food for miles around, I think I answered the Major's troubled look by letting my mouth sag open, but I'm not sure, because I was in a state of shock. "*Our* lunch" and "Hugh" at once crystalized and justified all that fleeting uneasiness of the last day or so. I knew with a sudden sickening finality that Miss Peckham was planning to marry the Major.

I stood gazing after them till they vanished into the Tavern. Then, still half stupefied, I crossed the street without looking either way and narrowly escaped being run down by a wrathful truck driver. I went on to the school office, presented my receipt, accepted my late pass, picked up my books which I had left there, and went on to my next class—algebra—like an automaton.

I don't remember much about that class except that the teacher was annoyed with me and that toward the end of it I heard Bozo baying outside the school. I spent most of the time reproaching myself for having put the Major in his present peril. If it hadn't been for my "loony schemes" he probably wouldn't have gotten Still Waters, but he wouldn't have gotten Miss Peckham either. Now, once the contract was signed, he would be too polite to refuse to marry her; he would be defenseless. But the contract wouldn't be signed till four o'clock. Perhaps there was still time to undo the damage I had done. Just how, I didn't know, but Bozo's baying reminded me that I was not without an ally.

When I left the Morgue, my mind was made up. There was no time to be lost; so I was going to cut my next class (which was my last period study with Miss Norcross), even though our principal was campaigning against cutting just then and had imposed excessive penalties for it.

I thought I could duck through the Emerson Street door while classes were changing without attracting any attention, but I was mistaken. As I put my hand on it, an authoritative voice said, "Philip!" and I turned around and found Miss Norcross's tortoiseshells directed toward me. She was standing in the office doorway, the bank deposit receipt in her hand. "That's not the way to my room," she said.

"But I've *got* to get home," I blurted out desperately. "It's terribly important."

"I heard Bozo a few minutes ago," said Miss Norcross, with her ghost of a smile.

"Oh, it's not just Bozo," I protested. "It's much more than that. I've made an awful mistake that affects somebody else, and I've got to do something about it right away. I only just found out about it coming back from the bank."

Miss Norcross looked at me intently for a moment and then said, "Very well; I'll excuse you." As assistant principal, she's the only teacher who *can* excuse students unless they've broken a leg or something. "The office will notify your homeroom teacher," she added.

I thanked her hurriedly and made my escape. I whistled Bozo from the Mapes Street door, and we started for home at top speed. As we ran, my mind was searching frantically for some way to save the Major. The only hope now was for him to displease Miss Peckham severely, and there was no time for a buildup; it would have to be done in one decisive stroke. I did once waver and consider postponing my effort till after the signing of the contract so that the Major would get Still Waters; but as I recalled Miss Peckham's voice saying "*our* lunch" and "Hugh," I dismissed any such notion as too risky. Once the Major had Still Waters, I suddenly realized, Miss Peckham would never let him go; for by marrying him, she'd get the farm back for nothing. And I also realized for the first time that my efforts to save Still Waters had been largely selfish. True, the Major did not want to leave; but he would be able eventually to find another farm in another town that would suit him just as well; and he'd have Caleb and Bozo and the stock. He really didn't need Jane and me; he could replace us too.

These dismal reflections probably interfered with my thoughts about what to do next, because by the time I got home the only plan that seemed at all feasible was to get Bozo to nip Miss Peckham this very afternoon before the four o'clock appointment. Of course nipping Dolores would have the same effect, but it would be too hard to persuade Bozo to do that. Even Miss Peckham he wouldn't attack readily, because he'd been trained to keep away from her, and anyhow Bozo just isn't a biting dog. But even a modest nip in time might be enough to turn the trick. To carry out this plan, I had to get the recorder as quickly as possible, give Bozo his instructions, and then ride like mad with him to Miss Peckham's and wait for her to come out and get bitten.

I noted with relief as I loped down our drive that Mother's Volkswagen was out; I wouldn't have to explain what I was doing home so early. Bozo and I dashed on into the house and upstairs to my room unimpeded. If I had had my wits about me, I would have wondered where Jane was, but I had forgotten she was not in school.

I was hot and winded after my long run, and my room felt close even though the dormer window was open. I got the recorder from my desk and flopped down on the windowseat to catch my breath, while Bozo sat on the floor in front of me, panting and looking at me inquiringly. As soon as I could blow, I started playing and giving Bozo his instructions, but as I feared, he would not readily accept the idea of biting Miss Peckham. I got him to the point of repeating the picture of the St. Bernard advancing upon Miss Peckham; but at the last moment the picture went blank and he bayed most dismally.

Time was getting short and I was getting desperate

when the cowbell clanged outside my door and startled us both so that I dropped the recorder and Bozo bayed. I sat for a moment frozen by the recollection that Jane had not gone to school. What if she wanted the recorder now? Well, she just wouldn't get it this time. With Bozo baying by the open window, I couldn't very well pretend I wasn't there; I'd just have to get rid of Jane somehow as quickly as possible.

Accordingly I picked up the recorder and thumped out of my room to glower down the stairwell. Bozo came along and peered through the railing. It was Jane at the bottom all right. She was dressed in blue jeans and a sweatshirt, her face rosy and with little wisps of curls clinging damply around it.

"I thought you were sick," I said sternly, and then added as an afterthought, "And if you're coming down with chicken pox, you shouldn't use the recorder; you'd contaminate it."

"I don't want your precious recorder; I'm tired of it," said Jane and surprisingly started to giggle. Then she went on, "Anyhow, I told you it was Peckham pox I had, not chicken pox. And now that I've cooked her goose, I'm cured."

"Cooked Peckham's goose?" I asked.

"I sure did," said Jane, "for good and all."

"Oh, lord, what've you done now?" I asked. "I hope you haven't made things any worse. You don't know how serious the situation is. That woman is determined to *marry* the Major."

"Not now, she's not, Sir Hippo," replied Jane. "I tell you I've polished her off for good—though I admit I had some help. I hurried home to tell you about it, but if you're not interested, I'll leave you to your recorder." She sounded miffed, and yet I could see she was almost laughing again.

"Don't be stuffy," I said. "Of course I'm interested. In fact I've *got* to know what you've done, but for Pete's sake be quick. I'm in an awful hurry."

But Jane had a story to tell, of which she was the heroine, and she spared no details. She came up and sat on my bed and related the following, while I sat on the edge of the Morris chair and listened impatiently: "I stayed in bed all morning, sort of mulling things over, trying to decide what was wrong at the Major's, and I remembered Peckham's sickening behavior at that tea on the porch and then again yesterday when she fainted and had to be helped home; and suddenly I knew what she had in mind. By the way, how did *you* find out?"

"Never mind now," I replied. "Just tell me what you did."

"Well," continued Jane, "after lunch Mother said I could lie out in a deck chair with a blanket over me, and then she went to a Hospital Auxiliary meeting. So I just jumped on Jones and rode right over to the Major's to see what I could do about squelching Peckham's plans. I was so upset I wasn't even hungry, though all I got for lunch was clear soup, dry toast, and junket. I'm awfully hungry now though. You don't happen to have anything to eat up here, do you?"

"Keep talking," I said, but I got a chocolate bar from my desk, ripped off the paper, and thrust it into Jane's hand, begging her to take small bites so she wouldn't have to interrupt her story.

"When I rode in the dooryard," she went on, "there

was that awful Peckham smirking at the Major and he was just giving her a bunch of his best chrysanthemums with the utmost politeness as usual. The sight of it made me simply furious. I know now what people mean by seeing red. I don't know whether I dug my heels into Jones or what, but before I knew it he gave a piercing whinny and charged right at her. Of course he just brushed past her at the last moment the way he always does, but she was scared blue and screamed and dropped the chrysanthemums.

"Jones's charge carried us on to the barn, but I turned him there and started back, supposing I'd have to apologize for him since the Major was there, though I certainly didn't feel like it. But as we got near Peckham again, I heard her say, 'I don't see how you can stand those unmannerly children about so much, my dear Major. That little girl is the rudest child I ever met, and as for her brother, I believe he's mentally deranged—that balloon business, you know, and then he keeps lurking around playing on that little pipe of his with his eyes closed, and in the strangest places. You can't tell me he's normal.' " Here Jane got giggling so hysterically that I had to shake her to get her going again.

"Well, give me credit," she said. "I didn't laugh at the time; I was too mad. I put on my stoniest face and walked Jones up to her as if we were in a funeral march and said, 'I may be the rudest child you ever met, Miss Peckham, and maybe Phil hasn't all his buttons, but neither of us would ever be mean enough to shoot a nice, friendly dog like Bozo—or any dog, for that matter. You know perfectly well he'd never chase Dolores. He just smiles and swings his tail around whenever he sees her.'

"You should have seen old Peckham. She was so flustered she snapped right back at me, 'Well, he was still trespassing on my property!'

" 'Trespassing!' I said, and then I looked at the Major and decided we'd both said enough. He looked terribly shocked. Even when she tried to wiggle out of it by saying it was only a BB gun, I didn't say a word, though of course I was dying to point out what damage the BB gun had done, and how she had never owned up and had made the Major pay Dolores's bill. From the Major's face I knew I didn't need to. He never said a word, but finished picking up the scattered chrysanthemums and handed them to old Peckham with a kind of bow. She knew she was licked. 'Good-bye, Major Featherstone,' she said stiffly. Then she turned slowly so that she could take in the whole scene—the pond, the house, the workshop, the stable, and the pasture; and she murmured something mushy about 'the dear old place,' but you could see she was getting madder all the time. When she'd looked everything over, she gave the chrysanthemums an angry jerk and said with a sniff—she really did sniff—'I wish you joy of dear Grandpa's farm—you and your young friends.' As she said 'young friends' she gave Jones and me an awful glare.

"Then, just as she was turning to walk away, Jones reached over and grabbed a couple of chrysanthemums from her bouquet and began munching the stems so that the heads kept bobbing up and down as if he was waving them at her. I tried not to grin, but I don't suppose I looked exactly sad. Anyhow Jones and I got a glare to end all glares; she'd have killed us on the spot if she could have. She didn't say anything though; she just stalked off down the drive and never looked back. Jones snorted when she finally disappeared, and that was the end of that. It was lovely," Jane concluded with a reminiscent grin.

I drew a deep breath and sank back in the Morris chair. "I've got to hand it to you, Jane," I said. "You've rescued the Major from the awful fate I had prepared for him with my appeasement policy. I'd have made a mess of trying to save him myself. We'll miss him—and Bozo—and Caleb—terribly, but at least we'll know he's escaped that awful woman."

"Miss him?" said Jane, looking surprised. Then she exclaimed, "Oh! You hurried me so, I forgot to tell you. I met Caleb in the truck on my way over, and he stopped and told me that the farm had already been bought and paid for. Peckham changed the time from four to eleven so that she and the Major could have lunch in town together and make one trip of it. Caleb was pleased, of course, but he sounded sort of woebegone when he added that Miss Peckham had gone on home, but was coming back to get some chrysanthemums the Major was picking for her. I bet he'll feel better when he gets home and hears how things turned out."

For a moment I just stared at Jane, stunned; then as a wild joy surged through me and demanded expression, I jumped to my feet, bent my elbows and began running in place. Jane promptly bounced off the bed and faced me in the same attitude. I didn't know whether she'd remember our war dance, or rather our joy dance; she was only seven the last time we did it. That was when we heard that Mother was coming home from the hospital in Boston, where she'd been for weeks as the result of an automobile accident. It's a very noisy dance with a lot of stamping and whooping, and that time it had frightened the wits out of the poor woman who was taking care of us. But this time Bozo was our only audience, and he just backed into the kneehole of my desk and accompanied us with solemn drumbeats from his revolving tail.

26. A Song Without Words

Though I felt on the top of the world for the rest of the day, I had a restless night and woke unusually early the next morning, feeling shivery and generally miserable. I pulled up more bedclothes and tried to doze off again, but I just couldn't get comfortable. Finally I decided I might as well get up and crept into the bathroom to wash. When I caught sight of myself in the bathroom mirror, the awful truth dawned upon me: chicken pox had invaded the high school and I, the smallest and youngest freshman, was the first—perhaps the only—victim. I examined my spots disgustedly and returned to bed without bothering to wash them.

When Mother rang the cowbell to summon me downstairs, I went to the stairwell and announced my condition. "Get right back into bed, dear," said Mother. "I'll be up to take your temperature as soon as I get breakfast on the table. I suppose you're hungry, anyhow?"

"Not very," I replied.

Mother peered up at me in a worried way and said, "Get into bed *immediately,* dear, and stay there."

I did have some fever and was glad enough to stay in bed for a couple of days. I slept fitfully and dreamed disturbing dreams, mostly about Miss Peckham. In one she had caught Pounce and put him in a cage in her back yard; and then the cage was bigger and Jane was in it, too, and, try as I would, I couldn't get it open. Jane said, "Get Jones to kick it open," but I replied, "I can't find him. She must have got him, too." Then Jane began to cry and said, "She'll get you too; she'll get us all. We shouldn't have meddled." In another dream I saw Miss Peckham taking aim at the Major's stock with a rifle.

The third morning I felt much better and had a real breakfast. When Mother brought it up, she announced that Jane was down with chicken pox, too. "Good!" I replied.

"Good!" said Mother. "What's good about that, for heaven's sake?"

"It's ignominious enough in any case for me to have chicken pox at my age," I replied, "but if I can blame it on her, it's not quite so bad. And besides," I added as I realized Mother didn't see the force of this argument, "we'll have to stay home from school awhile, and Jane will be company."

"You two!" said Mother. "To hear you talk, anybody'd think I had a pair of horribly ill-natured children. Jane said that if she had to have chicken pox, she was glad you had it, too; but when I asked her why, she said, 'It won't be so lonely with Phil around.' "

We grinned at each other then, and I suggested that I get up after breakfast; but I still had a little fever and was doomed, as it turned out, to two more days in bed. The first one I spent mostly reading, or at least trying to read; my dreams about Miss Peckham still kept haunting me and distracted my attention. Uneasily I recalled Jane's account of Peckham's venomous glare as she left Still Waters. She really could cause us a lot of trouble, I reflected, and what might become of poor Pounce if he persisted in his attentions to her, I couldn't bear to consider. I tried to concentrate on the Major's triumph, but I could not recapture Thursday's exultation; Peckham could make it hot for him, too, if she chose. What if that bear, or whatever it was, did some more damage and she decided that it was the Major's stock instead of Tom Vickery's? She'd worry the life out of him; he'd be a much easier victim than Tom.

The next day, I felt fine and spent a good part of my time propped up on my pillows practicing on the recorder. I did this the more diligently because I had nothing new to read, and every time I let my thoughts wander, they hovered uneasily about Miss Peckham and the Major. In my zeal I mastered several exercises in the music book, and got to play a complicated air fairly well. But you can't play a recorder all day long; so I finally dug up some old dog magazines and amused myself by reading articles I'd skipped when they were new. After dinner I was just finishing a history of Pekingese (which turned out to be unexpectedly interesting) in one of them, when Father came into my room and asked, "If you came down to the second floor for a few minutes, would you have the strength to struggle back to bed again?"

"I think I might," I answered with a grin.

"Come on then," he said. "I thought you might like to hear the first telephone call received by the new recorder; it's historic. And your mother says you're to wear both socks and slippers and a bathrobe because it's cold in the open attic."

By some miracle I assembled all the required equipment promptly and followed Father on down to my parents' bedroom where Jane and Mother were waiting. Jane giggled when she saw my face; she had only a couple of spots on hers and had had, she announced smugly, hardly any fever. I sat down beside her on Father's bed, wondering all the while what could be so wonderful about the first recorded message that the whole family was assembled to hear it.

Father tinkered a little with the playback and then, after a bit of preliminary scratching and rustling, a strangely squeaky but familiar voice said, "Important message for H. Philip Birdsong: Miss Elvira Peckham, formerly of this town, has sold her estate on Foothill Road and her famous glass chariot to Mr. Richard E. Paine, Realtor. For further details, phone Samuel S. Paine III."

"Hooray!" cried Jane, bouncing on the bed.

"Be my guest," said Father, pointing to the phone.

I dialed Sam's number, and he answered. My whole family gathered around and listened shamelessly to our conversation. "H. Philip Birdsong speaking," I said. "Thanks for your message. I'm calling for further details."

"Say, Hippo," said Sam. "Is it really true you've got chicken pox?"

"Yes, it is," I replied coldly.

"But I thought it was a disease of little children," said Sam.

"Adults get it sometimes," I replied. "The further details, please."

"Well, you remember I told you the chariot has six forward speeds and three reverse?"

"Yes," I said, "but—"

"That's how Dad was able to buy it so cheap—that and offering to get Elvira's furniture moved to Boston. I can drive it on private roads."

"What are you talking about?" I demanded.

"Why, the chariot," said Sam. "I thought all those speeds were funny on such an old model, and you know what? Elvira thought she had sold it for a fancy price to an old-car buff, and he came all the way from Boston to get it and found it had been modernized."

"Modernized!" I exclaimed. "Are you crazy?"

"Not at all," said Sam. "It had new works put in it in the 1920's, and he wouldn't take it. He was mad as hops—said Elvira'd told him it was a bona fide 1910 model. Of course it's still valuable, but I guess Elvira got discouraged and let Dad have it for practically nothing."

"Well, congratulations and all that," I said, "but please

get on with the details. How did all this happen to come about?"

"Well, Elvira arrived at our house in an awful state Thursday evening. She had suitcases and hat boxes—and Dolores, of course—and she was going to Boston. She would stay at her cousin's (one on her mother's side) for a day or two, she said; but as soon as possible she'd get an apartment, and she wanted Dad to put her house on the market. That knocked us for a loop because she's always been so soupy about her dear little house and all. Mother thinks she's really flipped her lid. According to Elvira, the country's become too dangerous to live in. She says there's a conspiracy of the animals against her—all of them, tame and wild. She went on quite hysterically about your ponies and the weasel and a bear she claims haunts the neighborhood, but most of all about what she called 'that black demon wildcat.' I didn't know wildcats were black, did you?"

"Perhaps it was a panther," I said, grinning around at the family. "Had it done anything recently?"

"You bet it had," said Sam. "When Elvira got back from the Major's Thursday, very sad and upset to see the farm in what she called 'alien hands,' the cat flew past her out an open window. It had knocked everything off her tables and her bureau and had sent Dolores into a wild rage—apparently Dolores had been left home for once. Elvira sat down among the ruins and, finding a scratch on Dolores's nose, decided that that was the end. She couldn't survive such another terrible day, she said. I guess something else must have happened, too, because she rambled on about some cruel disappointment she'd suffered, but we couldn't make head or tail of that.

Mother didn't think we ought to let her go off alone in such a state, but there was no stopping her. Bill drove her to the airport, and she left her keys and her chariot with us.

"I guess she did all right, because she located that old-car buff right off and got herself an apartment near the Public Garden where she can walk Dolores in safety—or so she thinks. Father flew up today and closed the deal with her about the house. We knew the title was clear, and he wasn't taking any chances on her changing her mind."

"What's your father going to do with the house?" I asked.

"Bill's buying it," replied Sam. "He's getting married next month, you know, and they'll live there. He says I can keep the chariot there; Dad's selling *me* that—on the installment plan. Do you think the Major would let me drive it on the racetrack?"

"Probably," I replied, "when the stock is safely out of the way. But do you know Miss Peckham's address?"

"I could find out easy enough," said Sam. "You want to correspond with her?" This question was accompanied by a snort.

"Not exactly," I said, "but there's an article in an old dog magazine I'd like to have her read. It's about Sleeve Pekes; they weigh up to six pounds and are considered very select. I'm sure Dolores is or could be one if she could keep her weight down. Would you send it to Miss Peckham and not mention it's from me?"

"Well, sure, if you like. But since when have you been so crazy about Dolores?"

"Oh, I just got kind of sorry for her," I said. "It's wicked to let a dog get so fat, and I think perhaps if your second cousin once removed knows she's got a Sleeve Peke, she might keep her slim. The article tells about Sleeve Peke clubs; there's probably one in Boston that would welcome Dolores and Miss Peckham with open arms."

"No kidding," said Sam. "There really are such clubs?"

"Sure," I said. "There are clubs for everything—probably even for owners of 1910 electric cars with 1920 innards. Perhaps you could join one by correspondence."

Sam snorted again at that and said I was pretty cocky for a little boy with chicken pox. I replied that the prospect of a vacation from school made me cheerful and closed the conversation by wishing him a happy algebra test.

While Sam and I were talking, I was aware of intermittent whispering between Jane and my parents. As I hung up, Jane turned to me and said triumphantly, "I heard every word Sam said and passed it on just like in the United Nations. And isn't it just perfect? I was sort of worried about Peck—uh, Miss Peckham."

"So was I," said Father, giving Jane a significant look.

"I've been keeping Pounce in the cellar at night lately, when I could catch him," confessed Mother. "I'm so glad he can go free again. I only hope he doesn't keep haunting Miss Peckham's place when Bill moves in."

"He won't; it was Miss Peckham he was after," I said.

Father gave me a funny look, but turned toward Jane as she announced blissfully, "I never felt so peaceful before. I just feel like sleeping and sleeping."

"Me, too," I said, stretching luxuriously.

"What a refreshingly inactive program for a change!" said Father. "You'd better get off my bed and get right at it."

We said good night and Jane went to her room, while I stepped onto the attic stairway and closed the door. However, since Jane had mouthed the word "Wait!" at me in the hall, I lingered on the first step till I heard our parents go downstairs. Then I quietly followed Jane.

She was sitting on her bed waiting too. "I just thought you'd like to know that I phoned the Major today and everything's O.K. there," she whispered.

"Weren't you forbidden to get out of bed?" I asked.

"No," said Jane. "I could go to the bathroom, and the phone was just as near, but I thought maybe I'd better not mention it to Mother. Anyhow, the Major answered me from the workshop. He's got his stove up and he's had a phone extension put in, and he's working on the Christmas toys. He says he and Caleb have both had chicken pox, so we can go to Still Waters as soon as Mother'll let us. That ought to be by Friday anyhow, don't you think?"

"Sure," I said. "I'm getting up tomorrow and I suppose you will the next day."

"And guess who's taken to calling at Still Waters?" said Jane.

"Sam?" I asked.

"No," replied Jane. "Houdini and Spook, that new poodle of the Molloys. They showed up Friday morning, their tongues hanging out and Spook covered with burs. They both dived into the pond and had a drink and got all muddy. Then they hobnobbed with Bozo and inspected the stock and had a nap in the barn. The Major put them in the harness room and called Mrs. Molloy, but by the time she got there, they'd disappeared somehow. She said if they didn't bother the Major, he wasn't to bother about *them* if they returned. 'They'll come home for dinner,' she said. So now they come every day. And Spook has taught one of the kids—Starbuck, I think—how to get out of the pasture, and they go running around everywhere together. But she always brings him to the back door and barks before she leaves. And Bozo escorts both dogs to the crossroad and sits in the middle of the road baying good-bye till they're up the hill."

"Oh boy!" I said. "I thought things might be sort of quiet on Foothill Road now that Peckham's gone, but I guess not. I can't wait to get back there."

"Well, I can—for a while," said Jane, "because I really am awfully sleepy. Good night."

I replied, "Good night," and was just tiptoeing out of the room when Jane whispered again, "Phil, you'd better call the Major first thing in the morning and tell him about Peckham. He thinks she's just gone on a visit. I don't suppose he'll be as relieved as we are, but Caleb will be."

"O.K.," I replied and this time really got to bed and slept and slept.

We had a heavy frost that night, but the next day was still and sunny. Of course I wanted to go out, and at last it was agreed that I could, for a half-hour after lunch. "But don't go into the paddock, dear," said Mother. "Give the ponies their sugar and then go lie in a deck chair in the clothes yard; you'll be out of any drafts there, and I'll give you a rug so you'll be warm enough."

This program didn't sound very attractive, but it was better than nothing. I had a joyful reunion with the ponies, which lasted till Mother called to me from the back porch. Then, with a parting whinny, I shuffled through fallen leaves to the clothes yard and sank into a deck chair, where I lay for a few minutes enjoying the stillness and idly gazing up into the clear, delicate blue of the sky. The few pure white clouds that were moving across it must have been very high, for down below there wasn't a breath of wind. I automatically checked for interesting arrangements, but the shapes I saw suggested nothing to me except for one curiously thin and angular section of a jet trail that looked like a tray at eye level. One look at that was enough; so I came back to earth and pulled the recorder out of my game pocket, where I had put it as a provision against boredom.

I tried playing the tune I had practiced yesterday, but I kept making mistakes. So I soon gave up and, lying back in the deck chair, let my fingers ripple as they would over the holes while I blew steadily into the beak. After a few random notes a high, unearthly trill quivered in the still air. And then, as I listened with mounting wonder and excitement, there followed a joyous, cascading warble, and then the trill again. It was the mysterious bird song of my birthday night—the song that Father partly knew but didn't know he knew. And now *I* knew it was mine. I had played it on the recorder, but it had welled up from somewhere deep within me, and within me I heard and felt its echo as I held my breath and listened.

Then abruptly the quiet of early afternoon was shattered by a bloodhound howl as Bozo came lolloping through the open gate toward me. Almost simultaneously Pounce landed on my shoulder and Jones gave a prolonged whinny from the other side of the rose hedge. I was fully occupied for the next few moments delightedly shaking Bozo's paw, stroking Pounce, and replying to Jones's whinny; yet all the time my mind was groping here and there trying to find out why I had that queer feeling of having seen and done all this before. On my birthday night, of course, Bozo, Pounce, and Jones had all hailed me after that song; but I felt it was something more than that that I half remembered. A pony, a dog, a cat. . . . I rubbed my head thoughtfully and, leaning back once more, gazed again at the sky.

The clouds had regrouped themselves, and right above me I made out a pony with a small rider holding something like a short straight stick before him. And beside him was a large dog with a cat on his back. It was Hilary Philip Birdsong himself, playing his flute to his familiars as he rode through the air to Shropshire! Could I hail him? Could I play our call again?

I sat up and put the recorder to my lips, aware as I fumbled for the first high note of the trill that Pounce, who had dropped onto the big spool, interrupted a bath he was taking to stare at me, that Bozo's tail stopped rotating and that Jones was standing still, peering fixedly at me through a bare spot in the hedge. But before I could find that note, a familiar giggle broke the spell, and a voice called, "You look just like Pan in the stained-glass window. All you need is a lamb at your feet." The sewing room window is the only one that overlooks the clothes yard. It was open, and Jane was standing at it in her bathrobe.

"Why can't you exercise your imagination on something else?" I yelled back disgustedly. "There are some good clouds; why don't you try *them?*"

Jane leaned out of the window and squinted up at the sky. "Well, I see the patients' table," she called.

"*What?*" I answered.

"The patients' table," she repeated, "and Father beside it looking through a telescope."

I thought I couldn't have heard her right, and curiosity impelled me to run over nearer the house where we could talk more easily and where, perhaps, I could see what she meant. As I looked up, I realized that the pony-and-rider-cat-and-dog group was dissolving and had collided with that piece of jet trail that looked like a tray. The cat and dog had contributed a sort of stump to the tray so that it did look something like the patients' table, and the pony's head was just a blob on top of it. The only survivor of the group was the rider, who seemed now to stand behind the table with his flute still in his hand.

As I was taking this in, Jane corrected herself. "No, it can't be Father; it's too tall. Why, for heaven's sake, it must be *you!* You're awfully tall—perhaps you're grown up—but I'd know that hair anywhere; it sticks right up in a ridge." She looked down at me for a moment, then back up, and added, "So it's not a telescope, but the recorder. And you're playing it to that lamb on the table. I know it's a lamb; it's got its legs folded under it. And its mouth is open. It must be bleat—"

Jane's last syllable was lost as she disappeared back into the sewing room and Mother's voice took over. "You don't have to hang out the window by your toes to get a little fresh air, Jane," she said. "You've had quite enough for one day. Now get right back to your room." Then, before she shut the window, Mother looked down at me and said, "It's time you were in too, Phil."

As Bozo and I paused on our way upstairs for a little snack in the kitchen, Mother came in with the mail in her hands. "There's a letter for Jane which you can take up to her when you go," she said, "and here's your invention magazine, dear."

What Mother calls my "invention magazine" is just an ordinary science journal that includes information on new inventions. I guess she thinks that's all I read in it, and of course I do give that section special attention. But instead of turning to the inventions today, I gazed fascinated at the cover. In big letters I read, "ESP, FACT OR FANCY?" Then below in smaller letters, "Concise summary of all available data by leading scientists. Complete bibliography."

I didn't open the magazine in the kitchen, but gave Bozo the rest of my cookie, grabbed my apple, and made for my room. Mother called me back to get Jane's letter, which I had forgotten. Bozo and I delivered it promptly and were hurrying out of Jane's room when she said, "Hey! What's your hurry?" and then added plaintively, "I thought maybe you'd play a game of parcheesi with me."

"I will later," I promised, "but you've got your letter now, and I'm going to be very busy for a while. I've got to study."

"Study what?" asked Jane. "You wouldn't be in such a hurry about algebra."

"It's science," I replied. "I'm starting a special research program into something that's just come up."

Jane looked puzzled. "Cloud pictures?" she said, "or recorders? or how to grow tall?"

I looked back at her thoughtfully from the doorway a moment. "It's a wide field," I said. "It just might include all three."

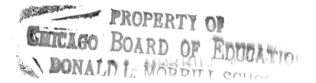